I0545938

FAMILY MATTERS

M K TURNER

Copyright © M K Turner

This edition published 2021 by 127 Publishing

The rights of M K Turner to be identified as the author of this
work have been asserted in accordance with the Copyright,
Designs and Patents Act 1988.

All rights reserved. No part of this publication may be
reproduced, stored in a retrieval system, or transmitted in any form
or by any means, electronic, mechanical, photocopying, recording
or otherwise without the permission of the publisher.

This novel is entirely a work of fiction. The names, characters and
incidents portrayed are entirely the work of the author's
imagination. Any resemblance to actual persons, living or dead, or
events is entirely co-incidental.

All rights reserved.

ISBN: 978-1-9996734-3-7

By M K Turner

Meredith & Hodge Series

The Making of Meredith

Misplaced Loyalty

Ill Conceived

The Wrong Shoes

Tin Soldiers

One Secret Too Many

Mistaken Beliefs

Quite by Chance

Family Matters

Not If You Paid Me

Bearing Witness Series

Witness for Wendy

An Unexpected Gift

Terms of Affection

The Murder Tour Series

Who Killed Charlie Birch?

Others

The Cuban Conundrum

Murderous Mishaps

The Recruitment of Lucy James

ACKNOWLEDGMENTS

Editing by Sharon Kelly

Cover Design by www.behance.net/lwpmarshala1e9

Photography by: Mario Klassen and Katie Harp
Park Street - Bristol

.

1

Alan Jenkins loosened his tie. Leaning back in his chair, he checked his watch again. Increasingly irritated, he drummed his fingers on the box in front of him. How long did it take to get rid of a bag of bloody clothing? As he pondered whether to make a call, he heard movement outside the door and sat upright.

"About bloody time. What took you so long?" Pointing to the chair in front of the desk, he snapped. "Sit."

Jenkins' nephew Max Deegan shrugged as he dropped his heavy frame into the chair opposite. "It was covered in blood. I couldn't just dump it. I had to burn it, needed to make sure it was done properly. Took ages, that was my favourite T-shirt too."

"Well then you shouldn't have let yourself get carried away. A slap would have done. I've bloody warned you about your temper."

"Yeah, well, he pissed me off. It was my favourite—"

"Yes, you said. Because of your handiwork with that knife, you'll have to take care of Meredith. I was hoping to drag that out." Sliding the box across the desk, Jenkins shook his head. "I'd not finished with him, but I've got another load coming in shortly and the house needs sorting." Rubbing his brow in an attempt to disperse the headache he knew was coming, Jenkins tried not to think about it. He pointed at the box. "That's got a silencer. Use it, I don't want to draw any more attention."

"Why?" Frowning, Deegan tried to remember the minimum sentence for killing a police officer, bent or otherwise.

"Why don't I want attention? Fuck me, Max, I know you're not the brightest spark, but please!"

"No. Why kill Meredith? I thought that was the whole point of getting him roped in." His frown deepened. "I thought you had *big plans* for Meredith." Trying to imitate Jenkins' voice and failing miserably, he tried again. "What I'm trying to say is, killing him might be the wrong move. After all, he can hardly run to the police himself, can he? And, that's if he finds out what happened to his mate."

"Who knows? I'm not prepared to wait and see. As things stand he doesn't know who we are or that we were involved, and I want to keep it that way." Jenkins glanced at the screen of the laptop to his left. "Shame, I wanted to play with him a bit, they're pretty girls. I wanted to see his face when he watched the tape."

Remembering why this wouldn't be possible, his face contorted, and he saw Deegan flinch. "And that's your fault. You've denied me" Slamming his hands on the desk, he nudged the box closer for good measure. "Now do as you're told and get it done. Don't cock it up. You're sure you're up to this, aren't you?" Jenkins hadn't missed Deegan's reluctance to take the box.

"Of course." Deegan was anything but confident, but he didn't want his uncle to know that. Jerking his thumb to the screen of the laptop, Deegan smirked. "You can still have fun with those two, can't you?"

"Possibly. Won't be as much fun now Meredith won't get to see it. Go on, fuck off. I can't look at your stupid mug a minute longer."

Pushing back the chair, Deegan got to his feet and lifted the box. "How do I find him though?"

"We know where his mother lives, and I'm tracking his phone. Take this." Lifting a mobile phone from the top drawer he tossed it to Deegan.

"It's all set up. He's nearly in Bristol. Before you set off, two things. First, drop my car off to Alex, tell him I want it spotless and to make sure there's not a trace of blood left. If it stains I'll need to get both the front seats recovered, and you'll be paying. When you've done that, go to Bristol, and torch the car in the layby on your way. Don't want the police picking up your prints and coming back to me."

Waiting until the door shut behind Deegan, Jenkins pulled the laptop closer. Meredith's woman was a looker, but his daughter was the one he wanted. She looked like Meredith, and seeing her fear, her agony, would give him great pleasure.

2

Meredith stubbed out his cigarette and dropped it into the bin. He was nervous, a feeling he wasn't familiar with. He couldn't remember being nervous on previous occasions. Grinning, he turned to Louie Trump.

"Do you know, Trump, I actually feel happy."

Trump grinned. "I should think so too, here, let—"

"Hang on a minute." Dave Rawlings pulled his phone from his pocket. "This I have to record." He tapped the screen before holding it towards Meredith. "And again, Gov. I can play it when you're back to normal, and I need reminding it's possible."

Meredith's eyes narrowed. "It won't take much to change to that status. And I'm not your Gov, not until next week." He smiled. "I can't wait though, there is a limit to . . ." He glanced to Rawlings' right. "Tom looks very smart. New suit?"

The others turned to watch Seaton's approach. Tom Seaton was on the phone. Frowning, he listened intently to the caller. Raising a hand to acknowledge them he stopped walking to complete the call.

"I bet you're all going to be called away." Meredith watched Seaton hold a finger up, asking them to give him a moment. He glanced at his watch. "We'd better wait and see before we go in."

Tom Seaton terminated the call and tapped out a message, before hurrying over to the group. He rubbed his hands together and had to force his smile.

"Come on then, let's get in there. The bridal party will be here soon."

"You mean you're not going to be called away?" Meredith patted him on the back. "You looked so serious then, I thought I'd have to get married with no back-up. Nice suit."

"New for the occasion. You'll be married, and there will be back-up. Time to go in." Throwing his arm around Meredith's shoulders he led him towards the door of the registry office. Pulling it open he allowed Meredith to enter.

"I need a quick word with Trump, and I'll be with you. Dave, make sure he doesn't do a runner."

Rawlings looked up from his phone, he too forced a smile.

"Will do." He stepped between Meredith and Seaton. "Come on, Gov. Not long and you'll be an honest man." He spotted his wife. "There's Eve, that means the rest of them won't be far behind."

Meredith, usually perceptive, didn't pick up on the tension building within his old team, and walked happily into the registry office. The door closed and he nudged Rawlings. "Can't wait to see what Loopy is wearing. She told Trump she was an unofficial bridesmaid."

"Not long now, and we'll find out." Rawlings placed his hand in the small of Meredith's back and pushed him forward.

Finally, Meredith caught on. "Is something going on I should know about?"

Rawlings' laugh was nervous. "Like what? We've had the stag do, no one is going to shave your eyebrows off today."

Meredith ground to a halt. "Now I know something's wrong. Tell me, Dave. I don't want to have to walk back out of here."

Rawlings looked him in the eye. "Do you trust me?"

"I did." Meredith pursed his lips. "Relevance?"

"Do you want to marry Patsy?"

"I do. Fuck me, Dave, spit it out. You're making me even more nervous."

"Then shut up, stay in here, and marry the poor girl." Rawlings held his arm towards the registry office. "I'm saying nothing until you've put a ring on her finger."

"I'm not . . ."

"You are! Don't make me fall out with you, Gov. Not here, not today. Move."

Meredith's mouth snapped shut. At a total loss as to what was going on, he had no idea how he should react. If it were any other occasion he would have insisted on the truth. He'd have marched back outside to see what was going on. But today he was marrying Patsy Hodge. Today he couldn't get it wrong. Five minutes before, he'd been as happy as he could remember feeling, now his chest was tight, and his stomach somersaulted.

"Okay, just tell me Patsy is okay."

This time Rawlings' smile was genuine. "Patsy is perfect, which is why you're marrying her. In there. Now."

3

Patsy Hodge entered the building followed by the rest of their guests. She looked down the corridor to where Meredith waited with Tom and the registrar, and smiled as she walked towards him.

"We made it." It was almost a whisper as she reached him.

Meredith looked her up and down. Her hair was piled on top of her head, tiny white flowers were dotted amongst the falling curls. She had applied more makeup than he was used to seeing, but the smoky grey powder on her eyelids made the blue of her eyes more intense.

"We did. You look better than beautiful, Hodge. Thanks for turning up." His voice was husky.

"You're welcome. Same to you." A little nervous herself, Patsy pulled on the edge of the satin bolero and drew in a breath. "I thought something would happen to stop this."

"Not this time." Meredith held out his hand.

Rawlings glanced at the clock. "Shall we get on with it?"

Meredith's head snapped around to look at him, and when Rawlings jerked his thumb towards the open doors of the ceremony room, Meredith turned back to Patsy.

"Shall we?"

"Yes. But you go in first. Dad wants to walk me in." She turned to face the guests and smiled at her father. "You lot follow Meredith. I'm ready, Dad."

Her father held out his arm as the last of the guests settled. Standing in front of the desk, Meredith watched him escort Patsy towards him. His eyes quickly skimmed the guests. Trump and Seaton hadn't reappeared, and when Rawlings closed the doors behind Patsy, rather than take a seat, he stood guard in front of them. Managing a smile for his sister, Julia, who blew him a kiss, Meredith turned away. He needed to concentrate, then he could find out what was going on.

The registrar straightened his tie, and rearranged his pen as he waited for Patsy to reach the desk, smiling as Meredith took Patsy's hand.

"Welcome. We are here today to witness the marriage of Patsy Hodge and John Meredith . . ."

His voice was low and melodious, perfect for his chosen profession, and as he spoke Patsy looked into Meredith's eyes. Meredith raised his eyebrows to show his amazement that they'd actually made it, and Patsy grinned. Standing side on to the desk, Meredith caught the movement of Rawlings pulling his phone from his pocket. He might simply be checking it was on silent, Meredith reasoned, and brought his attention back to the registrar.

"Do you, John Meredith take Patsy Hodge to be your lawful wedded wife?"

"I do."

"Repeat after me. I, John Meredith . . ."

Meredith attempted to relax, but when he fumbled his words, raising a murmur of amusement from the guests, they assumed he was nervous for totally the wrong reason.

* * *

Outside, Trump and Seaton guarded the main entrance. They allowed no one in without official identification, and flashed their own if anyone complained.

Seaton paced back and forward. "They should be done by now. How long does this take?"

"About twenty minutes. They come outside for the photographs," Trump glanced at his watch. "It shouldn't be long. The plan is what? He'll know something is wrong, I can't see how we can avoid a scene." He grimaced. "Poor Patsy."

"I don't have a plan. I only found out myself on the way here. Try and get them to go straight to the hotel? Where would you want to be arrested?"

"Point taken. We should get him to go to the station."

"Good luck with that. Oh shit, this looks like them."

Trump and Seaton stood shoulder to shoulder in front of the sturdy double doors. Two men in crumpled suits marched purposefully towards them. The taller of the two pulled out his warrant card as they approached.

"Excuse us, gents."

"Sorry, but you can't go in at the moment. It won't be long. Why don't you take a seat?" Trump smiled and pointed to a bench on a small grassed area.

"Not sure who you are, sir, but this is police business." The smaller one held his card higher to reinforce their authority.

Seaton peered at it. "Snap, Sergeant Exton." He pulled out his own warrant card. "You're here for our governor. Not that he knows yet. He's getting married. Give him ten minutes."

The two officers exchanged glances. The taller one took charge. "Former governor. I understand he's a civvy now. A private dick taking advantage."

"Only until next week. And a word of warning, a bit of respect is in order. Your information is wrong, and you don't want to get on the wrong side of him. He's got a long memory."

"The Chief Super has cleared this, so step out of the way. Let's not have a scene." DS Exton took a step forward.

"Uncle David knows? Then why didn't he call? Two minutes." Trump pulled out his phone and called Chief Superintendent David Ashworth.

"Who the hell is Uncle David? Is he taking the piss?" The taller one joined his partner.

"The Chief Super. He doesn't usually do this, he avoids him, which shows how important this is."

Trump stepped away and had a brief conversation with his uncle. He turned back with a smile. "He didn't realise Meredith was getting married. No one told him. He says to wait, try and avoid a scene. And be polite."

"And I'm supposed to just believe you, am I?" Exton snorted a laugh which died as Trump put the phone back to his ear.

"They don't believe me, sir. Perhaps you'd be kind enough to have a word." He handed the phone to the tall one.

"Sergeant Paisley, who am I speaking to? Right . . . Yes sir. Will do." Handing the phone back to Trump he rolled his eyes at Exton. "Come on, let's take a seat." He walked to the bench and pulled out a packet of cigarettes.

Seaton walked over to join them. "You'll be glad you waited. What exactly is it you think he's done? I wasn't given much detail; only told you were coming."

"No disrespect, but we'll talk to Meredith first." Paisley smirked. "He's not got an uncle too, has he?"

"No, but then, he doesn't need one." Seaton glanced over his shoulder. "Here they come, give him five minutes. Then he'll probably want a moment with Patsy."

Trump pulled open the door and kept his eyes trained on Patsy, unwilling to look at Meredith.

"Patsy you look radiant."

"She always does. What's going on?" Meredith demanded.

"Merriwinkle, get out of the doorway, I need a hug. You buggers made me cry." Peggy Green, an unrelated, but self-appointed matriarch of the disjointed Meredith clan, elbowed her way forward. She hugged Patsy, then grabbed Meredith's face and planted a noisy kiss on each cheek. "I couldn't have been prouder if you were my own. Well done, Merriwinkle." She pulled a tissue from her pocket and blew her nose. Pulling a small camera from her bag, she added, "Now smile, let's get some photos."

Handing Trump the camera, she pulled the newly wedded couple away from the door, and standing between them, she linked arms with them. "Smile. This is one for the mantelpiece."

Meredith jerked his lips into a smile and Patsy giggled.

"My turn." Patsy's father stepped up and stood next to his daughter.

"Throw the bouquet!" Scooping up the hem of her flowing cerise coloured dress, Linda hurried forward.

"Not so fast, Linda. I want a photo with these two before the first row." Winking at her father, Amanda, Meredith's daughter from a previous marriage, stepped into position.

Meredith obliged, then made a mumbled excuse and walked over to Trump.

"Now tell me what's going on. Where's Seaton?"

"He's over there, sir."

Meredith glanced at the men sitting on the bench. "Who are they?"

Trump took his elbow and walked him further away from the guests. "Police officers, they've come to arrest you."

"To what?" Meredith's laugh was genuine. "As Rawlings pointed out, the stag do was a while ago." The smile disappeared when Trump didn't respond. "You're serious, aren't you?"

"I'm afraid so. It's obviously . . ."

Meredith was already marching towards the men who jumped to their feet. He didn't waste time.

"What for?"

"Impersonating a police officer, robbery, demanding money with menaces, GBH. It's a long list. Better discussed at the station."

Meredith shook his head and looked at Seaton. "Did you know about this?"

"Only as I arrived, and not any details. I thought it best to wait until you'd said I do before I told you. I didn't want you going off on one and the wedding getting cancelled. Congratulations by the way." Seaton pointed over Meredith's shoulder. "Talking of which, the lovely Mrs Meredith is watching."

They looked across to the assembled guests where Patsy watched them despite her smiles and nods at the guests. When Linda demanded the bouquet be thrown for the third time, Patsy shooed the women into a group. Turning her back to them, she flung the bouquet over her shoulder not stopping to see who caught it. With tradition satisfied, she made a beeline for the group of men.

"Gents, let's give them a moment."

Exton opened his mouth to protest, but Seaton grabbed him by the arm and pulled him to his feet.

"Now move. He's not going anywhere." He led the men away.

Meredith stared at the ground. With no idea what was going on, he had to try and explain to Patsy why her day was about to get ruined.

"Meredith, Louie said you might want to talk to me." She placed her hand on his shoulder and he turned to face her.

"Good old Trump. What else did he say?"

"Not much. I don't like your expression. What's happened?"

Meredith pointed to Seaton and the two officers waiting to formally arrest him. "They've come to arrest me, for impersonating a police officer, amongst other things on a very long list."

"For impersonating a . . ." Patsy called to Seaton. "Tom, what the hell is going on?"

Tom walked towards her and the two officers followed a couple of yards behind. "I have no idea. I received a call from the Chief Super as I arrived. I'm sorry, Patsy, but the Gov is going to have to go in and sort it out."

"Someone will pay dearly for this." Meredith pulled Patsy back to face him and looped his arms around her. "I'm sorry. But we did it, Mrs Meredith." His kiss was tender. "Take the guests to the reception. I'll leave it up to you as to what you tell them. But the sooner I go, the sooner I can get back to you."

"Why is life never simple with you?" Patsy blinked rapidly. "Would you like me to call a solicitor?"

"No, Hodge, I wouldn't. This is a huge, by bloody gigantic proportions, mistake. So, why would I need a solicitor? Oh shit, Peggy's on her way." He looked at the two officers waiting for him. "Shall we go, before you embarrass me any further?"

One of them slipped his hands into his pocket.

Meredith pointed at him. "You've not arrested me, so unless that's a packet of cigarettes, keep it in there. I won't be wearing cuffs." He looked back at Patsy as an empty hand reappeared. "I love you, Hodge. I'll call as soon as I can." Kissing her briefly, he strode away ignoring Peggy's calls.

"And it's Meredith now. Not Hodge," Patsy called after him.

"I'm sure he won't be long, Patsy. Shall I go with him, or come with you?" Tom Seaton placed a hand on her shoulder.

"Go with him, please, Tom. Someone needs to keep an eye on him and let me know what's happening." She pecked Tom on the cheek and turned to Peggy who had reached them and was demanding to know where Meredith was going. "Peggy, there's been a change of plan, Meredith won't be joining us at the reception."

"But I haven't doused him in confetti yet. Where is more important than your wedding reception?"

"Police business. Come on. We'd better tell the others." Patsy linked her arm through Peggy's and looked at their guests milling around and waiting for the photographs. "This is going to be a bloody nightmare, Peggy. Can I rely on you?"

"Always. But he's not a copper again yet, is he?"

"No. He's not. It's a different type of business apparently." She smiled as Trump strode across to them.

"Are we still going to the hotel, Patsy?" When she nodded, he smiled with his lips, although the rest of his face remained serious. "Splendid. I'll round them up and send them on their way. You go ahead."

Patsy and Peggy changed direction, Amanda and Linda ran to catch them.

"Where's Dad going?" Amanda looked from one to the other. "This is serious, isn't it? Is he okay, he's not ill, is he?"

Meredith did little to stay healthy, usually ignoring signs from his body that things weren't right. He had only recently recovered from a pulmonary embolism. Before that was discovered, he'd taken a leave of absence from the police force, which was dragged out due to his illness, and he was now a week away from returning to work.

"Nope. Police business. Apparently, a need-to-know thing." Peggy held out her hand. "So, we're babysitting Patsy while he sorts it out."

"But he's not—"

"A copper, that's what I said. It seems there is more than one type of police business." Peggy narrowed her eyes at Patsy. "She won't tell us."

"I'm sure it will all be fine. You know what they're like by now, Patsy." Linda beamed at her. "I caught the bouquet. We're going to have to set a date now, it must be a law somewhere."

"Only because you elbowed me out of the way." Amanda looked at Linda's happy face and smiled. "Lovely dress, how many layers of chiffon?"

"Six. Took me ages to find. What's this police matter all about anyway? Must be serious if Meredith isn't attending his own reception."

"It is, but too long a story." Glancing back and seeing Meredith had gone, Patsy increased her pace.

Amanda could see Patsy had no intention of adding further information, and taking Peggy's hand, she fell into step with them.

4

Meredith walked along the familiar corridor. The two officers had said little on the journey and his temper was simmering. He stopped as he reached the rank of interview rooms.

"Which one? Three is my personal favourite, a bit bigger and closer to the fire escape should I need a smoke."

"That will do nicely." Exton agreed. He was feeling extremely uncomfortable. Meredith had been greeted and exchanged a word with everyone they'd seen so far. It was ridiculous that the Chief Super had told them to go to Meredith's old station. They should have been allowed to take him to Plymouth.

Meredith paused as he opened the door. By habit he always took a seat on the right side of the table, it made little difference, but he dithered which raised his blood pressure another notch. Gritting his teeth, he took his normal seat. Watching while Exton and Paisley settled themselves, and a stack of files was placed on the corner of the table.

Paisley cleared his throat and, flipping the button on the recorder, cautioned Meredith.

Meredith confirmed he'd refused legal representation. "Can we get on with it now? What have you got?"

"Quite a lot, and it's still coming in." Exton flipped open a file. "Where were you on November the thirtieth, late afternoon?"

"At home. Next question." Meredith linked his fingers and leaning back in the chair rested them on his stomach.

"December the fifth, one thirty . . ." Exton made a pretence of reading the file. "Three."

"One thirty-three you say? Um, that would be home, again. Look shall we stop mucking about, where do you think I was and why?"

"You seem very certain of your whereabouts, would you like time to check a diary or something?" Paisley smiled. "These are serious allegations, Mr Meredith, they need serious consideration."

"What are?"

"What are, what?"

"What are serious allegations? You forgot to formally arrest me, so I have no idea what allegations are serious." Meredith frowned. "How did you make sergeant making such stupid mistakes?"

"Would your answer be different if you had been arrested?" Exton began tapping his pen on the table.

"Nope. But at least I'd know what, and more importantly, why you think I'm involved. Tell me what you think you have on me."

The two officers ignored him. Paisley opened a second file. "Tell me about your shopping trip to the Orchard Shopping Centre."

"Never heard of it. Where is it? I don't mean to be rude, fuck it, I do. Why am I here?" Meredith got to his feet. "You've not arrested me, you're not telling me why you interrupted my wedding, I'm off for a slice of cake."

One stride and his hand was on the door handle. He looked at the two men jostling to reach him. "You are a waste of space. You'll regret ruining this day for me. Now go and speak to someone who knows what they're doing, and if you really do have an investigation start working on it."

"Humour me. Watch this." Exton waved a disc at Meredith, who paused. "Five minutes and you'll see why we're here, then we can have a meaningful discussion."

"And if I don't?"

"I'll arrest you and have you in the cells waiting for your brief."

Meredith's interest overpowered his irritation. He held out his hand. "Give it to me. It's a bit temperamental." He was already walking over to the DVD player.

5

Trump tapped his champagne flute with a butter knife, and a hush fell over the room.

"Ladies and gentlemen, Mrs Meredith would like a word." He smiled at the ripple of applause.

Patsy took another gulp from her glass and looked out at the small gathering of their friends. "Thank you so much for coming, Meredith is . . . well, Meredith is being Meredith, and he'll either turn up or not. He sends his apologies and has promised to join us as soon as he can."

She held up her hand at the small ripple of speculation. "It's not his health. Meredith is now as fit as a fiddle. As you know he goes back to work next week, and this is police business which couldn't be avoided." Lifting her hand, she spread her fingers and wiggled the one holding the bright, new wedding band. "But we still did it. We finally got married, and, with or without him, I intend to celebrate." She snatched up her glass. "Cheers."

Trump lifted his glass. "Ladies and gentlemen, please raise your glasses to the bride, Mrs Patsy Meredith." The room toasted Patsy, and he added, "Now find your seats as we will be served in five minutes."

Patsy grabbed his arm and said quietly, "Do you really not know what this is about?"

"Afraid not, Patsy. Those two officers are from Devon and Cornwall, but as far as Tom could make out it's to do with something in Somerset too, so all very confusing. Clearly a mistake, fingers crossed he'll be here before we've finished eating."

He wasn't, and Patsy asked the caterers to put a meal aside for him.

Meredith was not good on an empty stomach. But watching her father glance from his watch to the door for the fifth time in ten minutes, Patsy decided to go home.

They weren't having a formal evening reception as they'd only decided to book the wedding five weeks before, agreeing that it should be on the earliest possible date. Once booked, they found it impossible to find a suitable venue for an evening reception. A buffet arranged at their local pub was the best they could manage.

Patsy got to her feet and was about to announce her departure when Meredith strode into the room. He paused to take the half-finished pint from Dave Rawlings hand, and emptied it in one. His eyes found Patsy's and he smiled.

"About bloody time." Patsy's father appeared by her side. "Tell him to sit down and shut up. I'm going to have my say now."

"Okay, Dad. Give us two minutes." She walked to Meredith who pulled her into his arms. "I take it everything is sorted."

"Not really. I just watched myself talking to the owner of a jewellers who had been robbed in Taunton. Only it wasn't me. I've also been speaking to the owners of a lot of similar shops in Exeter and Plymouth, all had been robbed. Four so far and counting. But the bit that really grates was seeing myself . . . Oh bollocks, I need a drink."

"Yourself? Someone who looks like you, you mean."

"Of course. It wasn't bloody me, was it? But there I was flashing what has to be assumed a false warrant card though. I can understand why they thought it was me."

"What happens now?"

"I spoke to Ashworth, who agreed I could leave as long as I appear at the station by eight in the morning, bringing the necessary evidence to show I was elsewhere at the time of the robberies. He knows there's an explanation but has to play the game. I think he was miffed he didn't get an invite to the wedding. For what it's worth he sends his apologies for disrupting our special day. Bloody understatement." He smiled as Dave Rawlings appeared with his beer. "Cheers, Dave." He took a sip. "I'd better apologise to your dad."

"No need. Sit down, I'll tell them to bring your food. Let him make his speech. I have no idea what he's going to say, but he needs to get it off his chest. He's been watching the door for the last hour."

"Okay, but I'll apologise anyway." Meredith turned to leave, and she grabbed his arm.

"How much like you was this man? How good were the images?"

"Mirror." Meredith grimaced. "Actually, not true. He wasn't as good-looking as me, but not far off. And he had a badly cut suit I wouldn't be seen dead in, but it was bloody spooky, and explains why they came after me." He kissed her forehead. "Let's get this done, and then we can talk."

"Okay, but the only explanation must be that it's your brother. I can't think of anything else, can you?"

Meredith's father had left his mother with three young children when Meredith was six years old. It had ruined his mother's life, and as a consequence her children's childhood. When his father appeared years later, he revealed he'd had a son with the woman he'd left them for, but Meredith hadn't been interested, and had ended up throwing his father out of the house.

"That was my guess. It was interesting explaining I had no idea what his name was, other than Meredith of course, I'll have a word with Julia once I've sorted your dad out. They're looking into it." This time he did step away, and holding out his hand, he walked towards her father. "Mr Hodge, I am so sorry about this. Unavoidable. I'm hoping you've got some sort of speech ready, because I need a moment to sort myself out."

Jim Hodge beamed. "I've told you before, John, call me Jim. Sit yourself down and get something to eat, and as soon as this lot have settled, I'll give it my best shot."

Twenty minutes later, he reminded Meredith for the fifth time how lucky he was, and caused Meredith to choke on his drink when he ended his speech by saying he'd not yet given up on having a grandchild.

Speeches over, Julia rested her head on Meredith's shoulder as he pulled her into a hug. "Why is nothing ever simple with you, John?"

"No idea, stops life getting boring though. Have you ever met our half-brother?"

Their father had not only left their home, but also left their mother without any financial support. As they grew older, Meredith and his two younger sisters had to watch their mother's downward spiral into alcoholism. Meredith never forgave his father, and had no interest in the half-brother resulting from his father's betrayal. As a result, to the best of his knowledge, his sisters hadn't either.

Pushing him away, Julia stared at him. "Where did that come from?

Did you invite him? Or are you getting soft in your old age?"

"No, I didn't invite him. The only person missing is Ann, but Canada is long way away. You didn't answer the question."

"I haven't met him, I didn't know our father, wherever he is, and did think about looking them up when the boys were small but never got around to it. Why are you asking?"

"Because I think he's turned up, and not in a good way."

"That's why you disappeared?"

"Yep. I think he's going to keep me busy for the foreseeable."

"I'd like to meet him, after all, just because our father was a total waste of space, doesn't mean he is. He is family, and family matters, even to you John. You've got it right this time, you've met your match, your padlock." She smiled at the reference to her first conversation with Patsy.

"I know I have, and yes he matters, very much at the moment, but not in the way you mean."

"Oh God, is he in trouble?"

"He will be when I catch up with him."

"Be gentle, John. Don't burn your bridges too soon. There might be a perfectly good explanation. What's his name by the way?"

"DCI John Meredith, apparently." Meredith shrugged. "His real name? No idea, yet."

"Oh boy, I need a drink."

"Good idea."

After another hour, the party moved onto the pub, and the newly married Mr and Mrs Meredith slipped away a little after eight o'clock. They headed for the hotel they had booked for the night. Two hours after they arrived, and lying in the large four-poster bed on the verge of sleep, Meredith's phone rang.

"Ignore it," Patsy murmured into his chest.

"I intend to. I'm not even going to see who it was." Meredith pulled her closer as the ringing stopped. "I doubt they'll find us here. Whatever it is can wait."

After a few seconds silence it rang again.

"I'm still ignoring it." Meredith was now fully awake again but didn't move. "I'll put it on silent if it rings again."

"Good, I . . . Oh. There goes mine, perhaps we should . . ."

Meredith threw back the duvet and swung his legs off the bed. "One bloody day, one bloody day, Hodge. That's all we asked."

Snatching up his phone he stared at the screen and showed it to Patsy. "Amanda. I think we should find out what's so urgent."

Returning Amanda's call, he paced to the window and stared out at the lights illuminating Bristol. "This had better be good," he snapped as Amanda greeted him.

6

Amanda handed Jim Hodge two glasses of water, and happy he and Barbara, his new wife, had everything they needed, said goodnight and went back downstairs.

The house was a little chaotic following the activities in preparation for the wedding, and as she was on an early shift the next day, she wanted to make sure it was in order before Patsy returned the next morning. It didn't take long, and tying a knot in the plastic refuse bag she headed for the bin. As she closed the bin, she heard someone walking up the front path, and went down the side of the house to investigate.

"Hello?" she called hesitantly, squinting at her watch, it was a little after ten thirty, and too late for visitors. She turned the corner to see a tall figure step up to the front door. "Can I help you?"

Amanda stopped walking, and remained at the corner of the house. She smiled as her father turned to look at her. "Dad! What are you doing here? Where's Patsy? Don't tell me you've had a row already, that would be impressive even for you."

"I'm sorry?" Ed Meredith turned to face Amanda as she walked forward.

"I asked where Patsy was. Why are you here?" Frowning she looked at the crumpled trousers and creased shirt. "What are you wearing?" She rubbed her hands up and down her upper arms. "Open the door, it's chilly standing here."

"I . . . I can't." Ed held out his hand. "Meredith—"

"How much had you had to drink? No keys and an introduction.

Bloody hell, Dad. Patsy must be fuming." Amanda turned away, "Come on, the back door is open. I'll make you a coffee."

Ed Meredith followed her. "I'm not your father"

Amanda's step faltered but she kept walking. "I think that one has been done to death. This is beginning to irritate now."

When Amanda was a child, to hurt Meredith, her mother had lied and told him that Amanda wasn't his daughter. It had caused them to lose touch for too many years, and it still hurt when she thought about it.

Her tone was sharp, and Ed increased his pace to catch up with her. He grabbed her arm. "I don't know what that means, but I'm your uncle, not your father."

Amanda caught the difference in his voice, and spun around. She peered into the face of the uncle she didn't know existed. He was the image of her father. Perhaps a few less lines at the corners of his eyes, which appeared less intense than her father's, but it was a startling sight.

Amanda grinned. "Well, hello, Uncle. Come in, I need to see this in the light." Hurrying him into the house, and standing in the bright light of the kitchen spotlights, she studied him again, her grin remained. "Uncanny. I can't believe the likeness."

She stepped closer to him. "You're a little shorter than Dad, and your hair is thinner, but . . . I'm almost lost for words. Have a seat. Can I get you a drink? Dad's not here. He won't be back until tomorrow. He got married today. Did you know? Or are you really, really, late for the wedding? Was he expecting you? Why don't I . . ." She laughed. "I'm sorry. It's the shock, I'm a little freaked out. So, drink?"

"Coffee, thank you. I need to speak to your father, it's urgent."

"Not tonight, I'm afraid. We have a spare room though, you can stay there until tomorrow." Amanda pointed the teaspoon at him. "Why don't I know about you? Are you the black sheep? Will I get in trouble if I let you stay here?" There was laughter in her voice, but she had a niggle inside that all was not right. "Was Dad expecting you?"

"We've never met. Listen, Amanda, I need you to call him. It could be a matter of life and death." Ed pinched the bridge of his nose, and Amanda gasped. "What?"

"Your mannerisms, it's weird seeing another version of my father sitting at the table. How come you've never met?" Amanda went to collect the milk from the fridge, but spun to face him. "How do you know my name?" She tutted. "Because you speak to him, I suppose. Sorry I was being dense."

"Nope, never spoken to the man. I only know I look like him because I've been mistaken for him more than a couple of times. All but one of them caused me grief."

"Never . . . why? How did you know . . ." Amanda frowned. "This isn't going to be good news, is it?"

Ed shook his head. "No. Do you know how to get hold of him? Can you give me a number?"

"Wait there, I'll try and call him. What's your name by the way?"

"Edward, Ed will do."

"Well, Uncle Ed, you wait right there, and I'll do my best."

Leaving Ed in the kitchen, Amanda went into the sitting room to call her father. After several attempts she gave up and tried Patsy. Patsy didn't answer either and she went back to the kitchen. As she explained to Ed that she'd failed to reach them, her phone rang. Stopping mid-sentence, she turned and walked back into the sitting room.

"Hi Dad, I think you're going to be surprised when I tell you who's sitting in the kitchen."

"It's my wedding night, Amanda, can you get to the point."

"I have an uncle apparently. He looks like you, he has the same mannerisms as you, but he's polite. At the moment, anyway. He insisted I call, he said it could be a matter of life and death. Shall I tell him you're not interested?"

"I'd ask you to tell me you were joking, but I know you're not. Hang on." Meredith's arm fell to his side and he turned to Patsy. "He's at the house."

"Who is?"

"My brother."

"Bloody hell!"

"Quite. I have to go, you know that."

Patsy had climbed out of bed, and pulled her robe around her naked body. "Dad and Barbara are there. You're bound to wake them. Can't he come here?"

"The hotel or the honeymoon suite?" Meredith's tone was sarcastic.

"Meredith, our life has been anything but simple. Our wedding was a fiasco. But our marriage has been consummated." Patsy allowed herself a smile. "So, if you can get this sorted without my father getting involved, I would appreciate it. He still likes you." Her smile became a grin. "We have a suite, you can see him in there." She pointed at the door which led to the comfortable lounge area.

It took only a few seconds for Meredith to agree. He lifted the phone. "Can you bring him here?"

"Not really. Well I can in a taxi, but I can't drive I've been drinking remember."

"Actually, that's a better idea, although he got there somehow, maybe he's got a car. Tell him where we are, and Patsy will meet him in the lobby."

Amanda hung up and walked back to the kitchen, a little miffed she wouldn't be in on the conversation. Ed looked at her expectantly.

"Dad says you can go to the hotel. It's not far, it's in town. Do you know Bristol? He's staying at the Marriott Royal on College Green."

"I know it. I don't know how I'll get there though. My car ran out of petrol, I walked the last couple of miles."

"You'll have to get a taxi. I'd drive you, but I've been drinking."

"If I had money, I'd have put some petrol in the car. I left in a hurry, forgot my wallet. Can I borrow your car?"

His smile was as disarming as her father's, but Amanda was wary. "I'm not insured for other drivers. I'll lend you the money for a taxi. I'll call one now." Pulling a magnetic card for a local taxi firm from the fridge door, she ordered a taxi. "Here in ten minutes. I'll get my purse."

As she climbed the stairs, she remembered she had barely five pounds in cash. She hesitated outside her father's bedroom door, wondering whether to disturb Jim and Barbara. Deciding against it, she went into her own bedroom, stripped off her dress and changed into jeans and a sweatshirt. Grabbing her purse, she hurried back to her uncle.

"I've not got enough cash, I'll come with you and we'll stop at a cashpoint." Her phone beeped and she glanced at the screen. "Taxi's here. Let's go."

* * *

Ed Meredith had the same stride as his brother, and Amanda hurried to keep up with him as they walked past the Cathedral towards the hotel. Ed glanced at the newly renamed City Hall.

"It's a long time since I've seen the Council House. I heard they

26

renamed it. There's always someone who thinks the past needs updating." He held his hands out. "I don't see the point. The past is the past, what happened, happened, nothing's going to change it."

"That depends on what you're talking about, I suppose. There are some issues which are politically sensitive, so it's nice that someone listens and changes with public opinion."

"You're a liberal?" Ed stopped at the impressive entrance to the hotel and looked at the façade. "But I think that's a conversation for another day. What's your dad like?"

Amanda laughed. "Unique. I don't have enough words or time. To summarise, he's a good man, but it takes some people a while to get there."

"A good man," Ed mumbled as he allowed Amanda to enter the hotel in front of him.

"There's Patsy. Oh, she's seen you."

Amanda grinned as an open-mouthed Patsy approached, her eyes glued to Ed's face. Her mouth closed as she reached them. She held out her hand.

"Patsy H . . . Meredith. Pleased to meet you."

"Ed. You too." His smile was lopsided as he appraised her quickly.

Patsy blinked. He was scruffy, looked like he needed a shower, but he was a slightly younger version of her new husband. She jerked her thumb over her shoulder. "The lift's this way." Ed nodded and strode towards it, clearly in a hurry to get to his brother.

Patsy grabbed Amanda's arm. "Are you as freaked out as I am?"

"I was, I thought it was Dad at first."

"Why are you here by the way, does Meredith know you were coming?"

"He's got no transport, no money, and no coat. What you see is it. I didn't think Dad would fork out to put him up here, so I came to escort him home."

"He lives in Bristol?"

"No idea. I'll ask."

Ed was watching the numbers change above the lift door. Amanda went to stand next to him.

"Do you live in Bristol, Uncle Ed?"

He glanced down at her. "That sounds odd. But I'm sure I'll get used to it." The lift doors opened, and he stepped aside to allow them to enter. "Which floor?" He held his finger over the pad.

Patsy didn't miss the fact he'd not answered the question. "Six."

The three remained silent for the short journey, and Patsy stepped out first. "This way." They walked to the end of the corridor and Patsy opened the door.

Meredith was standing with his back to them looking down on College Green, he turned slowly.

Patsy ushered Ed in. "Meredith, this is Ed. Ed, Meredith . . . er, John."

"Meredith will do."

The two men appraised each other.

Meredith hadn't moved, so Ed stepped forward his hand held out in greeting. Meredith ignored it, and as his brother reached him, and without warning, he pulled back his right arm and punched Ed in the face. Ed teetered for a second before his knees buckled. The two women dashed forward and saved him the indignity of hitting the floor.

"Dad! What on earth has come over you?" Amanda settled Ed onto the small sofa.

"What are you doing here? I thought you were putting him in a taxi?"

"No cash. Why did—"

"I take it you know." Ed grimaced as he moved his lower jaw from side to side.

"I do, and I can guess why. But what I'm really interested in, is why you're here?" Meredith looked down at his half-brother.

"I'm in trouble, deep shit trouble, and I had nowhere else to go. I came to explain."

"Well, that would have been nice if you had done it before I was arrested, and before our wedding was ruined."

"You were arrested?" Amanda removed her hand from her uncle's shoulder. "Because of Uncle Ed?" She stepped in front of Ed. "What's been going on?"

Taking her by the shoulders, Meredith pushed her towards a chair. "I'll do the questions." He looked at his half-sibling, still shocked at the resemblance. "Why did you think I'd help you?"

"I didn't. But I thought it was a safe bet you wouldn't kill me, turn me in perhaps, but not kill me."

"No. Still don't understand." Meredith glanced at Patsy. "Is there any alcohol in the fridge, I need a drink?" He looked back at his brother. "Carry on, I'm all ears."

"I've been stupid." Ed held up his hand to silence Meredith. "Which I know you know, it's a long story," His eyes darted between Patsy and Amanda, clearly not comfortable speaking in front of them. "And I want out, but it seems I'm considered too valuable. I thought if I came to you, you'd hand me over, testify against me, and bang - I'm locked up through no fault of my own. Done, over, ended." He lifted one shoulder as though that explained all.

"Six months for impersonating a police officer, then the added charges for robbery, assault, and whatever else you've been up to, my guess is that's a five stretch minimum. The fact you thought it was the better option is interesting though. You're right by the way, I will be handing you over, whose idea was this?"

"I don't know who's at the top of the chain, but you know the bloke who got me into it." Ed shrugged. "He certainly knew you well."

"Name." Meredith rolled his eyes as Patsy handed Ed a beer.

"Tony Beresford."

"Uncle Tony is involved in this . . . whatever this is?" Amanda looked at her father.

"Ah, so he's related. I should have guessed." Ed took a swig from the bottle. "I thought he knew a lot about you for it to have been a professional relationship."

Tony Beresford had been a good friend of Meredith's when they were teenagers, their closeness lasted only until his affair with Meredith's first wife was revealed. It deteriorated further when they moved away from Bristol taking Amanda with them.

"Not related, no. He was once a mate, and he was Amanda's stepfather for a while. Last I heard he was in Dartmouth."

"He said he'd been inside a couple of times."

"So how did you meet?"

"My . . . *our* father died a couple of months back." Pausing, Ed looked at Meredith but there was no reaction. "I can see you're moved."

"Good riddance. Get on with it."

"I went down to Exmouth for the funeral. My mother took his loss badly, and I stayed on for a while. I was in a bar one night and Tony marches up to me, held out his hand and said something about burying the past, it was nice to see me, and asked how Amanda was." Tipping back his head, Ed emptied the bottle. "Any chance of another?"

Patsy collected fresh drinks. Ed winked his thanks as she handed him the bottle and her breath caught in her throat. She could see why everyone had been taken in.

"Thanks, much appreciated. Apologies about the wedding, I didn't know."

"Accepted. Life with Meredith is never—"

"Can we get on with it?" Meredith interrupted. "Where is Beresford now? I'd like a few words." Meredith watched Ed's shoulders jerk as he asked the question, it was almost as though he wasn't expecting it. "Do you know?"

"Can I speak to you alone?" Glancing at the women, Ed twitched a smile. "Sorry, ladies, no offence."

Patsy looked at Meredith, it was an odd question given how much they already knew. She didn't want to be dismissed.

Meredith shrugged. "Why?" He didn't care one way or another, but he wanted to make Ed feel uncomfortable. "I'm happy for them to stay."

"It's sensitive." Ed glared at him. "Best not discussed in front of ladies."

"Patsy is as tough as old boots, and Amanda is my daughter, so unless they want to leave, get on with it and stop pissing about."

"He's in the boot of his car," Ed snapped, and drew a finger along his throat. His eyes locked onto Meredith.

"Oh, you've cut his throat, have you?"

"Not me."

Amanda gasped. "Are you serious?"

"Deadly."

"And you know this how?" Meredith dropped into a chair, and lifted a hotel notepad and pencil from the small ornate coffee table.

"I saw it happen. I saw them bundle him in, and as it was the only form of transport, immediately they'd gone, I had to take the car to get away. They didn't know I was there." He looked at his feet. "It's why I had to come to you."

"No more buggering about . . . what did you say your name was?" Ed snorted amusement. "Ed."

"Right, Ed, straight answers. Where is the car now? Who are they?"

"The car is on one of the streets off the Portway, not sure if it's Seamills or Shirehampton, but I can take you there. I ran out of petrol."

He held out empty hands. "Had to leave without my wallet."

"And they . . ."

"No idea. As I said, it was a need-to-know operation, and I didn't need to know. The bloke who killed him was a bruiser. Six foot plus, eighteen stone. Tony put up a good fight, but he had no chance."

"You didn't help him?"

"Nope. Didn't know the bloke had a knife, I thought it was a punch-up at first. As I didn't know why they were fighting, I didn't feel it was my place. Then the bruiser pulls the knife from a holster on his ankle and it was over in seconds. There was little point then."

"Where were you? And what were they driving? You must have some useful information."

"In a disused layby on the road to Chudleigh. There's a sign stating the layby is closed. It's overgrown, so if you do drive in you can't be seen from the road. They weren't there when we arrived, and I stepped into the bushes to take a pee. I didn't see them arrive, I heard them. I heard shouting, went to see what was happening, and it was done. They were driving a Mercedes SLK on a sixty-six plate. Anything else?"

"You can drop the fucking attitude for a start. You come to me, when I'm already pissed off with you, and ask for help. You tell me an old mate is dead in the back of an abandoned car, and you take that tone. Don't push me, pal."

Meredith was jabbing his finger, he'd given up on Tony Beresford long ago, but the thought of his old friend being murdered and stuffed into the back of a car and abandoned, upset him.

Patsy could see he was ready to blow, and she put her hand on his shoulder. "I think the first thing to do, is recover Tony's body. Then Ed can explain to the officers who arrested you what's been going on."

"What officers? When did all this happen?" Ed seemed genuinely concerned.

"This afternoon, I didn't make my wedding reception thanks to you." Meredith had calmed a little, but his tone was still sarcastic. "I can't believe you don't know more than that. How did Tony rope you in? Why did you agree? Who knows you wanted out? Was that why Tony was killed? Because if so, they'll be after you too. Are you sure you weren't followed? Because if you were, as well as ruining our wedding, you've put my family at risk. Not acceptable."

"I wasn't followed. If I was, they'd have picked me up as soon as I had to abandon the car. For the record, *again*, I don't know who else was involved. I got all my information from Tony."

"You cretin!" Meredith shook his head in disgust and Ed jumped to his feet, it was his turn to jab his finger.

"Don't start insulting me, I took that punch because I deserved it. Enough now."

"Or what?" Meredith also got to his feet. "Because let me tell you something, from where I'm standing—"

"Can we find Uncle Tony please? I know he was a bastard to Mum in the end, but is anyone else comfortable with him being out there somewhere?" Bottom lip, quivering, Amanda flipped her hand towards the window. "Dad, you have to call this in, he was family – sort of."

"I know, and I will, but before I hand him over to those idiots, I want to know what I'm dealing with." A thought occurred to him and he took a step closer to Ed. "If Tony was holding all the cards, did these mysterious men you didn't ask the names of, know you weren't really a copper?"

Ed shrugged. "I've no i—" Sentence unfinished, Ed slumped back onto the sofa as Meredith punched him again.

Shouting for him to stop, Patsy grabbed a handful of tissues and handed them to Ed. "Meredith! Stop it! Ed use these, I'll go and get a towel." Patsy gave Meredith a warning glance before hurrying to the bathroom.

Pushing the tissues into his nostrils, Ed glared at Meredith. "It was quick easy money." His voice sounded odd. "No one got . . ." He gagged as the blood trickled back down his throat and pushing Meredith aside, ran to the bathroom, ignoring Patsy who was returning with the towel.

Meredith followed him and watched him while he retched and spat blood into the basin.

When he'd regained control, Ed splashed water over his face, and lifting a face towel from the stack, gingerly cleaned away the blood. He turned to Meredith, his anger barely under control. "Last fucking one. I came to you. I don't think a copper is allowed to assault a suspect, is he?"

"Last one when I decide. And for the record, I'm not currently a copper, so it makes no difference." Meredith had to turn away, it was a surreal experience looking at this man, his half-brother, and seeing himself. "Come and sit down, and if you don't give me any more shit answers, I might stop hitting you."

"Oh for God's sake, Meredith. I know he dropped you in it, but he's here now. Let's accept yours is the biggest and move on, shall we? What now?" Patsy stood, hands on hips, glaring at the men.

Ed was about to sit down when his hand flew to his pocket. "My phone's ringing," he announced shocked.

"And that is unusual because . . . you have no friends or acquaintances who would want to call you?"

"Because this is the phone Tony gave me. My own is still at my mother's. I've only ever had a call from Tony on this." His hand dropped to his side. "It's stopped."

"Yes, we know. Stop stating the bloody obvious and find out who it was." Meredith held out his hand. "You're sure Tony was dead?"

"I'm not an idiot! Have you ever seen a man have his throat cut? I hadn't, but it doesn't take long to bleed out. He was dead before they put him in the car."

"Did you check?" Amanda asked.

"I promise you I didn't need to." He handed the phone to Meredith.

Meredith looked at the screen. "No caller ID." The phone beeped. "But they left a message." He held the phone to his ear.

His frown became a snarl and Patsy noticed his free hand make a fist. She stepped forward. "Ed, sit down." She looked at Meredith. "Not good news I take it."

"Nope. They've tracked this phone. They want to meet tomorrow, and . . ." Meredith held up his hand for silence. "Ha! They also say where and when."

"Where?" Ed looked concerned.

"It doesn't matter, you won't be there".

"You're going to meet them? Well I'd suggest you take back-up, and watch the bruiser, he's carrying."

"Shut up." Switching off the phone, and removing the sim card, Meredith slid the phone into his pocket. "We need to get a move on." He went to the bedroom and collected his own phone. He tried first Seaton, and then Trump, but finally got an answer from Dave Rawlings. "Why is no one answering?" he demanded. He listened to the answer. His eyes closed and his sigh was deep. "Shit! I forgot. Round them up and meet me at the bar in The Royal." He rolled his eyes at Patsy. "Yes, I'm aware it's my wedding night. My duties are fulfilled, and I have someone I want you to meet. Oh, and Dave, find an all-night chemist on the way, I think there's one on the centre, and grab me some hair dye . . . No, I don't care what colour. Just do it! Call me when you get here."

"Who was that?" Ed's eyes followed Meredith as he paced back into the bedroom.

"Friends. Coppers to you, we need to check your story before they take you in."

Patsy watched the relief flood through Ed Meredith. His shoulders slumped and his chin rested on his chest. She stepped forward and patted his back. "Meredith will get this sorted." She gave him a warm smile as he looked up at her, and studied the detail of his face. "I have to confess, I'm finding the likeness a little off-putting."

"I would imagine you do, it took Tony . . ." He looked away, his lips pursed. "Well, Tony struggled with it too."

Meredith reappeared, now dressed in shirt and trousers, he waved his finger at Patsy.

"Don't start feeling sorry for him. He's a conniving little shit who ruined our wedding day."

"Dad, there might be a perfectly good explanation." Amanda went to collect the kettle and took it to the bathroom. She grimaced as she caught Ed's response.

"No, there's not."

7

Meredith knocked back the remainder of his beer as Rawlings and Trump ambled into the bar. Sliding from the stool he jerked his thumb towards the lifts. "This way."

"Thank you for coming, chaps. Can I get you a drink for your trouble?" Dave Rawlings called as he and Trump followed Meredith. "Seaton won't be joining us, too drunk."

"Well you've all been drinking all day. But thanks for coming, you'll be glad you did."

Meredith hit the button and looked at the two men. Trump's eyes were not quite looking in the same direction, and Rawlings' shirt tail poked out below his jacket. He clasped a bag in one hand and swung it towards Meredith.

"I've got it." He grinned. "Hope you like the colour."

Meredith caught the bag and peered inside, he smiled for the first time since Amanda's call. "Perfect."

"What's if for, sir? We've been trying to work it out." Trump almost looked at the bag.

"You'll see." Meredith stepped into the lift. As the doors opened on the top floor, his lips twitched. "Brace yourselves." Throwing open the door to the room, he waved the men forward. "After you."

The two men greeted Patsy and Amanda, Trump began thanking them for a wonderful party, when Ed appeared in the bathroom door, and raised a hesitant hand in greeting.

"Good Lord." Trump pointed at him.

"Fuck me." Rawlings looked at the coffee pot ordered from room service. "I think I need one of those."

Patsy laughed. "It's a little spooky, isn't it?" She gestured to the sofa. "Sit down, Dave, you look a little wobbly."

"Thanks." He grabbed Trump's still outstretched arm and pulled him forward. "Black." Once seated, he glanced back and forth between the Meredith brothers. "Is this what the dye was for?"

"It was. I know I'm the better looking, and if we were side by side even an idiot could tell us apart, but until this thing is done, and as I want to spend as little time with him as possible, I need him to look different, this is the quickest way." He waved the bag.

"I am not dying my hair." Ed pushed his fringe away from his forehead.

"You are, and from where I stand you have little choice." Meredith pulled an upright chair away from the desk and set it next to the coffee table. "Have a seat. While we're making you look beautiful you can start at the beginning and talk us through how Amanda's stepfather ended up in the back of your car with his throat cut."

"Throat cut?" Trump got to his feet. "I think I need some cold water splashing." He fanned his face with his hands. "I need to be soberer than this – is that a word? Of all the days to turn up." Slipping out of his jacket, he dropped it on the sofa and headed for the bathroom.

"Which one of you ladies would like to do the honours?" Meredith asked.

"I'll do it. I've done mine a few times." Amanda took the bag and removed the box. "Good brand, Dave. Uncle Ed, you need to take off your shirt, it might get ruined otherwise."

"He needs to take off everything." Meredith jerked his thumb towards the bedroom. "This way."

Ed didn't move. "Dye my hair and strip off? I'm not about to do a runner, even with my clothes on."

"Evidence, you dolt. Move it." Meredith held the door open.

The pair returned minutes later. Meredith carried a hotel laundry bag containing Ed's clothes which he placed by the door. Ed wore a pair of Meredith's jeans and hotel slippers, his torso remained naked.

"Your dad doesn't want dye on his tee shirt," Ed explained to Amanda, who slipped a towel around his shoulders, before pulling on the plastic gloves supplied with the dye. "What colour is it?"

"Umm, red." Removing the lid from the tube she tilted his head back.

"As in auburn? I'm not sure it will suit me."

"Possibly . . ." Amanda applied the first of the dye along Ed's parting and began to work it in with a brush.

"From the beginning," Meredith instructed, his lips twitched as Amanda made another parting in Ed's hair, and applied a second row of dye. "Red is red. Not auburn." He smirked as Ed's eyes narrowed.

"More coffee?" Trump lifted the pot. "I'm ready. Mr—"

"Ed. His name is Ed," Meredith warned. "Don't start calling him Meredith." Perching on the side of the chair he looked his brother in the eye. "From the beginning. We'll decide what is and isn't relevant. Kick off with meeting Tony."

"As I said earlier, I was in Exmouth for our father's funeral. I went—"

"When was this?"

Meredith turned to look at Trump who had snorted.

"You don't know when your own father died?" Trump was incredulous.

"No. Don't care. Didn't know him, can we get on?"

"Sorry, of course, sir." Trump smiled at Ed. "Continue."

"It was in November." He turned to Meredith and Amanda pulled his head back to the former position, continuing to brush the dye into his hair. "If you're not a copper, why's he calling you, sir?"

"Because I'm important. Get on with it."

"Dad died in October, buried on the twelfth of November, and it was about a week later. I went into a bar on the High Street in Exeter, took a perch and chatted to the barmaid. I was aware he'd been staring at me, but I wasn't looking for trouble, so I avoided eye contact."

He shrugged and Amanda tutted as she repositioned his head. "He went to the gents and detoured on his way back. He held out his hand and said we should put the past behind us. Bygones et cetera. I told him I didn't have a clue what he was talking about, but he persisted."

Meredith put his phone on record and placed it on the coffee table.

"Speak slowly and clearly. Talk us through from the first meeting to the part where you abandon his body." He ignored Ed's protest. "Get on with it."

37

8 CHAPTER NAME

Tony Beresford placed his empty glass on the bar and looked at Meredith. He knew Meredith had seen him and was surprised he hadn't even acknowledged his presence. Deciding to challenge him, he walked to the other end of the bar.

"Come on, Meredith, I know you clocked me. It was a long time ago, let me buy you a pint."

"You can if you like, Peroni, cheers." Ed handed him his glass. "I saw you staring, but I don't have a clue who you are."

"I know I've lost a bit of hair . . . okay, a lot, but it's Tony." Tony shook his head as Meredith raised his eyebrows. "Meredith, have you got dementia? Tony Beresford. I was with Karen, your ex. Your daughter Amanda lived with us."

It was clear Meredith had no idea what he was referring to, so he tried a different approach. Lowering his voice, Tony leaned forward, "You fucked my mother when we were at school."

Ed pulled his head back and grinned. "I don't think I did. That I would remember."

"She's dead now. Cancer. For some reason, she felt the need to confess all before she went. You weren't the first, nor the last. Seems she taught half my mates the facts of life." His shoulders twitched. "Long time ago."

The barmaid returned with their drinks. And he chinked his glass against Ed's.

"Cheers. Sorry . . . Tony did you say? But you have the wrong man."

"I do not. Are you expecting me to believe you're not John Meredith?"

"I am. Because I'm Ed Meredith. I understand I have an older half-brother, and some half-sisters. Never met 'em though."

Tony climbed onto the next stool. "Bugger me, you're serious. Ha! Well, let me tell you, Ed, you are the spitting image of your brother. I doubt your mother would be able to tell you apart."

"I'm sure she would. How long since you've seen him?"

"Best part of twenty years. But I've seen his photo in the papers, and he's been on Crimebusters a couple of times. You are identical." Tony studied Ed's features again. It occurred to him this might be Meredith stringing him along for some reason.

"Crimebusters? What did he do?" Now interested, Ed leaned forward.

"Appeal for witnesses. He's a copper." Tony turned his nose up.

"You don't approve?"

"Not in my line of work. Moved away from Bristol to keep out of his way, still ended up inside though." Tony finished his pint. "Your round."

Ed called the order to the barmaid, then asked, "Inside? What did you do?"

"There's a list, but to keep it simple, I used to borrow things."

"Without the owner's permission, and never returned them, I'm guessing." Ed smiled and paid the barmaid.

"Correct." Tony looked at him from the corner of his eye. "You're not a copper, are you?"

"No." Ed laughed. "I've borrowed a few things myself in the past, but needs must and what have you. By trade I'm a landscape gardener."

"Have you done time?" He glanced at Ed's hands. They were a worker's hands. His nails were bitten, his fingers calloused, Meredith would not have hands like that. He smiled again as he tried to work out how he could use Ed's likeness to Meredith for his own gain.

"No, I'm minor league, it wasn't a career choice. I got a slap on the wrist once. It wasn't regular, how should I . . . I was an opportunist in times of need."

"But now you're gardening."

"Yep. More of a live-in handyman. I've not needed to borrow anything for a long time."

"Do you live locally?"

"No, I'm staying with my mother for a couple of weeks. We buried my dad last week."

"And Meredith wasn't there?"

"No. As I said, I've never met him. They weren't close."

"That much is clear. I don't think I ever met his old man. Had to help sort his mother a couple of times though, she liked a drink." Tony got off his stool and moved closer. "If I can find a use for you which pays well, do you fancy making some easy money?"

"I might. Depends what you want me to do. I have no intentions of residing at Her Majesty's pleasure."

Tony slapped him on the back. "Good man, I'll keep you safe. I've got to see a man about an opportunity, let me have your number." He tapped the number into his phone as Ed dictated. "I'll be in touch." Emptying his glass, he got to his feet. "Give me a couple of hours."

"I'll be around," Ed glanced at his watch. "Sarah finishes in half an hour." He smiled at the barmaid who blushed.

"Chip off the old block. Still can't get over it." A grin and another slap on the back for Ed, and Tony left with his phone clamped to his ear.

Two hours later, Beresford watched Ed saunter back into the bar. He lifted his drink in salute.

"Sorry to interrupt your evening." He smirked as he handed Ed his drink. "It will be worth it."

"You didn't interrupt." Ed even had the same twinkle in his eyes when he smiled. "I was waiting for my taxi when you called. I simply diverted it. What will be worth it?"

"How does a thousand quid for half an hour's work grab you?"

Ed sipped his beer before responding. "Go on."

"The details are being finalised, but as we've only just met, and Meredith is your brother, first I need to know I can trust you."

"And I you. What do you suggest?"

"I was just thinking about that. I need you to break the law."

"How seriously? Like I said, I have no urge to get banged up."

Tony grinned. "I need proof you've borrowed something. I need something to hold against you if you are playing me."

Ed looked around the bar and lifted his glass to his lips and emptied it. "Get your phone ready." He instructed and beckoned over the barman who had replaced Sarah. "I'll try a pint of the real ale." He pointed to a pump and turned to Tony. "What can I get you?"

"I'll stick with the lager. Ta." Tony's glass joined Ed's on the bar.

"The barrel's gone on the ale. I'll have to whip down to the cellar." The barman removed the empty glasses and disappeared through a door at the rear of the bar.

"Ready?" Ed slid off his stool and walked swiftly but calmly to the hatch at the end of the bar. Ducking under it, he walked to the till and lifted the card tucked between a box of straws and the cash register. He swiped the card, opened the till and lifted out a wad of notes. He paused only to smile at Tony's phone before returning to his seat.

There were a handful of customers dotted around the bar, but none so much as glanced over. Tony nodded his approval as Ed returned.

"Do I get half of that? How did you know the barrel had gone?" Tony slid the phone back into his pocket.

"Nope, you get the memory. I knew because I was watching him, last customer changed to a different beer. Now, what is it you're proposing?"

"I've been to see a contact who has a couple of little jobs lined up. He's working on the detail, so I can't tell you what or where yet, all you need to know, is that you have to impersonate your brother."

"As a copper?"

"Of course as a copper." Tony rolled his eyes. "Otherwise we could use anyone."

"What do I have to do?" Ed smiled at the barman as he returned. "Only a half, thanks." He called.

"Not sure yet. He didn't say."

"Who's *he*?" Ed pulled a note from the wad he'd taken from the till and handed it to the barman. "Keep the change."

Tony waited until the barman had busied himself at the other end of the bar. "Need-to-know. You don't. It goes without saying, he's a bad man, and the further away you are the better."

"Yet you still do business with him?" Ed's eyes narrowed. "Why would that be, if he's best given a wide berth? I have to say you're not selling this well."

"You're as sharp as your brother, I'll give you that." Tony rubbed his hand over his face. "Ah, bollocks. In for a penny. I pissed him off, you don't need the detail, but now I owe him. You are my payment, so don't cock up."

"What? You don't know me. You don't know what I'm capable of, or if it's even possible for me to carry this off, and yet you are placing so much trust in me. That's dangerous. Now I'm definitely worried if I can trust you. You're a risk taker with a bad record, I'm not sure I need that in my life."

"You're right. I'm fucking desperate. I admit it. I need you to do this. I'll tell you what, I'll stick another five hundred a pop on for you." Tony forced his grin.

"Which tells me you're also going to be earning out of this mysterious thing you want to drag me into. So, what do I have to do, or is that a secret too?" Ed sipped the real ale and grimaced. "That's disgusting, I'll have another pint of lager."

He studied Beresford and decided even though the money was good, it wasn't worth the risk, not for someone he didn't know, and who clearly had cocked-up in the past. He chinked his fresh drink against Tony's. "Cheers. No offence, but I don't think this is going to work out. Thanks for the consideration though."

Tony grabbed his arm. "Don't be hasty, mate. Wait and hear what you have to do first, I bet it'll be of interest."

"And your role . . . is what?"

"Gofer. The boss man knows Meredith, the real one, and he doesn't want him to know he's involved. I'm to be the go-between. He tells me, I tell Meredith, or you as it happens."

"Are you telling me, this big, bad boss man, who you're afraid of, doesn't know I'm not my brother?"

Tony shrugged. "No. Look, mate, if I'd told him that, I'd have been cut out of the loop, and my debt would go unpaid. I wouldn't be needed, think about it, it makes sense."

"For you." Ed began to shake his head. "No, no. Sorry, Tony, the more you tell me the less I like it."

"It's good money, and I'm doing you a favour by being involved. If he thinks it's Meredith, and he's at arm's length, he has no hold over you. When you're done, you're done, you can walk away without fear of it catching up with you. Look, why don't you see what he wants and then decide. You've nothing to lose."

"When will I know? I've got a job to get back to." Ed was already sliding from the stool. He held out his hand. "Give me a call tomorrow, if I don't hear from you, I'll assume it's gone pear-shaped, and get myself home. If you do call, I'm making no promises."

"Deal. Where is home by the way?" Tony shook his hand.

"Not sure that's relevant." Ed pulled a twenty-pound note from the wad and dropped it on the bar. "Have a drink on me." Smiling, he turned and walked out of the bar.

* * *

Tony Beresford received the call the next morning. He called Ed, and they arranged to meet in the same bar for lunch. This time Tony chose to sit at a table in the corner. He ordered the drinks and asked for a couple of menus. It was the same barman as the night before.

"Coming right up. You were in here last night, weren't you?"

"I was. Why?"

"We had some money go missing from the till and I wondered if you saw anything?"

"No, sorry mate. Don't you have cameras?" Tony cast his eyes around the walls of the bar.

"Only on the outside. Thanks anyway. I'll get you those menus." He glanced at the door as it opened. "Here's your friend, I'll ask him too."

Ed shook his head frowning. "Never saw a thing, and I didn't leave the bar. How much was it?"

"Couple of hundred. Bloody thieves, I hate 'em. Soup of the day is parsnip, and the special is steak pie." Collecting some menus, he placed them on the table. "Give me a shout when you're ready."

Ed pulled out a chair. "So, what does he want me to do?"

"Let's order first. I like the sound of the pie."

Orders placed, Tony spoke quietly and quickly. "There are some jobs lined up. Robbing jewellery shops mainly, and you've solved a major problem for them. If you'll do it, he's upped the price to three thousand."

Ed frowned. "I'm not robbing anyone. Those places have high tech security, nah, not for me, my friend."

"You don't have to rob them idiot. They have been watching these places for months, they know the procedures on opening and closing, the alarm systems, everything. Their problem was how to disable the cameras—"

"I can't do that either. I can mess about with electrical—"

"If you would shut up for just one minute and hear me out, you'll find out what you do have to do! God, you're hard work. Must run in the family." Tony took a large draught of his drink.

44

"We're not family, simply related. Carry on, I won't interrupt."

"Anyway, they know the type of systems used in the places they're interested in, and he's got a list of four where the equipment has yet to go digital, so there are hard copies of the recordings. Your job – as a policeman – will be to collect those." Tony clapped his hands. "Simple!"

"So that would be twelve grand." Ed pursed his lips. "Keep talking." Added to his savings, that would give him enough to put down a deposit on his own place, and all for a couple of hours' work.

"It would. Long story short, we won't be told the exact location until an hour before the job, then we need to have you in position, so you can catch their exit and go in and deal with the staff. You'll say you saw them running, flash your warrant card, pretend to call it in, take the recordings and be away sharpish."

"My warrant card?"

"Getting it sorted, once we've finished here. You're in then?"

"Probably, I still don't understand why they need me, anyone with an ounce of savvy could imitate a copper."

"They don't know you're imitating him, remember?" Tony rolled his eyes. "Keep up, Ed. When this moves it's going to go fast so I need you to process a little faster." He wound his index finger in circles against his temple.

"I'm thinking just fine, thanks. Is this top bloke thick?"

"No, why?"

"Because any sensible person would know it would only be a matter of time before," Ed counted the reasons off on his fingers, "one, it goes wrong on the job, two, someone realises it's my brother taking the recordings, three, I'm caught on external cameras . . . I could go on."

"That's why he likes it. Even if none of that happens, he's got Meredith by the short and curlies. He likes that. So, in answer to your objections, one, don't cock up, two, who cares, you're not your brother, and three, who cares, you're not your brother."

Ed smiled. "I like those odds, I'm not prone to cocking up. What happens now?"

"We wait for the call. They're getting everything lined up. By the way these jobs are not necessarily local, have you got transport?"

"A bike."

"Push?" Tony was joking, but his smile fell away.

"Yep. Cycle everywhere. Good for your health and the environment."

"Shit, I didn't think you people actually existed. What do you do if it rains?"

"Get wet. No such thing as bad weather, only bad clothing." Ed pushed his glass to one side to allow the waiter to place their meals on the table. "If I am picked up on some camera or other no one would expect me to get away on a bike."

"You're serious, aren't you?"

"-ish. I take it you have transport?" Ed waited for Tony to nod, "Then that's how you could earn your cut. I'm starving let me eat while I have a think."

There was little else Ed could question without more detail. But he liked the idea of the money, and it would be his brother and not him in the firing line. Meal finished, he went with Tony to get his photograph taken, before cycling back to his mother's house to await the call. She was delighted he'd be staying a little longer.

* * *

"So, without a thought to Meredith, and what impact it might have on him and his family you decided to do it." Patsy stood in front of Ed, she had intended to mop up the dye running down his forehead but decided it could stain.

"I didn't know him. I needed the money." Ed shrugged. "I'm here now."

Meredith poured himself more coffee. "Keep talking. This bloke clearly knows me well enough to want something on me, but I'm no nearer working out who it is." He pointed at the plastic bag encasing Ed's hair. "How much longer?"

"About twenty minutes." Amanda yawned. "Then he needs to shampoo it. I'm exhausted."

"There's no need for you to stay. Get yourself off home. We'll catch you in the morning."

"I'm going nowhere until someone has recovered Uncle Tony's body."

Meredith could see there was little point in arguing so he returned his attention to Ed. "Get on with it."

9

Tony called Ed a little before midnight. "First one is tomorrow morning at eight. I'll have your warrant card when I pick you up. Don't forget smart suit, clean shoes. You have to dress the part too, don't forget."

"Ah."

"What does 'ah' mean?"

"I have shoes which I could clean, but I don't have a suit."

"Everyone has a suit. What did you wear to the funeral for God's sake?"

"Trousers, white shirt, black tie. I've never had the need of a suit, I wasn't going to waste the money for a twenty-minute funeral service."

"Shit, shit, shit!" Each word increased in volume. "We don't have time to buy you one. We have to be in Exeter by eight." Tony fell silent for a moment. "I think Tesco opens early. I'll check. You'd better keep your fingers crossed or you'll be wearing mine, and your trousers will be arguing with your ankles. I can't believe you didn't wear a suit to your father's funeral."

"What time are you picking me up?" Ed ignored the criticism.

"Seven. Be ready, and at least wear your funeral outfit in case."

* * *

The next morning, dressed in a black shiny polyester suit which gave off bursts of static every now and again, Ed sat with Tony in the window of McDonald's watching the High Street. They were the only customers opting to eat in, everyone else chose to hurry away with their breakfast choices.

Tony checked his watch for the umpteenth time, and looked at Ed. "Any minute now. The assistant usually arrives on the number twenty-three bus. After it goes past, she'll be here in seconds. Our blokes will be ready to escort her in. Then it will take no longer than ten minutes." He laughed. "Meredith would have refused to do this job, purely based on what you're wearing."

"Vain, is he?"

"Umm, not really. Arrogant, fussy, opinionated, but he did like nice clothes. He's a sharp dresser."

"Well good for him." Ed looked down. "This is shit though. I'm sweating buckets dressed in this plastic thing."

"Beggars and choosers, mate. For twenty quid, what did you . . . here comes the bus. Sit tight." Tony pushed the tray in front of him into the centre of the table, his food barely touched. His eyes focused on the jeweller's opposite. "You know what to say."

"I do. Now I know to be arrogant too. Is that her?" He watched a young woman, in her mid-twenties walk up the hill towards the shop. She was searching in her handbag. "Looking for the keys, do you – oh, her phone."

Jenny Harris dialled her boss. She did the same every day. The rule was she could only open up if he was within five minutes of her. She had yet to work out why he didn't simply leave earlier. He was the one with the car, he never had to stand in the cold and the rain awaiting her arrival. Call complete, she dropped the phone into her handbag and pulled the keys from her pocket. He was parking the car.

Stooping, she turned the key in the lock that held the shutter in place, and with a little flick of her foot it slid up revealing the shop front. The displays were empty except for the cheapest items which weren't considered worth the effort of locking away each night.

Inserting the key into the front door, Jenny didn't notice the two workmen increase their pace. Pushing the door open, she winced at the high-pitched bleeping as the alarm detected her presence. Opening the door to the cupboard on her right, she punched in the code and the bleeping stopped.

"Jesus Christ!" she screamed as she turned to find a burly figure, wearing a high visibility jacket and a balaclava, standing behind her.

"Oh, no. Please—"

Her plea was silenced as a gloved hand was clamped over her mouth.

"Shut it, and you'll be fine." He took the keys from her hand and tossed them to a second, identically dressed accomplice. "Let's put the kettle on for the boss."

Pulling her close, he marched her to the rear door, where he waited until the other man had secured the front door and hurried to unlock the rear door. Once the door had closed behind them, he demanded, "How long before he gets here?"

"Now. He was in the car park. Five minutes. I don't know, please don't hurt me."

A chair was pulled forward and she was bound to it before tape was fixed across her eyes and her mouth.

"Sit tight. Don't move and you'll be just fine." He turned as a bell sounded, telling him Simon Evans had arrived. He wheeled Jenny to the far side of the small office area. "Come on, Simon, don't keep us waiting."

The door opened.

"Jenny, I hope you've put the—" Simon Evans dropped to the floor as he was coshed from behind. He was still unconscious as they taped his wrists and ankles and blindfolded him.

"Right, quick now."

It took seconds to unlock the secured room at the rear of the premises, and no longer than seven minutes to fill several black bags with the most expensive selection of jewellery on the shelves. By this time Simon Evans was conscious and groaning. The key sat in the lock of a smaller safe located within the secure room.

The first man walked out to him. "Good. I was thinking I'd need a bucket of water. Code please, Simon."

"I can't remember."

"Perhaps this will help" The man lifted his foot and tapped it against Simon's groin.

"I don't, honest. Give me five minutes. I can't think straight."

This time the foot was drawn back and it found its mark with a dull thud. Simon Evans yelled his agony and attempted to roll onto his front. The foot was placed on his chest and pinned him in position.

"If you ever want to use your old man again, give me the code."

"I really don't remember. Please."

The foot lifted from his chest. "Shame. I hope you don't want kids. Three, two—"

"Seven, five, three, two, eight."

"Good man."

In the other room the code was entered, the safe opened and emptied in two seconds. Less than fifteen minutes after entering the shop the two men were ready to leave. They paused only to send a text.

Tony's phone vibrated and he nodded to Ed. "Off you go, I'll be in the car park."

Ed stood and ran his fingers through his hair. "Wish me luck."

"It's all set up. You don't need luck. Move it. There they go."

As Ed crossed the road, he watched the two men saunter towards a pickup truck. Slinging their loot into the back as though it were rubbish. No one gave them a second glance. He nodded approval. Clever. He blew out his nervousness as he pushed open the door and entered the shop, slipping the lock as it closed behind him.

"Hello," he called, and when he had no reply, he shouted, "HELLO THIS IS THE POLICE. IS EVERYTHING OKAY?" He walked to the back door and pushed it open. "Shit! I knew something was wrong."

He pulled Simon Evans into a sitting position and pulled off his blindfold. He flashed the warrant card. "DI Meredith, I saw two men jump into a car outside. They chucked some holdalls into the boot. I knew it wasn't right."

"No, they robbed us." Simon caught sight of Jenny for the first time. "Are you okay, Jen?" Jenny grunted into her gag. "Can you untie her?"

"Yes, first let me call this in. Were they armed?"

"I never saw, they hit me with something, don't know what."

"But they never said they had a gun?" Ed walked over to Jenny, and removed the blindfold and gag as gently as he could. "Did you see any weapons?"

Tears of relief flowed, and Jenny shook her head.

"Two seconds." Ed pulled out his phone and called Tony. "It's Meredith. I'm on the High Street, there's been a robbery at the jewellers. Saw them jump into a fifty-six plate BMW three series. What? Hang on." He turned to Simon. "Sorry, didn't notice the name, what's the shop called?"

Having completed the fictitious call, he released the two victims from their bindings.

"Someone will be here to take a full statement soon, cars will be out looking for the BMW. Did they say anything that would indicate who they were?" He watched as they shook their heads. "What were they wearing? Did they have gloves?"

"I saw nothing. I was blindfolded while I was unconscious. What about you, Jen?"

"Gloves. They were dressed all in black, except they had high-vis jackets on, and balaclavas. Oh, and they knew your name." Wary eyes looked at Simon.

"They clearly did their homework. How much has gone?" Ed followed Simon and looked at the near empty shelves.

"Just about everything. That's hundreds of thousands. Fuck. I hope my insurance company doesn't mess me about. I'm wiped out." There was a catch in his voice.

Ed turned to Jenny and smiled. "Put the kettle on, Jen. I need to get back to the station and start work on this. Where do the recordings end up?" He pointed at the camera in the corner of the room.

Simon Evans took him into the small kitchen where Jenny was making tea. He handed over the discs which held the recordings for the last six months.

"I only keep six months' worth. Will they help do you think, if they were disguised, what use are they?"

"They knew the layout somehow, might be able to work out who and when they did that." Ed turned away. "I need to get this started. Sit down and have a cup of tea." He winked at Jenny and left them to it.

Dropping the discs into the footwell he looked at Tony. "Three grand for this one, but I want a bigger cut on the next one. Hundreds of thousands, he said, and I'm the only one with my neck on the line."

"Meredith is. Not you."

Ed slapped his own cheeks. "I'm sitting here because of this. My neck on the line. Mine."

"Shit. I'll make a call. They've lined up another one for closing time in Plymouth. He won't be happy."

"Tough. Do you want me to speak to him?"

"NO." Tony waited for the barrier to lift and drove away from the high street. "You do as you're told."

Ed's fee was doubled. And over the next two days, they did three almost identical jobs to the first. All went without a hitch. On the fourth job, Ed found out that the haul was over half a million. The owner of the shop was planning an exhibition of handmade jewellery by local craftsmen and had more than the usual amount of stock in the building. He'd wept as he explained this to Ed.

At the time Ed had felt guilty, but the guilt had eased when he'd found out the proprietor was less than honest himself. Close to thirty thousand pounds in cash had been in the safe, a fact he forgot to mention to Ed.

On the following Saturday, a further job was planned, but one of the crew had broken his leg playing football with his son, and Tony was called in at the last moment.

"He spoke to me like I knew nothing, the bastard." He handed his keys over to Ed. "You scratch my baby and you'll be paying for the repairs." He stroked the bonnet. "First brand new car I've ever had."

"Can we stick to the job? I don't know Taunton well. Yes, I know our rendezvous is in the satnav, but if anything happens, I'll drive to the Taunton Deane services and call you from there."

"Happens? Like what? Why would anything happen, the other jobs have gone like a . . . Oh, I get it, because I'm involved. You listen to me—"

"Get a grip. We've always ended up in the same car before. If anything went wrong we'd know what was what. I'm simply saying we need a contingency, should either of us not make the rendezvous as planned."

Tony's eyes narrowed. "I'm going to say yes, because I don't need to be wound up any more than I already am."

The pickup truck pulled into a space on the other side of the road.

"He's here. I'll text you when we're on the way out." He tapped the roof of the car. "Remember what I said."

Ed nodded and climbed into the car, dropping his newspaper on the passenger seat. He only had to drive a mile to the job, which was scheduled to take place at eight fifteen when the owner arrived. That was almost an hour away, but he decided to get into position early. He had no idea what the traffic would be like if he left it any later.

The shop in question, *Precious*, was on the pedestrianised High Street. It sold designer everything but clothes, and had an extensive selection of unique jewellery. Ed followed the satnav to the car park in

Old Pig Market, situated to the rear of the High Street. He bought his pay and display ticket and parked the car to face the exit. Placing his phone on the dashboard, he opened his newspaper and tried to care about the latest nonsense being spewed out by what appeared to be half the politicians in the western world.

Unable to concentrate on a story about the possibility of a nuclear war, he poked around in the glove compartment, and sucked a mint as he scanned the contents. He was startled when his phone peeped a little while later. Snatching it up he read the message from Tony.

In position

Ed checked the time. They were a good twenty minutes early. Wondering if they had new information, he shoved the contents of the glove compartment back in, and with his fingers drumming the steering wheel, he watched other cars drive into the car park.

After five minutes, he found he was getting nervous, so got out of the car. The driver's door clipped the wall and as he brushed away the brick dust, he rolled his eyes. That would give Tony something else to moan about. Lighting a cigarette, he walked slowly towards the exit.

If Tony's instructions were correct, if he looked to the left, he would see a gap between the buildings which would lead him onto the High Street. It was there. Walking in the opposite direction to fill the time, as it wouldn't do to be on the street too early, the cool breeze calmed him. He reached the top of the hill and turned back. Halfway back down his phone beeped. They were going in. He rechecked the time and slowed his pace.

It was five hundred yards to the High Street, go through the gap, turn right and it was the second shop after the department store. The jobs took ten to fifteen minutes, this one was a little different as it wasn't simply jewellery they were after, so Ed guessed it would be a little longer. Stopping, he lit another cigarette, and leaning against a lamppost he pretended to scroll through his phone.

Ten minutes after the first message, the second confirming they'd completed the job came through. Grinding out his cigarette with his heel, Ed frowned. That was far too quick, he hurried towards the shop trying to work out what could have gone wrong. When he got there the door was ajar, and someone inside was wailing.

He stepped inside, holding out his fake warrant card. "Hello, I'm DI Meredith, is everything okay in here?" He closed the door behind him and slipped the catch to lock it.

A middle-aged woman appeared from the rear door. Ed was shocked to see blood on her hands, the wailing continued somewhere behind her.

"Are you a policeman? We've been robbed!" She choked on a sob and flapped her bloody hands to compose herself. "Sorry. It was so scary. So bloody scary, they didn't need to do that to her. She was frightened, that was all. She wasn't doing anything." Turning, the woman went back the way she had come. "It's okay, Sue. The police are here, the ambulance won't be long."

Ed's step faltered as he followed her. "Ambulance?"

Going through a second door he found the source of the wailing. A female was sitting on the floor, her back against the wall holding a towel to her face. The once grey towelling was now mostly red, and there was a splatter of blood on the wall above her.

"What happened? Keep it short, I'll get some uniforms down to take full statements, the quicker I start looking for these robbers, the more likely we are to catch them."

"They came as we opened up. Just pushed us into the shop and made me unlock the back room." The middle-aged woman indicated the door which led to the safe. "Then one of them had a gun, you know a long one, like a rifle but shorter—"

"A shotgun." Ed suggested.

"Exactly. We were so scared already, but that shook Sue, didn't it?" She paused to look at Sue, whose wailing had been reduced to a whimper.

Sue nodded.

"Sue screamed and when he pointed it at her, she became . . . sorry, Sue, hysterical, and he hit her in the face with it. Her face sort of exploded." She clasped her hands to her cheeks. "Show him, Sue."

Ed braced himself, thinking Sue was going to move the towel. She didn't, she lowered one hand and opened it. Ed stepped closer, three bloody teeth sat in the middle of her palm. He grimaced.

"She's trying to save them, in case they can get them back in. I've called an ambulance, I think they broke her nose too. Did they call you?"

"Put them in a glass of milk." Ed looked away, the emergency service would have dispatched a car. Time to make a move. "Where are the recordings? I'd better get them to the station."

"What recordings?"

54

"From the security cameras." Ed wanted to get out of there, he doubted it would take long for the police to arrive.

"The cameras are everywhere. Come, I'll show you."

"It isn't the cameras I need, it's the recordings they make." Ed's eyes scanned the room. There were two cameras in this little room alone.

"I don't know where they go. Not here." The woman looked around puzzled. "I didn't think to ask, they only finished installing the new digital ones a few days ago. My husband took care of it."

"A new system?" Ed was cursing silently, he lowered his face a little. It was a futile gesture, every camera in the place would have already captured his image.

"Yes, but I don't—"

"Not to worry." Ed was already moving back into the main shop. He stepped over a toppled display in an effort to avoid the camera to his right. "I'll go and make some calls and see where the ambulance is." He'd reached the door and fumbled as he tried to open it.

"Don't you want my husband's number?" The woman walked towards him as he struggled with the catch. "Did you lock the door?"

Ed didn't answer. Door open, he stepped out into the sunshine, and hurried back to the car park. He called Tony as he waited impatiently at the first set of red lights. The call went to an answer service.

"What the fuck happened? They got this one wrong, there were no recordings, they've gone digital. If this light ever changes, I'm on my way." He threw the phone onto the passenger seat.

Tony was pacing back and forth when Ed pulled into the supermarket car park. Ed was already lighting a cigarette as he climbed out of the car.

"I'll have one." Tony stepped forward and his hand shook as he pulled a cigarette from the packet. "I picked up your message." He took a long drag on the cigarette. "Trying to work out how to tell him."

"What happened? Why was the girl hit?"

"Because she wouldn't stop screaming. It wasn't meant to be that hard. I couldn't concentrate, silly bitch."

"It was *you!*" Ed shook his head. "I'm done. Pay me my cut for this one, and I'm gone. I don't do hitting women, and they've got my mugshot on about a million fucking cameras. I'm out."

"Don't be hasty, they haven't got you, they've got Meredith. It's different. Wait and see what the . . . right, shut it. This is him."

Tony answered the call and began pacing again. "I had n-n-no choice—" He was cut off abruptly. He listened, all the while shaking his head.

Ed couldn't make out the words, but he could hear the volume. He watched the colour rise in Tony's cheeks. Eventually, Tony was allowed to speak.

"I'm sorry. It won't happen again." There was another burst of shouting and he rolled his eyes at Ed. "Listen, there's something I need to tell you. Two things actually, the first is that they went digital. There were no recordings in the shop, and the second, as a result of that, Meredith wants out."

He winced and held the phone away from his ear as the shouting erupted again. Ed could now hear the words clearly.

"I don't give a fuck what Meredith wants. He's out when I say he's out. You can tell him to keep his nerve, keep his head down, and I'll be in touch. He doesn't want to get on the wrong side of me again, or he'll regret it. Wait for my call."

The line went dead, and Tony sighed. "Well there's your answer."

"I don't need an answer, I'm off." Ed was already walking back to the car.

"You can't just disappear. He'll find you."

"No, he won't, he'll find my brother."

Tony held out his hand. "That's harsh when you don't even know him."

Ed laughed. "Says the man who came up with the plan in the first place. And, no, I'll drive. I don't trust you."

Tony's car was immaculate, with the exception of the damage to the edge of the door. He rarely smoked, and certainly not in the car, but today he was making an exception. He dropped Ed's phone into his hand and slung the newspaper onto the back seat.

"Give me another smoke."

Ed handed him the packet. He saw Tony's hands were still shaking. "Calm down, he can't expect you to be able to control me. Or I should say my brother. I'm guessing he's no pushover."

"The fucking opposite, and that's what worries me. Do me a favour, I'll pay you all of my cut, if you hang around until he calls back. Listen to what he has to say before you make your decision."

"Nope. You said no cameras and no violence. I got both in spades.

Sorry, Tony, no can do."

"I'll give you three grand to hang around until he calls."

"Plus your cut as promised earlier?" Ed wavered. Prior to this job, he'd been prepared to carry on, and now the money was threatening to dry up he was tempted.

"No. That includes it."

"Then nothing doing." Ed floored the accelerator. "Hold on, the sooner I'm out of here the better."

"Slow down. Okay, but you'll be wiping me out."

"I'll be doing you a favour."

They didn't speak until they reached the post box on the corner, three streets away from his mother's home. Ed had made that arrangement from the beginning. He was always waiting when Tony arrived, and took a convoluted route back to his mother's once Tony had driven away.

"I'm docking the petrol money by the way. It's cost me a fortune driving all over the country. I'll call you as soon as I hear anything."

Ed didn't respond, he simply waved as Tony drove away. He waited until he'd turned the corner at the bottom of the hill before setting off at a jog. To the best of his knowledge, Tony had never tried to follow him.

Tony wasn't as stupid as he looked. He'd simply checked the electoral register for the name Meredith, and he knew exactly where Ed was staying. Ed discovered this when Tony called three hours later. Ed was dozing and yawned a greeting.

"Come on. You're needed." Tony sounded more relaxed than he had earlier.

"Okay, give me ten minutes." Ed pulled himself up out of the armchair and stretched.

"We haven't got that long. I'm outside."

"What the . . ."

Ed was at the window in two strides. Sure enough, there was Tony's car. Without a word to his mother, who had appeared in the hall drying her hands on a tea towel, he ran out of the house slamming the door behind him. He yanked open the passenger door and got in, aware his mother would now be watching from the window.

"How long have you known?"

"Day after I first picked you up." The engine was running, and Tony pulled away. "I'm not stupid."

"Stop the car. I'm going nowhere until you tell me what's happening."

"No can do. We can't be late." Tony turned onto the main road.

"Stop the fucking car! I've got no wallet, no keys, I've not even got my own phone."

Tony looked him up and down. Ed was wearing the polyester suit trousers, and his funeral shirt.

"It wouldn't have helped. Trust me. You don't need anything, we've got a meeting with the big man. It's in a layby, no one will see you." Tony held his hand out. "Have you got a smoke?"

"No. Meeting about what?"

"He wants to convince you it will be worth your while to stick around. You need to start practising sarcasm, not too heavy, but enough to convince him you're the real deal. Oh yes and roll your eyes if he's sarcastic but don't bite. Meredith wouldn't give him the pleasure . . . what else? You already do the nose pinching thing."

"What nose pinching thing?"

"This." Tony pinched the bridge of his nose and looked down. "You both do it when you're trying to temper your response to something."

"I don't think I do." Ed frowned. It seemed he had more in common with his brother than just looks. His mother had spent most of his teenage years telling him to stop rolling his eyes. "Now I'm getting to meet this mysterious big man, what's his name?"

"He wants to surprise you."

"Yes, I get that, but as I am not my brother, if he knows him, he'll expect me to recognise him." Ed rolled his eyes.

"That's it. You've got the tone and the mannerisms. Keep that level of irritation and he'll never know the difference. I'm . . ." Tony glanced at the display in the dash as his phone rang. "Keep quiet." Pressing a button on the steering he drew in a breath. "Hello. We're on our way."

"Meredith is with you?" The voice was deep and the volume louder than necessary.

"He is. I'm on hands free if you want a word."

"See you soon, Meredith. It's been too long."

"I'm not . . . He's hung up, hasn't he?" Ed's comment was unnecessary as the muted voice of a radio presenter returned.

"He's a man of few words."

"Probably just as well. Where are we going?"

"To meet him in a layby."

"Very cloak and dagger. Not sure I like that."

"Given this morning's little mishaps, he probably didn't think it wise to be seen with you in public. Anyway, he used it before for . . . you don't want to know. He's comfortable there."

"True. If you see a service station, pull in or I'm going to pee myself."

"No need, nearly there. Was that . . . hush." Tony turned the radio up.

". . . was brutally attacked in the raid. She is currently in hospital where doctors are attempting to repair the damage which included the loss of three teeth. A man posing as a police officer was on the scene seconds after the men made off with goods valued at over half a million pounds. Police have issued images from the shop's security system in a hope someone will recognise any of the men. You can see these images on our website at . . ."

Tony switched off the radio. "Bollocks."

"I don't know what you're worried about. Your face was covered. I really do need to—"

"We're here. Stop moaning. Remember, arrogance, eye rolling, sarcasm, nose pinching the full works."

Tony ignored the sign advising the layby was closed, and cursed as his car brushed through the overgrown brambles. He stopped in a less vegetated spot.

"He's not here yet."

"No shit, Sherlock. I'm going for a pee."

Ed got out and wandered away from the car. Seeing a gap in the hedgerow he stepped onto the verge and into the void. Unzipping his trousers, he heard a vehicle drive past him. Some of the tension left him as he relieved himself, and he inclined his head as he heard a car door slam and Tony call a greeting. The flow faltered as raised voices reached him, but nature was determined to take its course and he remained where he was. Once done, he zipped his trousers and took a step forward. Tony was jabbing his finger at a hulk of a man.

"Don't give me that. You know what I know, don't you forget it," Tony yelled.

"Is that a threat?" The man lifted a heavily tattooed arm and formed a fist. "Because that wouldn't be wise."

"Not a threat no. I'm saying you can fucking trust me." Tony stepped to one side and looked towards the Mercedes. "I'm going to have a word."

As he stepped away, the large man grabbed him by the arm and swung him round. "Oh no. I asked you a question and I got threats, now I want an answer."

Tony had stumbled and was down on one knee cursing. With a roar he threw himself forward and his head rammed the stomach of his opponent, who, winded, stumbled backwards, arms flailing. Ed smiled, perhaps Tony had more gumption than he'd given him credit for. Taking advantage of his surprise attack, Tony righted himself and landed a decent right hook on the chin, followed by a punch to the stomach. Taking several steps back, Tony caught his breath.

"I think that's enough. Now—"

"You're right. Don't get so lippy in future." Leaning down, hands on knees, the man panted. Looking up from that position he held out his hand. "You've got a decent punch; shall we start again?"

A relieved Tony nodded and stepped forward his arm outstretched. He didn't see the other hand slip lower, or the blade hidden behind the leg of the man as he straightened himself. Taking hold of the proffered hand, he pulled the man upward.

In an explosion of movement, Tony was yanked forward, twisted around, and the blade of the knife sliced into his neck from left to right. A thin red line appeared as his assailant released him and stepped away. Tony's hands reached for his throat before his knees buckled.

Ed froze for a second and took a half step back. What the fuck had just happened? He peered through the branches as someone climbed out of the Mercedes and walked to where Tony lay.

"A bit unnecessary."

"You said to get rid." The big man looked worried.

"But not here, not now, you idiot. Put him in here." He walked to Tony's car and pushed his knuckle against the button to release the boot, before peering in the window. "Keys are in the ignition. Lock it and dump 'em."

Leaving the big man to it, he stepped back to watch. Tony was heaved into a sitting position, his shirt now crimson, and his head lolled to one side as his body was dragged to his car. With a grunt he was lifted higher and the top of his body pushed into the boot. It took some force to get the body into a position to allow enough room for the legs. The boot was slammed shut, and wiping his hands on his jeans, his murderer retrieved the keys from the ignition, locked the car, and taking a step back lobbed the keys over the hedge into the field beyond.

"Done," he announced.

"Not quite," his companion answered. "We've got to sort Meredith out first. Then it'll be done." He glanced at his watch. "I'm starving, let's get back."

10

There was silence for a few moments, as the group in the bridal suite considered Ed's story. It was Patsy who spoke first.

"I take it you found the keys and drove the car to Bristol?"

"I did. Believe it or not it only took ten minutes or so to find them."

"And you came straight here?"

"Nope. I drove to my mother's, packed a bag, stopped for a burger, went to the bank and got my savings. Of course, I came straight here. I didn't want to put her at risk."

"Well, she clearly is. Although, of course, whoever is behind this believes you are me. And, therefore, that I'm still living in Bristol, and have been driving up and down the M5 on a daily basis, which means my family are at risk." Meredith glanced at Amanda.

"Agreed. But it might be worth getting your mother to go and stay somewhere else until this is sorted." Patsy nodded. "Yes, that would be safest."

"I wonder what the question was that Tony didn't answer. Surely it wasn't worth dying for." Amanda sighed. "I have an early shift tomorrow. It's almost midnight, I'd like to know his body has been recovered before I try and get some sleep."

Ed merely nodded. He knew exactly what had been said, but he wasn't going to tell them Tony had died because of him. He had no idea why. Perhaps Tony didn't like the man, the way the question was being asked, or perhaps he knew it would put Ed in danger. But that question was the reason Ed hadn't shown himself, or gone to Tony's aid, not that he could have done much. Whatever the reason Tony didn't tell him that Ed was taking a pee, it didn't alter the facts, and he saw little point in sharing that information.

"I can show you where I left the car." Ed got to his feet and stretched.

"Not like that." Meredith pointed to the polythene on Ed's head. "Can it come off now?"

Amanda grimaced. "Uh, yes. Quickly Uncle Ed, it's been on a bit longer than necessary, but I'm sure it's okay."

"I hope you're right. I'll take a shower. It'll be easier." He walked into the bathroom and slammed the door.

"We find the car and the body, and, I'm assuming, sir, give both over to the chaps who ruined the wedding?" Trump smiled his thanks as Patsy topped up his coffee.

"Nope. We find the car and the body, and I find out who's after me and make sure they get what's coming." Meredith looked disappointed in Trump. "Would you trust those two to sort this out before I go the way of Tony?"

"But—" Dave Rawlings got to his feet.

"No buts, Dave. I'm not trusting the safety of me or my family to those two." He glanced at his watch. "We'd better get a move on. I've got to be at the station at eight." Catching the look exchanged between Trump and Rawlings, he pointed at the door. "You two don't need to be part of this. I wanted you to hear it from the horse's mouth, so if I disappear for a few days, you'll know I'm not choosing the new Mrs Meredith a wedding gift." He smiled at Patsy.

"Well, the new Mrs Meredith isn't happy with it either. Jesus, Meredith, you are a copper through and through, and yet in your world you're the only one who's allowed to break the rules and not trust the force to sort any issues out. One has to assume they don't know of Tony's involvement, therefore the investigation into his murder will be local, and it will probably be assigned to your team. If you think I'm going to agree to you running off around the . . . Oh dear." She forced her mouth shut as Ed came out of the bathroom. Her lips quivered as she held back the smile.

Meredith grinned. "Suits you. Now get that T-shirt on, and let's get going." He turned to the others. "Are you two ready?"

Rawlings burst out laughing. Ed ignored him, and struggling to control his temper, he strode straight to the bedroom where he collected Meredith's shirt. He was still pulling it on when he returned.

"I'm pleased to be of entertainment value to you. Shall we go and find the bloke with his throat cut, or shall we stay here awhile longer and laugh at my almost fluorescent red hair." He turned to Amanda. "I'll expect you to do something about this soonest."

The laughter and smiles disappeared.

"I'll do my best." Amanda stepped forward and patted his arm. "But can we find Tony please?"

Meredith looked at Trump. "I take it you'll be going home to bed. I'll text you once I confirm everything is as he says it is."

"I rather thought I'd come with you." Trump pulled on his jacket.

"And then what? Do as I ask you, or do what you need to as a serving officer?"

"That's not fair, Gov. If you're going to go all maverick on us again, why call? We're coming with you."

"Nope. I can't allow you to compromise yourself. Go home the pair of you, I'll be in touch. Promise."

The two men reluctantly agreed, and everyone trooped into the lift. They ignored the startled look from the night porter. Trump and Rawlings headed for the exit to get a taxi, and Meredith and the others took the half flight of stairs down to the car park. The Meredith brothers in the front, Patsy and Amanda in the back.

"Do you remember the name of the street you abandoned him in?" asked Meredith as he headed for the A4.

"I didn't abandon him. I ran out of petrol. No money, no card, no anything."

"I asked for a street name, not an excuse."

"No. But I know where it is. I'll shout when we get there." Ed drummed his fingers on his knees, his brother was an arrogant, irritating individual, but now was not the time to air his opinion.

Meredith drove away from town, and a little under the speed limit in case he needed to make a sudden manoeuvre. After a mile or so, Ed leaned forward.

"Turn right at these lights, I remember the car started playing up here and I turned off at the next exit. If I'm correct, the car is up there on the right. I turned into the first street."

Meredith did as instructed.

"This one. Not far up."

Pulling over, Meredith stopped the car.

"I don't see any point in you two coming with us. Particularly you,

Amanda. You don't need to see this."

"Okay, but I've seen a lot of dead bodies, Dad."

"Not ones you were connected to, and this fascination with Sherlock has got to stop."

Amanda was in her final year of training to become a doctor. Having been introduced to Frankie Callaghan, a senior medical examiner, whom her father nicknamed Sherlock, she was considering specialising in forensic pathology, much to her father's annoyance. He was also worried she might have a romantic interest in Frankie. Mixing work and pleasure rarely ended well, as he knew from his past misguided misadventures.

"Stay put please." He opened the car door. "Come on, Red, you've got the keys, I take it." Turning to Patsy, he added, "Patsy, we have to get this off the road. I'll drive it in and grab a cab. You take this one."

"Are you going home or to the hotel?" Patsy was already getting out of the car. "Wait a minute. How can you drive it anywhere without petrol?"

"Good point. Let's deal with that first."

They drove to the nearest petrol station and after an angry exchange when Ed pointed out he had no idea if diesel or petrol was required, Meredith took a guess and headed back to the car with five litres of petrol.

Meredith handed over the keys to Patsy. "See you soon. Keep the bed warm for me." He watched her drive away before turning to Ed. "A Beemer you say, Red?" He could see one ahead.

"Yep, that's it. And the name's Ed."

"Ed, Red, Shed. All the same." Meredith held out his hand. "Keys."

Ed pointed the key fob at the car, and as well as unlocking it, he managed to pop the boot open. "Oops, sorry."

"It had to be done at some stage." Meredith paused. "Sort the fuel out, I'll take a look." He wanted Ed busy, as he wasn't sure how he'd respond. He waited until Ed had opened the driver's door to release the fuel cap, and steeling himself for the sight of Tony's corpse, stepped up to the car.

Tony's body had certainly been shoved in. The top of his body rested on his right shoulder, his head out of view, his torso was twisted, unnaturally so, and his legs, bent at the knee, faced upward. Swallowing, Meredith pulled his phone out and switched on the torch. He held his breath as he leaned forward, the smell of congealed blood had already reached him. Ignoring the flap of skin under the chin, he focused the torch on the cheek. There it was. A large bean shaped birthmark a little in front of Tony's left ear. He slammed the boot, he'd seen enough.

"That'll do," Meredith called. "Let's go."

"It's the bloke you knew, I take it?" Ed screwed closed the petrol cap, and set the container in the footwell behind the driver's seat.

"Yep. You were right, he had no chance of surviving that wound, even if you'd known what you were doing."

"Did you think I lied?"

Meredith's hand shot up and he flicked at his ear. "Must be a bloody moth. Come on, let's get— Shit!" He dropped to his knees, grabbing Ed and yanking him down as the second bullet grazed the top of his arm. "I think you were wrong about not being followed."

Meredith peeped over the top of the boot. "Crawl around to the other side and get in. How good's your driving? They're in a car on the other side of the road, he's shooting through the sunroof of that Audi."

"I'm not a getaway driver, I doubt I could reverse fast enough to get away. They really want me dead. Shit! I don't think I can, they're shooting at us." His voice had gone up an octave.

"No, they want me dead, thanks to you, and you'll be driving towards them. Get in the bloody car, it's your fault we're here. On three, and keep your head down. They've got a bright target."

"Where are you going?"

"Just do it." Meredith hissed, and started the count. "One, two . . ."

Ed was already moving, and as he clambered into the car, Meredith pulled open the back door. Lying across the seat he opened the petrol canister, and called to Ed, "Start the engine and open the sunroof, don't put your head up until I say."

Squirming, he pulled the newspaper from underneath his body, rolled it into a cylinder and forced it into the canister. He lit the paper as the sunroof opened. Changing position, he held the flame away from his body as he screamed at Ed. "GO! GO!"

Ed floored the accelerator, glad the car was an automatic as he wasn't convinced he'd be able to change gear, and the car shot along the road. A bullet hit the windscreen and he lost vision before punching a hole in the crazed web of glass in front of him. He was still cursing as Meredith got to his feet, and as they passed the car, lobbed the burning canister in through the sunroof of the Audi. The flames singed his hair as he did so, and he dropped down slapping the side of his head.

"What now? I can barely see where I'm going." Ed called.

Meredith glanced out of the rear window. He could see one man running after them. "Take the next left, keep going. I've got a call to make." He held on to the seat in front as Ed threw the car around the corner, clipping a parked car as he did so.

"Tony would have gone ape shit. He loved this car."

Meredith ignored him and checked his phone to make sure he'd dialled correctly. Frankie Callaghan answered as he returned it to his ear.

"Meredith. I'd like to say what a pleasure, but I'm assuming you know it's one o'clock in the morning. I've not long gone to bed, cracking reception by the way. I don't think Tom Seaton will see much of tomorrow."

"If you're in bed I take it you're not working? In which case I'll need a favour." Meredith smiled at the sigh.

"Meredith, seriously? It's your wedding night. How can you possibly need another favour which isn't going through normal channels?"

"Long story, but I'm in a car with no windscreen, a dead body in the boot, and a gunman possibly in pursuit. Oh, and I'll need a plaster, the bastard got my arm." There was silence from the other end. "Sherlock, are you there?"

"Of . . . you're serious, aren't you?"

"Of course I am. It's my wedding night for God's sake. I wouldn't be calling you if I wasn't serious."

"But how . . . why . . . You never fail to surprise, Meredith, I'll give you that. What do you want?"

"I want you to meet me at the mortuary. Get someone to stand by the gates, I'll come in where they collect for burial. How long will you be? I reckon I'll be there in ten minutes." He squinted through the hole in the windscreen. "Left and then next right," he shouted to Ed.

"I'll be there shortly afterwards. I can't wait to hear this story."

"Good man. See you there." Meredith glanced out of the rear window. He was confident they weren't being followed. "Red, pull over. I'll drive now."

Ed needed no further encouragement. The car squealed to a halt and he jumped out, brushing bits of glass from his trousers. "I don't suppose you've got a ciggy, have you? I'd nearly given up before I met him." He looked at the boot.

Wincing at the pain, Meredith changed hands and pulled a pack from his top pocket. He lit one himself before tossing them to Ed. "Let's go, it might get breezy." Pulling off his shoe, he tapped the heel on the remaining windscreen until most it had been removed and used it to scrape away the glass which had landed on the driver's seat.

"Is this place safe?" Ed asked. "I reckon there must be a tracker on the car. How would they have found it otherwise?"

"I doubt it. They wouldn't have been looking for the car. It's more likely to be a phone. Probably checked it to see if the body had been discovered, and found it gone. What I can't work out is why wait there?" He pursed his lips. "Assuming they thought it was driven away by you . . . me, why wait there? Who in their right mind would abandon a car with a dead body in the boot and then go back to it?"

"We did."

"Hmm." Meredith glanced to his left. "You hungry?"

"Starving but no money."

"You can add it to the list of what you owe me."

Meredith pulled up outside a fried chicken outlet. Five minutes later, balancing the bucket of chips and chicken between them he drove towards the mortuary.

Frankie Callaghan paced up and down in front of the open gates to the car park. He glanced at his watch. Meredith had said ten minutes. It had now been twenty. He threw his hands into the air as Meredith appeared, driving a sorry looking BMW and waving a chicken drumstick at him.

"Not so much of an emergency that it would stop you eating," Frankie called as he waved them into the car park closing the gates behind them.

Despite his words, he took a drumstick when Meredith offered him the bucket. Ed was the last out of the car and Frankie looked from one to the other. Drumstick poised inches away from his lips. He lowered his arm. "Scottish cousin, Meredith?"

"Half-brother, Sherlock. He's the reason we're here. Shall we get on?"

"As soon as I've finished this." Frankie bit into the chicken. "Did you choose that colour by mistake?" He waved the bone towards Ed's head, and dropped it back into the box, wiped his hand on his scrubs and held it out. "Frankie Callaghan."

"Meredith. Ed."

"So, to business. Have either of you touched the body since it was placed there?" He spun to Meredith. "Hang on a minute, did he put the body in here?"

Ed spoke before Meredith had swallowed his food. "I'm not deaf. And I can speak for myself. The answer is no, I didn't. Nor did I kill him. I drove the car to Bristol. Full stop. End of."

"Neither of us have touched the body, Sherlock. I did touch the boot to shut it, but hopefully there will be some other useful prints." He looked at Ed. "I take it the one you call a bruiser wasn't wearing gloves?"

"No. You're right, his prints should be on there."

Frankie took several chips and ate them as he walked towards door of the building. "Two seconds." Punching the code to release the door, he disappeared inside.

Meredith held the bucket towards Ed. "Last chance. You won't want more once he opens the boot."

Ed helped himself and they watched Frankie and a young man in scrubs push out a trolley, on top of which sat a camera with a large flash. "Why did you call him Sherlock?"

"Because he's quite clever on the quiet. He's helped me solve several cases, and he's not afraid to step over blurred lines if the need dictates."

Frankie held out his hand as his assistant switched on a floodlight which momentarily blinded them.

"Keys." Taking the keys from Meredith, he opened the boot and peered inside. "A couple of shots in situ then we'll get the poor chap out of there."

Meredith took his phone from his pocket and walked back towards the gate. He pulled Ed with him. "Trust me, you don't want to see them unfold him."

Ed merely nodded and stared at his feet as Meredith made his call, and Frankie's camera repeatedly illuminated the boot of the car.

"Tom, it's Meredith. I recovered the car, but there was a welcoming party. They're armed and using a silencer. Seen too many Bond films I expect. Anyway, Tony Beresford is dead. I've handed him over to Sherlock. I suggest you start there while I try and find out if my long

70

lost and unwanted brother can ID anyone. Give me a shout if you need me." His second call was to Patsy, it was much the same, although he didn't mention the gun. She promised to update Amanda.

"Who's Tom?" Ed remained with his back to the car.

"A friend, police officer, why?"

"Because the two who came to the hotel were called Dave and Louie, how does this Tom know what's going on?"

Meredith smiled. "You're quite bright on the quiet, Red. He doesn't, he will when he's struggled out of bed, and sobered up enough to work out what I told him, then he'll call the others and they'll come here. A couple of hours at least I reckon, and that will be soon enough. The other two are probably still awake, if I called them they would be down here too soon." He glanced towards the car. Tony's body had been removed and was covered with a sheet. "Come on, let's see what Tony can tell us. The bin's over there."

Frankie closed the boot and looked to a second assistant who had appeared carrying a case. "Prints first please, from the outside in, and bring me what you find on the boot before you do the rest please, Chris"

Ed dropped the bucket into the bin and followed the others into the building and through to the examination room.

Frankie and his assistant lifted the body onto a stainless steel table, and Frankie pulled a microphone down, before throwing back the sheet.

Ed paled, making his hair look even brighter, and turned to face the other way.

"Do we have a name?" Frankie asked.

Meredith gave him both name and date of birth, Tony's birthday had been two days before his own. Frankie gave a summary of the situation into the microphone, while Meredith got the first-aid box and found a dressing for his arm.

"Can you do his clothes first. I need his phone and wallet sharpish."

"I rarely do a PM when the victim is clothed, Meredith." Frankie pulled the microphone closer. "Victim is wearing a zip up, navy blue fleece top. Two side pockets, one containing a packet of mints and a tissue, the other containing a Samsung mobile phone. Photograph please." He placed the items on a trolley next to the table and his assistant obliged. "DCI Meredith has taken the . . ." He switched off the microphone and looked at Meredith. "Are you a DCI?"

"I've never really not been, have I?" Meredith grinned and pressed the button to turn the phone on. The screen lit up for a few seconds before it faded. Trying again, Meredith shook his head. "Battery's dead." He slipped it into an evidence bag as Frankie carried on.

"DCI Meredith has taken the phone. The deceased is also wearing a Boss T-shirt." He lifted the scissors to cut away the shirt. As he methodically removed Tony's clothes, Frankie added a house key and a wallet to the evidence bag held by Meredith.

"Death appears to have been caused by a cut to the throat, severing the carotid arteries, the trachea and jugular. The cut appears to have been from left to right, suggesting a right-handed assailant positioned behind the victim. Death would have been quick. I am . . ." Frankie paused as the second assistant entered. "Any good?"

"I got quite a few prints from the boot, I'm running them now, do we have anyone to eliminate?"

"Me and him." Meredith pointed at Tony's body.

"Let's get that sorted first." Frankie switched off the microphone and supervised the collection of fingerprints. "Take the Meredith clan with you and process them. Thanks, Chris."

"Thank you, Sherlock. I'll get going once I've got that. The team will be in touch in the morning. Give me a shout if you find anything unusual."

"Will do. And it's already morning, Meredith. Early morning, but morning none the less."

It took almost an hour, but when everything had been processed and Meredith and Beresford's prints were taken out of the equation, they were left with two sets of unidentified prints. A search of the data base revealed only one set were on the system. They belonged to Max Deegan.

Ed leaned over Chris's shoulder. "That's him. That's who did it. Do you know him?"

"Well, that was easier than I thought it would be, and no, I don't think I do. Bugger. If he's now loose with a gun, I've got to call Trump. He needs to be apprehended sooner rather than later. Two seconds."

Walking away, Meredith called Trump and brought him up to date. "I'll be at the station at eight, get me the necessary info printed off. I'll see you there." He hung up before Trump could question him. His phone beeped as he was slipping it into his pocket. Reading the message, he looked at Ed. "Not a lot we can do for the moment. Patsy has reminded me to go to the hotel not home, you'd better come with me for the time being. I need some sleep, something tells me tomorrow is going to be a long day."

Sticking his head around the door, he thanked Frankie again, and asked to be kept informed.

Leaving by the front door, he flagged down a taxi. As he settled in for the short ride back to the hotel something occurred to him, and he turned to Ed. "How did you know where I lived?"

"Tony."

Ed was exhausted and didn't bother opening his eyes.

Meredith thumped his arm. "Wake up. But why?"

"I swear to God, if you hit me one more time . . . what do you mean, why?"

"Why did he give you my address? Why did you need it?"

"Oh, I see. He didn't. On the last job, the one where he hit the girl, I had to drive his car. I was early and had a poke around. He had some stuff in the glove compartment, photos and . . . SHIT!" He sat upright, his features frozen.

"What?"

"The photos. I've just realised. They were of Patsy and Amanda. Recent photos. I'm sorry. I never thought, it's been—"

"Shut up. Driver, turn around. Back to where you picked us up."

Meredith was phoning Frankie before the taxi had managed to do a U turn. He explained what he wanted and when they pulled up outside, Chris was standing there with an envelope. He handed it over as Meredith ran up the steps.

"Frankie asked if he should be concerned. To be honest, it's clear he already is. He also said he didn't think this was what you were after, but he has a spare room if the girls needed somewhere to go."

"Tell him I'll call him if I need him." Taking the envelope, Meredith was pulling out the contents before he'd closed the door of the taxi. "Now the hotel."

"Were they still there?" Ed tried to look at the documents as Meredith leafed through them.

Meredith held up one photograph of Amanda. Her hand lifted in greeting, she was smiling at someone, but not the photographer.

"Just one. It looks like it was taken in the car park at the hospital." He sorted through the papers and held another up. "Is this what you saw?" It was a typed sheet with Meredith's name, address, and car registration.

"No. It was handwritten on a sheet torn from a pad. There was no car registration either. What does this mean?"

"It means my girls are in danger." Lunging at Ed, Meredith grabbed his T-shirt and pulled him forward. "If your greed hurts my family in any way, I will do you serious damage."

The words were delivered slowly and calmly, and the look on his face told Ed he was deadly serious.

"I haven't done anything to put them in danger. When I saw the photos, I didn't know who they were. They were simply two nice looking girls. Although there was one of Patsy loading shopping into the boot of a car. I thought it was weird but put it down to a domestic. You know I thought Tony was having his wife followed or something."

"She's way out of his league." Meredith crumpled the sheet in his fist. "Now think. What other photographs were there, what were the girls doing, were they recent? What was the weather like?" He thumped the back of the seat in front. "Bollocks!"

"Oi!" The taxi driver half turned before looking back at the road. "Any more and you can walk."

Ignoring him, Meredith shoved the papers back into the envelope. "Think, Red, think. You've brought this shit to my door. What else was there?"

11

I t's where?" Alan Jenkins listened again, one hand covering his eyes, although he knew he'd heard correctly the first time. "You bloody fool!"

"Hardly my fault, boss. What was I supposed to do?" Deegan held the phone away from his mouth as he sighed.

"Let me think now. Follow Meredith and sort him out. The instruction was simple enough. Why were you sat watching the car? Why not torch it like you were supposed to and then go after Meredith?"

"I was following the signal, almost on top of him and saw him turn at the lights. They changed and I had to stop. As I pulled away, I glanced at the phone and saw he'd turned right, then it died. I haven't got a charger, I wasn't expecting to do this. So, I stayed with the car because I thought he'd come back to it. I thought he'd gone into one of the houses, so I waited. I wasn't expecting him to come in a different car and start firebombing me, was I? I managed to get one shot, but only grazed him." Deegan decided the whole truth was unnecessary. "My car must be a write-off."

"But if you'd torched it like you should've, there'd be less evidence, and you might have drawn Meredith out. For fuck's sake, Max, it's not that hard, surely? Where are you now?" When he heard the answer, he closed his eyes in disbelief and told himself to stay calm. "Did you leave prints? Did you touch the car?"

"I—"

"Of course you did!" bellowed Jenkins. "Because when you got knife happy and decided to slit his throat you weren't wearing gloves, so now they will link the car back to you, and you decide to sit outside waiting for them to spot you. You're a fucking liability. Disappear now. Get out of Bristol, don't come here, go somewhere you're not connected to, and I'll be in touch. But do it now. Clear anything personal out of the car. And go! Not in ten minutes, not after you've picked up some food, or had a pee. NOW!"

"How? Where do you want me to go?"

"Bus, train, just don't steal a car, as to where, I really, really don't care. Just disappear."

"Okay." Deegan had no idea where he should go or how, but wasn't brave enough to ask again. "What are you going to do?"

"Try and limit the damage somehow. I'll try and set up a meeting. You know the old saying, if you want a job done properly? Well it's true. Now get off the phone, get out of that hotel and buy a charger, and I'll call you if I need you. And I'm warning you, if you come anywhere near Plymouth without my clearance, I'll make you sorry. Family or no family." Hanging up, Jenkins threw the phone on to the sofa. "Shit!"

Storming into his bedroom, he slammed his hand against the light switch. Groaning, his wife pulled the duvet over her head.

"No use hiding, I've got to go away for a few days. Get your arse out of bed and pack me a bag. I'm going for a shower."

"A bloody please wouldn't go amiss." Kate Jenkins threw back the duvet and opened her eyes, wincing as the door to the en suite bathroom banged shut. Pushing herself up, she slid open the wardrobe and pulled out a small suitcase, dropping it onto the crumpled duvet. Was it big enough, come to that was it too big? How long was a few days?

Pushing open the bathroom door she called above the noise of the shower. "How long is a few days? Two, six? I don't know how many shirts to pack. Where are you going anyway? You realise it's only half two in the morning, don't you? And you'd better not have forgotten we have another lot coming in."

"Do you think I'm stupid?" The water stopped running and his hand groped for a towel. "I didn't wake up and think, I know, it's nice and dark, I've got nothing better to do, I'll go on a road trip." The water had washed away some of his irritation, and wrapping the towel around his waist, he smiled at her. "Let's say three days. If it turns out to be longer, I'll pop into Marks and Sparks and pick up a couple."

"Where are you going and why?" Kate was already walking back to the wardrobe.

Ignoring her, Jenkins ran his hand over his chin trying to decide whether to bother to shave. He decided against it, last time he had a beard, Kate said he looked younger, and he was certainly looking haggard and old at the moment. Opening the cupboard under the basin he pulled out a wash bag and checked the contents. Carrying it into the bedroom, he selected an aftershave and dropped it in, before placing it in the case.

"Did you hear me?"

"Hear what, my love?"

Knowing he'd heard, Kate chose a shirt she knew he didn't like and turned to face him.

"Is it another woman? Because if it is, I'll pack differently. You heard me." She rolled the shirts into a ball and dropped them in the suitcase. Returning to the wardrobe, she stooped and picked up a pair of shoes. Tossing one onto the shirts, she launched the other at her husband. "Pack your own suitcase." Taking little satisfaction from the look of shock on his face, she stormed out of the room.

Completing the packing, Jenkins left his case in the hall and went in search of his wife. She was standing on the back-door step, blowing smoke into the crisp darkness. On the breakfast bar were two mugs of tea and he smiled, taking a sip before approaching her. Slipping his arms around her waist, he leaned down and kissed the back of her neck.

"Why would I need another woman when I have you? You are my world you know that." He meant it too. There had been other women in the past, and there would be an odd dalliance here and there in the future, after all Jenkins had needs to be satisfied, but those liaisons meant nothing. His Kate was one in a million and he'd never let her go. Look at all she'd achieved while he'd been locked up. "I'm going away on business. Might take a day, might take a couple."

"Business? Why don't I know about it? What sort of business calls you in the middle of the night and gets you out of bed and packing a case? Your business, *our* business, is here, and I don't know anything about a trip." Turning she pushed him away. "Move. It's bloody freezing out here."

Kicking the door shut, he pulled out a stool and sat while he sipped his tea.

"You haven't answered me. I'm starting to get stroppy."

"Max has got himself in a spot of bother."

"That's because he's stupid. What's it got to do with you, and why does it involve staying away?"

"Because if he comes back, he'll get nicked. That'll bring it too close to home, and I don't want the filth sniffing around my business."

"But you're not involved in whatever he's done?" Hands on hips, she shook her head. "I don't want the police poking around either, but why should they? Are you sure you're not involved?"

"I'm not. But it won't stop them looking, and you know me, once they start poking around I'll lose my rag and then the shit will hit."

The hands remained in place. "So why go scooting off after him? Why the middle of the night? That just draws attention to yourself."

"Because he's family, our nephew, and closest thing we've got to a son since . . ." Seeing the look of horror on her face, he didn't finish the sentence. "His dad's still banged up. He works for me, and they'll think I'm involved. I'm simply tidying up to keep them at a distance. And the middle of the night, because it's when the stupid bastard called me. I got mad." Smiling, he winked. "Only you can tame my temper, you know that."

"No one is waiting for you?"

"Not a soul."

"I could cook you breakfast, put my face on and come with you? Aretta can deal with any business."

"Yes. Get the pan out. Although why you'd want to drive around endless streets looking for lowlifes is beyond me. But feel free. Hit the switch on the kettle." Gripping his mug, a little tighter, he tried to keep his tone light. Inside he was boiling, and he knew he might explode at the next question.

Dropping her hands to her sides she considered this. Was it a double bluff? She wasn't stupid, but if he was telling the truth, there was nothing she'd like less than to be dragged around clearing up after Max, bloody nuisance that he was. Alan did him so many favours it sometimes felt he was taking advantage, and he of all people should know better.

Bending to get a frying pan, she asked, "What's he done this time?"

Deciding to stick to as close to the truth as possible, he covered his face with his free hand. "Don't ask."

"I am asking." The frying pan was banged onto the hob and she walked to the fridge.

"Tried to shoot someone. Luckily, he missed, but it doesn't mean he's not in deep shit."

"*Shoot* someone?" Dropping the bacon and eggs onto the breakfast bar, Kate's hands were back on her hips. "You're behaving, aren't you? Even if you weren't, you don't do guns. Do you?"

"No, I don't. Nor does he as a rule, but he thought he'd been wronged and made a bad choice."

"Wronged? Wronged? Did someone look at that trollop he calls a wife in the wrong way? Did someone slap his cheek with a leather glove? Bloody hell, Alan, you don't go shooting people because you were wronged. If I did that, you and half your family would be dead. Shit!" Picking up the bacon, she dropped several rashers into the pan. "Why are you getting involved, it could be dangerous?"

"No. Just expensive. I'm glad he's a bad shot or it would cost me more. I need to grease a few palms that's all. Finding the right ones is what might take the time."

This rang true. Alan always managed to buy himself out of trouble. Or he had until he met Meredith, and that was her fault. She'd had no idea that speaking to Meredith would have the results it did. It wasn't only Alan sent to prison for armed robbery. When Kate had gone to see Meredith, she'd thought it was for the best, she'd thought Alan would only get done for receiving. She'd thought wrong.

Well, she'd sorted that whore Carol Plumb out, she never got to shag Alan again, but poor old Terry . . . Kate would have kept her mouth shut if she'd known he was involved. Screwing her eyes shut and tensing her body, she let the thought go. She blew out a breath as she turned back to Alan.

"Where will you find these palms? Which part of the country, I mean? I can tell it's not local."

"Bath, maybe Chippenham, up that way."

"But not Bristol?" The spatula was pointed at him.

"Not Bristol."

Turning back to the pan, she flipped over an egg. "That's good, because you promised me. You go back there and something bad will happen. Always does. We've done alright down here, we run a nice business which keeps us comfortable. You go back there, and all the old faces might tempt you back. And I'm not just talking about the gang of shits you call friends."

Sliding the bacon and egg onto a plate, she placed it in front of him. "And if you do that, we're over, done, finito. A promise, not a threat." Kate turned away. "I'm going back to bed."

"I thought you were coming with me." Grinning at her back, he shoved a forkful into his mouth.

"That was before. I want no part of this. But you keep in touch, take your charger, and buy a new one if you *lose* it." She made speech marks with her fingers as she left the kitchen. "You've tried that trick before and . . ."

Turning, she walked back into the kitchen, and yanked a plug from the socket by the toaster. Dropping the charger next to the plate, she took his face in her hands and kissed his forehead. "There you go. I just remembered we've got another lot tomorrow, so I'd better stick around." She tapped the charger. "No excuses. 'Night." Her slippers slapped the tiles as she left him to his breakfast.

"Love you, Kate." Despite the many lies he told, and his true intentions, it was the truth, and his smile was genuine.

"You'd better. Don't forget to lock the back door."

Pushing the plate away, Jenkins pulled out his phone. "It's me. Is the next lot guaranteed for tomorrow? Bollocks, they get it wrong sometimes, let's hope tomorrow is one of those days. I've got to go and sort Max out . . . Dickie, shut up and listen. If I'm not back in time, you know the procedure, help Kate if necessary. Any trouble Kate can't handle, call me. But only if absolutely necessary. If you cock up, I'll damage you." Hanging up, he went into the hall and lifted his coat from the banister, shoving his hands in the pocket he made sure his gloves were there. He was going to need them.

12

L et me see." Patsy spread the documents over the little coffee table and looked at Ed. "How many photographs?"

"About a dozen. Only one of you together though, outside your house. I'm sorry the relevance has only just occurred to me."

"What did you think they were?" Patsy was squinting at a receipt. "There's nothing else useful here." She looked at Meredith. "And you don't know Max Deegan?"

"No. I only had a quick glance, but he's only been done for minor stuff as far as I could see, mainly in Plymouth. We'll know more once I've seen Trump at the station. He's bringing his record with him. But in my experience, you don't go from knocking off an off licence to slitting someone's throat. He's just not been caught."

"Agreed. The most pressing thing to deal with is Amanda's safety. Whoever is behind all this is after you, and judging by the photos Ed saw, he doesn't care how he gets to you. Thank God Dad booked an early train."

"And your safety." Meredith gave her a weak smile. "I know this is my fault, so I'm sorry. I don't know who it is, but my only guess is it's someone I've pissed off big-time."

"Well that list would take a lifetime to work through." Getting to her feet, Patsy poured herself another coffee, and smiled as Ed sniggered.

"Hey, Red. Glad this amuses you, this neck-deep shit you've landed us in. My wife and daughter are at risk because of you." He threw Patsy a smile as he said wife, before turning back to his brother. "Think back to the layby. What did you hear? The Tony I knew wasn't frightened of getting physical, but he chose his moments and opponents carefully. Rarely started anything he couldn't finish, so my guess is, he either knew what might be coming, or Deegan said something which wound him up."

"Perhaps he's changed. I saw the damage he did to that poor girl. He said he panicked and couldn't think straight, but it was way out of order." Running his hand through his hair, Ed grimaced. "Can we not do something about this? Seriously, black, brown, grey if you like, but not this."

"I don't think the boys who will be interested in you inside will care, in fact they might like it." Yawning, Meredith looked at his watch. "I've got four hours before I have to be at the nick, I need a couple of hours' sleep, here's the plan. We'll go to bed, you can have the couch, Red. At half seven, Patsy, you get home and see your parents off, then stay with Amanda until you hear from me, preferably not at the house, and somewhere public. Me and Red will go to the station. God knows how long it will take, so keep in touch." Getting to his feet, he held out his hand which Patsy accepted. "Come on, bed."

"What about the doctor?" Ed shrugged. "He said he'd help."

"What doctor?"

"The one we took Tony to."

"Oh, Sherlock, what about him?"

"He said he'd help, isn't that what the bloke told you?"

"Your hearing is very good, you were in the taxi."

"What's that got to do with anything?"

Groaning, Meredith dropped back onto the sofa. "It's got a lot to do with you not hearing what went on in the layby. You've been lying, not that that surprises me, but why?"

"You don't even know how far away . . ." Ed paled. "Shit. I've just made another connection. You need to move Amanda. Now."

"Tell me." Springing to his feet, Meredith stepped over the table and grabbed Ed by the shoulder, his grip vice-like.

Knocking Meredith's hand away with a string of expletives, Ed stood nose to nose with him. "We can do this here, or I can tell you in the car on the way and stop wasting what could be precious minutes." A shiver ran up his spine and he looked away. "Come on. NOW!" He went to the door and pulled it open. "Patsy, is he always this awkward?"

"Pretty much." Patsy laced her trainer and went to join him. "You can tell me in the car. Then I might slap you."

Meredith snatched the keys off the arm of the chair. "You won't get far without these."

Earlier, Meredith had thought he might be able to sleep while standing, now, fear and adrenaline had taken hold, and he snarled at Ed, "We're in the car, tell me."

* * *

"I reckon those brambles scratched your car, Tony." Ed smirked as Tony's face screwed up at the thought.

"There's no one here."

"No shit, and there was me thinking I was missing something. I'm going for a pee."

"Hurry up, they'll be here soon."

Watching Ed wander off to a gap in the hedgerow, Tony drummed his fingers on the steering wheel, wondering why this was the meeting place, and willing himself not to get out and look at the damage to his car. Even when Jenkins' car pulled into the layby and he got out, he kept his chin high and refused to look.

The door of the other car opened, and Max Deegan got out.

"The boss not joining us?" Tony called, hoping he wouldn't be asked to get into the car.

Deegan marched up to him and looking over his shoulder peered in through the windscreen. "Where's Meredith? Please don't tell me you didn't bring him."

"Why?"

"Because he was supposed to be here. He was going on his final journey." Deegan smirked and jerked his head back to the car he'd vacated. "He won't be happy. And if he's not happy you'd better look out."

"What does that mean - final journey?" Staring Deegan straight in the eye to stop himself looking over at the hedge, Tony sounded calmer than he felt.

Deegan poked him in the chest. "How thick are you? You must know he's a dead man walking, the boss just wanted some fun with him first."

"Well I'm sorry about that, he didn't turn up. I'll have a word." He stepped to the side to pass Deegan, but Deegan stopped him.

"You stay there. I'll ask what he wants done. You silly man, you should have found Meredith and delivered him as instructed. You might also be a dead man walking now." Deegan grinned. "You might have become a liability. He doesn't like them. Where's Meredith?"

"Don't give me that. You know what I know, don't you forget it."

"Is that a threat?" Deegan lifted a heavily tattooed arm and formed a fist. "Because that wouldn't be wise."

"Not a threat, no. I'm saying you can fucking trust me." Tony stepped to one side and looked towards the Mercedes. "I am going to have a word."

As he stepped away, the large man grabbed him by the arm and swung him round. "Oh no. I asked you a question and I got threats, now I want an answer."

Tony had stumbled and was down on one knee cursing. "I don't know where Meredith is."

With a roar, he threw himself forward and his head rammed the stomach of his opponent, who, winded, stumbled backwards arms flailing. Ed nodded, perhaps Tony had more gumption than he'd given him credit for. He'd better step in and lend a hand. Taking advantage of his surprise attack, Tony righted himself and landed a decent right hook on the chin, followed by a punch to the stomach. Taking several steps back, Tony caught his breath.

Deegan's smile was evil. "Please yourself, but when he gets the girl, I'm going to enjoy showing her a new trick or two. Does she like it rough?"

Tony's confusion lasted a second. Realising they were talking about Amanda he launched himself again at Deegan. "You'd have to slap her around so she'd know you were there, I've heard your dick is so small she wouldn't even realise you were trying. Can't keep it up either, I've heard." His forehead found Deegan's nose, quickly followed by a roundhouse to the side of his head.

Deegan held his hand up. "I think that's enough."

Ed blew out a relieved breath and stopped walking as Tony replied.

"Agreed. But don't mention the girl again."

"You're right. Out of order. Don't get so lippy in future." Leaning forward, hands on knees, Deegan panted. Looking up from that position, he held out his hand. "You've got a decent punch. Shall we start again?"

A relieved Tony nodded and stepped forward his arm outstretched. He didn't see the other hand slip lower, or the blade hidden behind the leg of the man as he straightened himself. Taking hold of the proffered hand, he pulled the man upward.

In an explosion of movement, Tony was yanked forward, twisted around, and the blade of the knife sliced into his neck from left to right. A thin red line appeared as his assailant released him and stepped away. Tony's hands reached for his throat before his knees buckled.

As Tony's life ebbed away, Deegan stood over him. "I'm gonna get Meredith, and I'm gonna have the girl. Loser."

* * *

The car skidded to a halt as Ed finished updating the incident, and Meredith spun round in his seat. "And you've only just joined up the dots?"

Patsy placed a hand on his arm. "Meredith, calm down. It's all been a bit of a whirlwind."

Ed leaned forward, his face as angry as his brother's. "I'm a gardener. I talk to plants for a living. I'm not a shit-hot copper, nor am I a criminal – not really. My mind doesn't work that way! I watched a man die a few hours ago. He died protecting me, and, now I realise, defending Amanda. No, I didn't join those dots because that's not the way my mind works."

"But you realised the girls were in trouble, why didn't you mention that bit?" Meredith was not going to let it drop.

"Get out of the car." Patsy was already opening her door.

"What?" Meredith turned to watch her run around to the driver's side of the car.

Yanking open the door, Patsy could barely contain her temper. "Get out. I'll drive. Because while you're arguing with him about this, Amanda is possibly in danger. OUT!"

"Point taken. I won't say another word until we're home."

"Out. I hate you driving when you're mad." Patsy held the door until Meredith conceded and got in the passenger seat. Once she had pulled away, she added, "And we're not going to discuss it until Dad and Barbara have gone. All that needs to be achieved is we make sure Amanda is safe, and you get to the station on time. That's it. Not open for discussion."

"What time is their train?"

"Eight o'clock. You can give them a lift on your way to the station. Ed can help me babysit Amanda."

Meredith snorted. "Do you think he could fight his way out of a paper bag? Fat lot of use he'll be. No offence, Red."

"Sarcasm suits you." Ed leaned forward. "As it happens, I can handle myself. I had nothing to gain, and everything to lose once Deegan pulled a knife. You have no idea who I am or what I'm capable of."

85

"Assisting armed robbers. Impersonating a police officer. I know you're capable of that, and apologies, but does that put you at the top of the trust list? Afraid not. I'll have to get one of the boys around, and keep this meeting as short as possible."

"Right we're here. There's a light on upstairs, so they're up. End of conversation. Let me do the talking if anything other than niceties are necessary."

Jim Hodge was halfway down the stairs when Meredith opened the door.

"Hello, John, I wasn't expecting you. I thought you were Amanda. Who's that . . . Hello, love, and . . ." He looked from Meredith to Ed. "Is he—"

"What do you mean expecting Amanda? Has she not been home?" Even Meredith heard the panic in his voice.

"Of course. She tucked us up last night, you've not long missed her, she's on an early shift at the hospital. I thought she'd forgotten something."

Slapping his forehead, Meredith allowed himself a brief smile. "Of course. I'd forgotten. Excuse me a minute." Leaving the others in the hall, he went into the sitting room and called Amanda. Patsy stood with her ear to the door. "Amanda, it's too long a story but don't go to work, go to Sherlock. He's going to be expecting you, and stay with him until I tell you different . . . At last, thank you." Meredith hung up as soon as Amanda agreed.

His next call was to Frankie Callaghan.

Turning away, Patsy headed for the kitchen. "Tea is necessary I think, or would you prefer coffee, Ed? Dad this is Meredith's half-brother. His car broke down so he missed the wedding, but he found us in the end."

Shaking Ed's hand, Jim gave the usual greeting while staring at Ed's hair.

"Nice to meet you too, Jim." Ed pointed to his hair. "Girlfriend's idea of a joke, needless to say, she's not a girlfriend any more. Coffee please. Black with two."

"Same as John," Jim observed and led the way to the kitchen. "Patsy, I hope you didn't come home just to give us a lift. I've already called a taxi, it'll be here in a minute."

"Why? Your train isn't until eight. It's freezing on those platforms."

"Because I can't run with a suitcase. If we're on platform ten or above it's a long old march, and I've cut it fine before. I'm not running.

Anyway, there's that nice little café I was planning on having breakfast in."

"Ah, so now the truth emerges, this is all about a greasy spoon café." Patsy grinned at her father, who pushed her out of the way and placed the empty mug he was carrying in the dishwasher.

"As if." He looked out towards the hall. "What's wrong with John? He didn't look very happy."

Patsy lowered her voice. "He wasn't pleased Ed turned up."

Jim Hodge raised his eyebrows and looked at Ed. "Are you a wrong 'un then? Why wasn't he pleased?"

Ed held his hands up. "I have no idea. I'm hoping it's the hair, but it could be the fact our father ran off with my mother." His hands rose higher. "Neither were my fault, but what can you do?" He looked at the fridge. "Talking of breakfast, I've not eaten for a considerable time."

Meredith appeared behind him. "No, not since the bucket of fried chicken a couple of hours ago, you haven't."

Grinning, Ed turned to face him. "Are you hungry too?"

"You'd better not have eaten fried chicken. I thought you were sticking to all things healthy - I suppose that's only when I'm around." Patsy glanced at Ed. "Did he eat fried chicken?"

"Not really, I think he pinched a couple of chips. I can do healthy, as long as it's food and it fills a hole."

"Good. There's a box of cereal in the cupboard, and bread for toast in there." She pointed at the breadbin before looking at Meredith. "Did you get that problem sorted?"

"Yes, she's on her way to Sherlock. She didn't seem put out." He raised his lip in a snarl. "Getting too friendly those two."

"What will be, will be, Meredith. You know that." Smiling, Patsy lifted the kettle and went to fill it.

Her father refused a drink and was beginning to explain about the taxi again, when his phone beeped. "Oh dear. Taxi is here, I've not even brought the cases down."

"I'll do it. You get your coat on. Morning, Barbara." Meredith smiled at Patsy's stepmother and waited for her to clear the stairs. "Your taxi is here. I'll grab the cases."

Five minutes later, Patsy closed the front door. "They're gone." Stepping around Ed who was pouring cereal into a bowl, she dropped some bread into the toaster. "What's the plan?"

"I've got an hour before I need to be at the station, I'm taking Red in." Pulling out a chair, he pointed at the cereal box. "Pass the cornflakes, Red. God knows how long it will take. I'll have two slices of toast, please."

Ed took a seat at the table. "It might be better if I don't come with you."

"It might be better for you, it won't be for me. I need to get on and find out what you've unleashed on us."

"That's not quite true, is it?" Patsy put the first of the toast on the table. "They thought he was you. It's not him they are interested in."

"Why are you taking his side? Are you suggesting I let an armed robber walk free? I don't think so." Mouth full, Meredith cut the air with his hand indicating it was the end of the discussion.

"She is right. I know I did wrong, but it was all meant to be clean and harmless, other than the insurance companies, of course. I got greedy, I got carried away, and to be honest I quite enjoyed being you."

Meredith's lip twitched. "Did you? Why?"

"Because I'm a quiet sort of a bloke. Don't like fuss and bother, usually just blend into the crowd. I quite liked being pushy, arrogant and opinionated. Although I didn't need the last bit much, we were in and out on the jobs I was involved in."

Patsy looked from one to the other as she joined them, she said nothing, but knew, that like Meredith, Ed would not blend into the crowd.

"I am not pushy." Meredith shovelled cereal into his mouth.

"I'm not going to argue with you, but I might be some help in protecting the girls until we catch whoever this maniac is. That's all I'm saying. For instance, are you going to this meeting today? I would recommend not. Not now they've taken a shot at us, you'd be a sitting target. Look, I don't know . . ."

"WHAT?" Patsy banged her hand on the table and pointed at Meredith. "When were you going to mention that?"

"No one got hurt. But I've had another thought, what about your mother? We haven't sorted her out. Do they know where she lives?"

"Mum? I don't think they'll be interested in her. Tony knew where she lived, not sure about the others. I can't see that—"

"That's because you're not Meredith." Still angry, Patsy glared at Meredith. "This shooting thing isn't forgotten, but you're right. Unless they know your mother died, Ed's mum could be in danger. It's clear they're prepared to do anything to hurt you." Getting to her feet she pulled open a drawer and dropped a pad in front of Ed. "Address, telephone number, name."

"What are you going to do? Shall I call her?" Jotting down the information, Ed passed her the pad, as Meredith also got to his feet.

"You're not going down there on your own," he warned Patsy.

"I think you'll find you have other fish to fry, and correct me if I'm wrong, but that sounded like you thought you could tell me what to do. You who gets shot at without so much as a word."

Shaking her finger at Meredith's attempted response, she turned her attention back to Ed.

"It might be dodgy if I go to the house, they may have someone watching it. Call your mum, tell her it's too long a story, but to meet me somewhere . . . Is there a big department store, or somewhere else busy I could meet her?"

"Yes, Debenhams, but she won't go without me telling her why."

"She will." Patsy passed him her phone. "Ring the number and give it back." Turning to Meredith she looked him up and down. "I think you need to get ready."

Meredith knew he didn't have the time to talk her out of whatever plan she was concocting. Cursing silently, he left the kitchen, pausing to listen to Patsy greeting Fiona Meredith.

"Fiona Meredith? Sorry, did I wake you? Apologies, but I need you to listen to me, and listen very carefully. My name is Patsy, and I'm a friend of your son. He's in trouble, and he needs you."

There was a slight pause while she listened to Ed's mother's response. "Yes, his life might be in danger. Please get dressed, put a change of clothes in a shopping bag, no case, and I'll meet you in the ladies of Debenhams in . . ." She glanced at her watch. "An hour and a half. I'm driving from Bristol so don't worry if I'm a little late."

Listening to the demands of a seemingly distraught Fiona Meredith, she kept her authoritative tone. "I will explain all when we meet. I can't answer any more questions, I need to get going. I'll call you when I'm on the road, oh, and Fiona, don't answer the door, should anyone knock. Bye." Hanging up, she looked at Ed who had thrown his hands into the air.

"Was that necessary? She'll be terrified."

"Absolutely necessary. I need her to follow instructions not ask questions. I'm going to get changed. I'll find something more appropriate for you to wear. Make yourself useful and load that lot into the dishwasher."

When Meredith came down, he found Ed standing on the back door step smoking. Pulling a cigarette from the packet, he pushed Ed into the garden and held out his hand for the lighter.

"I would have asked, but you two seemed busy." Looking Meredith up and down, Ed whistled. "Nice suit."

"Oh, you heard. I was merely pointing out that I wasn't telling her, I was asking her." Blowing his smoke skyward, Meredith shrugged. "She didn't agree."

"Is she still going?"

"Apparently." Ignoring Ed's smirk, he flicked ash from his lapel. "We need to make a move. The sooner we get this sorted, the sooner I can find out who's after you."

"You."

"Us.

13

Fiona Meredith rolled over and sighed. Squinting at the clock she read the too bright digits. Six four five. Six bloody forty-five. What could they be rowing about this time of the morning? Ed would be moaning when he got up.

At the thought of her son, her eyes opened wide. She hadn't heard him come back last night. He always woke her up when he came in at night, he'd never been able to do anything quietly, it was the only reason she'd be happy when he went back home.

The banging started again, sitting up, she turned on the light and cocked her head. That wasn't the neighbours having a row. That was her door. Shoving her feet into her slippers, she pulled on her dressing gown. She hadn't heard him come home, because he hadn't taken any keys. No keys, no phone, no wallet. Idiot. He was up to something she was sure, but she'd kept quiet not wanting him to leave because she was interfering, but she'd have it out with him today.

"What was so important you . . . what the . . ."

No further words were possible as the large gloved hand caught hold of her cheeks and squeezed hard.

"Shut up. Get inside and you won't get hurt!" Kicking the door shut behind him, Alan Jenkins forced Fiona back into the hall. "Where's your son? Where's Meredith?"

Letting go of her face, he stood close, making her tilt her head to look at him. Massaging her cheeks with her fingertips, she shook her head.

"I don't know. I thought you were him. He didn't come home last night."

"I know that, he's in Bristol. What I want to know is where?"

"How would I know?"

"Because he's your son, you stupid bitch. Now think!" Jenkins jabbed his finger into her shoulder.

Having a temper of her own, Fiona would normally have had something to say. But now she was scared, this wasn't about her. This was about Ed. Her mind was all over the place as she tried to think what he'd been like yesterday afternoon. But there was nothing, he'd been dozing then answered his phone, jumped up and left. He never took a coat, never took anything. Something was very wrong.

She shook her head. "I don't know. Someone turned up yesterday afternoon, he got in the car and he's not been back."

"What sort of car?"

"A red one."

"Make, model?" Although his demands were sharp, Jenkins had a pretty good idea as to exactly what car it was, and the loss of Beresford's body was beginning to make sense.

"I don't know, I don't drive. A longish red one. Looked posh. Is he in trouble?"

"Shitloads."

"I bloody knew it. When he disappeared and I realised he'd not taken his wallet, I thought, something's wrong. He never goes out without his wallet." Her hand trembled as she pushed her hair away from her face. "What sort of trouble?"

"The sort that gets you killed. Where's his wallet?"

"On the table in the kitchen." Her eyes moved towards the kitchen door, and he shoved her forward.

"Show me." He spotted the wallet as he walked in and snatched it up. A healthy stack of twenties, his warrant card, and a visa card. The old girl was telling the truth, he had left in a hurry. "Ring him." He pointed at the phone on the table.

"I can't, that's his. How can I ring him if it's here?"

Dropping the wallet and picking up the phone, Jenkins pushed the home button. He was asked for the code. Slinging the phone to the floor, he pondered his next move. He knew Meredith was in Bristol, the pay as you go he'd given him had been switched off after he'd arranged to meet him Would he turn up? The only way to find out, to find him, was to go there. But what to do with the mother? She clearly didn't know about her son's extra-curricular activities, she might phone the police. Bollocks! He nodded as he realised she might be useful bait.

"I'm going to have to . . ." The phone in the hall started ringing, and he smiled. "I think that might be him." His smile disappeared quickly. "If it's not, say as little as possible and get rid of them, do you understand? Don't make me hurt you."

Returning to the hall, Fiona went to the table and looked at the phone. She pointed at the number flashing on the small screen. "It's not him. I don't know that number."

"Well it won't be his phone, you stupid cow, his phone's on the kitchen floor."

As Fiona stretched out her hand, he slapped it away. "Hang on, we'll do this on loud speaker. Don't do anything stupid." He hit the button, and a female voice filled the narrow hall.

"Fiona Meredith? Sorry, did I wake you? Apologies, but I need you to listen to me, and listen very carefully. My name is Patsy, and I'm a friend of your son. He's in trouble, and he needs you."

"What sort of trouble? Who did you say you were?"

Fiona's voice betrayed her nervousness, but Patsy mistook it for concern about her son, not because a muscular man had one hand holding the cord of the phone, and the other clenched into a fist. She gave Fiona instructions on where to meet, and hung up.

"She said his life was in danger! Why? Who is she?" Her knees had turned to jelly and pushing past Jenkins she plonked down on the stairs, burying her face in her hands. "I don't know what's going on. I don't understand."

"Get in here and shut up. I need to think." Jenkins jerked his thumb towards the small living room.

"I don't think I can walk. Who was that woman?"

"Get a grip." Yanking her up by the arm, Jenkins marched her into the living room, shoving her onto the couch. "Patsy Hodge is his girlfriend. You don't know much about your boy, do you?" He pointed at the photograph of John Meredith senior on the wall, a black bow tacked to the corner of the frame. "I heard he'd died. Condolences. He looks like his dad, was he a bad boy too?"

"He is not a bad boy. He's a hardworking, caring man. How dare you force yourself into my home and spout this crap." Fiona's temper had surfaced.

Jenkins smirked. "You'll be telling me next you didn't know you had a granddaughter."

Unable to believe him, Fiona shook her head. "That's a lie. Why would you say that?"

"Because it's true. Now button it. I was going to take you to Bristol, but now I might wait and get two for the price of one."

"I think I'm going to be sick."

"I said shut up."

"I'm serious."

Gagging, hand over mouth, Fiona ran from the room and up the stairs. Cursing, Jenkins waited on the landing while she heaved into the toilet. After a few minutes, the flush was pulled, and he heard running water. Pushing open the nearest bedroom door he looked inside.

It was Ed's room, and he walked in and looked around. Opening the wardrobe, he frowned at the quality of the few tee-shirts hanging there, and shrugged, Meredith didn't live here, they probably weren't his. He opened the drawers and seeing only a few pairs of socks and boxer shorts, decided he was right. Yawning, he looked at his reflection in the dressing table mirror. He looked old. Old and tired, Meredith had certainly put some years on him. The bathroom door opened and as he turned to look, something on top of the wardrobe caught his eye

"I'm going to get dressed. I'd appreciate some privacy." Standing in the doorway, Fiona's face was drained of colour, she looked frail.

"Get on with it. Three minutes." As she turned away, he reached up and grabbed the bag pushed towards the back of the wardrobe and dropped it on the bed. Unzipping it, he smiled, things had got a little bit better. Lifting out two of the bundles of twenty-pound notes, he guessed this was almost everything Meredith had picked up from the jobs. Dropping them back in, he jumped as Fiona reappeared.

"What are you doing going through . . . where did that come from?"

"I'd tell you, but you'd probably throw up again. Downstairs. Naughty, naughty Meredith, he's good at keeping secrets." Picking up the bag, he followed her downstairs.

14

Checking Amanda was safely occupied in the morgue with Frankie, Meredith kissed Patsy goodbye, biting back warnings to be careful. As her car pulled away, he looked Ed up and down. Wearing one of Meredith's least favourite suits and a freshly pressed shirt he looked very smart, or would have if it weren't for the hair.

Meredith grinned. "Very smart, Red. Although why Patsy thinks you need to be tidy to sit in a cell and then on to Horfield nick is beyond me."

"Prison. Today? Surely I have to have a trial first." Ed slammed the car door as the engine started. "Surely I'll get bail?"

"Let me think about that for a moment . . . Impersonating a police officer, armed robbery   . . . umm, no. Highly unlikely. Look on the bright side, you'll be running up credit for the sentence you eventually get."

"But I wasn't armed, nor were the other guys until Tony. Granted they threatened, but the worst that happened was a bit of hair removal with the tape." Closing his eyes, he thumped his head back against the rest and groaned. "Bollocks. Will you look after Mum for me?"

"Not personally, no, but I'm sure the police will until they catch whoever's behind this."

"What does that mean, you're sure? You don't know? I bet they'll help you keep your family safe." Thumping his head again, he cursed, "What a fucking mess."

"That's what happens when you're naughty." Glancing at Ed out of the corner of his eye, Meredith said, "I should have asked this before, but do you have a wife, boyfriend, partner, you know, a significant other, you haven't thought about?"

"Nope. Single. I have got this . . . thing with the woman I work for, but nothing formal and not even Tony knew where I worked. Only that I was a gardener."

"Will she miss you?"

"Of course." Doing his best to be an arrogant Meredith brother, Ed winked at him.

"I mean, is she not going to go looking for you?"

"Oh no. Her family wouldn't like it for one thing, and she has no idea where Mum lives."

Nodding his acceptance, Meredith remained silent for the remainder of the journey. Ed wanted to ask many questions, but his nerves were getting the better of him, and he remained silent. He sighed several times as he matched Meredith's stride into the police station. Punching in a code, Meredith pushed the door, which remained locked.

"Changed the code." As he pushed the bell, he looked at Ed. "Leave the talking to me. Follow my lead, got it?"

"With pleasure."

The duty sergeant smiled at Meredith as he signed in. "Nice to have you back, Meredith, I thought . . . oh boy! Are you related? Of course you are." George Davies held out his hand.

"George, and you are . . ."

"Red. Obvious reasons. Is the Super in?" Meredith tapped the signing-in book and Ed obliged.

"Rrrrred Merrrridith." George completed the name with a flourish of his tongue as well as the pen, and handed them visitors' passes. "When are you back properly? The place isn't the same without your smiling face. The Super is in the conference room. He's looking pained."

Already walking away, Meredith called, "No change there then. Back today hopefully."

By the time they'd walked past the third shocked face, Ed had his smile and nod off to perfection.

"Remember, button it, and if it's necessary to speak follow my lead." Meredith drew in his breath, knocked and pushed open the door.

Chief Superintendent David Ashworth didn't look up from the file he was studying but waved his pen in circles.

"Morning, sir."

Meredith indicated a chair, and Ed sat down. The two detectives from the day before were not in the room, so Meredith launched into the explanation he had prepared on the way to the station. "Sorry about all this bother and you being dragged up here, but you'll be pleased to hear that for once it's not my fault. But we do need to crack on, things have taken a sinister turn."

Not looking up, Ashworth snorted. "More sinister than armed robbery by a former detective, Meredith?"

"Much. This is my half-brother, Ed. I met him for the first time in—"

"Dear God." Ashworth allowed his glasses to slip down his nose and was staring at Ed. "Our armed robber, I presume?"

"Yes. But only under duress. Some low-life has it in for me, and a former friend, Tony Beresford, introduced him to Ed, although they've never met. Ed has been threatened, his mother has been threatened, Patsy and Amanda are under threat. He tried to appease them by doing what they wanted, but when that girl got injured, he said no more. Tony Beresford passed on the message and got his throat cut for the privilege. Ed naturally thought it was time we met, and drove Beresford's body to Bristol. It's now with Frankie Callaghan. I—"

"Why?" Ashford was now leaning back in his chair, arms folded across his chest.

"Why what, sir?"

"I'm talking to your brother. Why did you drive the body to Bristol?"

Still reeling from the fact that Meredith seemed to be protecting him, Ed had to organise his thoughts before speaking. "Because I was shit scared. Because I knew I needed the police to take over, but I don't know who I've been doing this for. Everything came through Tony. I thought if I could get hold of John, he'd know what to do. So, I—"

"Who's John?"

"Me, sir."

"Ah. Forget you have a first name sometimes. Carry on. One moment." Ashworth held his hand up, stopping Exton and Paisley from entering the room.

Looking over his shoulder, Meredith could see they were not best pleased, and saw Exton nod at Ed, clearly wondering who it was. Nudging Ed to continue, Meredith turned back to the table.

"May I?" Ed helped himself to a glass of water. "I didn't know who was who. The jobs they pulled went off without a hitch, and poor old Tony wasn't that bright. I didn't know if they had police help. After all, they thought I was a copper."

"Why?"

"Because Beresford told them he was me. Whoever set this up, knows me. Ed has seen pictures of Amanda, Patsy and his mother in Beresford's car. He heard a thug called Max Deegan tell Beresford he was going to enjoy watching Amanda's fear, right before he cut his throat."

Holding up a finger, Ed interrupted, "I would like to say at this point, I didn't know who Amanda and Patsy were then. We'd never met, I obviously knew my mother."

Ashworth rolled his eyes. "Okay. I think I understand. Is there anything else I should know before I let those two in? I don't like surprises."

"They're armed. Handgun with a silencer is my guess. When Ed took me to the body in the car they were lying in wait. Shot several rounds at us. We'll know more later. Frankie Callaghan's guys are working the car now, they'll have recovered the round that went through the windscreen."

"When the hell was this? Why don't I know about a shooting in Bristol?"

"Early hours, sir. I spoke to Trump and he took control. The public were unaware, as I said, they used a silencer. We should have their car now too, I . . ." Meredith cleared his throat. "I   firebombed it."

Ed grinned as the Chief Superintendent's eyes looked like they might pop out at any moment.

"Enough. I've heard enough, I'm content to let Louie deal with it at this end."

"About that, sir, is there any chance I can start back immediately? It's only a week early. I'm already heavily involved, albeit involuntarily, and that won't change. To my mind, it's only a question of whether it's made official or not."

"God, Meredith. Nothing is bloody simple with you. What do I do with those two? They have their own case to tie up."

"That's not a problem. The issue with Patsy and Amanda, and soon to be his mother, will be a local problem anyway. Tony's body is here, although if they want, they can take it back with them. We can share any leads we get in our respective patches. I can't see how they can have a problem with that."

"You can't? Roles reversed, you would."

"That's because I'm an awkward bastard." Meredith grinned as Ashworth looked down at his file to hide his smile.

"We can give it a go, I suppose. But I'm not sure you should head this up, you're too closely involved. I might keep one of them up here."

"Oh, come on. Spare me that. I'll take a back seat, let Trump have the case." Catching the slight incline of Ashworth's head, Meredith knew he was on to a winner. Ashworth was eager to see his nephew climb the ranks. "It's a local issue, sir. There's going to be all sorts of misunderstandings if you bring in an outside team."

Getting to his feet, Ashworth looked down on Meredith. "You are not coming back until your sick note expires. End of. Louie will be appointed OIC, and when you come back you will do so in an advisory capacity, unless another case comes up, if one does you'll be assigned to it. Clear?"

As Meredith confirmed the message had been received, Ashworth beckoned Exton and Paisley in. His outline of what Meredith had told him was brief. Exton kept looking from Ed to Meredith as Ashworth spoke; he held his tongue until he'd finished.

"What about him - Ed Meredith? He might have a brother on the job, and have a story about being forced to take part, but—"

"I'm a gardener. Not an armed robber. What would you do if your family was at risk?" Ed demanded, keen to enhance Meredith's version of his involvement.

"I'd go to the police like any sane person would. Whatever story you have to tell, you broke the law, not once, not twice, in fact . . . did you take money for your part of the operation, don't answer that, I can tell by the look on your face you did, that's not the action of an innocent person."

Turning back to Ashworth, Paisley demanded, "Whatever you allow to happen up here, you have to let us take him back with us. It's ridiculous to consider any other option."

That was his mistake. Making demands rather than requests was unwise, but suggesting Ashworth might be ridiculous, cemented Ashworth's decision.

"Really? You may charge Mr Meredith with whatever laws he has broken, you may arrange for him to appear before magistrates and they will decide whether or not Mr Meredith gets bail. I'm sure they will take his cooperation and assistance, not to mention the threat to his family, into consideration, and then, DS Paisley, then, when the matter comes to trial, a judge and jury will decide his fate. Would you like to tell me what's ridiculous about that?"

Meredith kept a straight face, but Ed's smile appeared as Paisley shook his head.

"Good, that's sorted. Now, if you'll all excuse me, I have a meeting to attend. Meredith take them somewhere to conclude this business and I want a daily report, however meagre you might consider it to be. Understood?"

On his feet, and already on the way to the door, Meredith agreed, "Yes, sir. Perfectly."

"Good. Tell DS Trump I'll see him in an hour.

Once outside, Meredith found Tom Seaton waiting for him. He held up a finger as Tom took in Ed's appearance, grinned and opened his mouth to speak.

"Two minutes before the questions, Tom. Red has some business to attend to first. Are any interview rooms free?"

"Yes, but—"

"Good." Turning to the three men trailing him, he waved his hand to hurry them. "Come on, we haven't got a lot of time. This way."

Not bothering to take the lift, he took the stairs at his usual pace, only slowing as he reached the doors leading to his former office and the adjacent interview rooms. "Tom, get the coffee on, and tell Trump to bring the file in. You three with me."

Closing the door behind him, he invited everyone to take a seat. When they'd done so, he pointed at the machine suspended from the ceiling. "I know you're not familiar, Red, so I'll bring you up to speed. In a moment, I'll hit the button, and this interview will be filmed and a copy kept here, and one provided to these chaps. You will be cautioned and charged, you will also be asked if you require legal representation. Do you?"

"I don't know, do I?"

"If I were a mate, and in normal circumstances, I'd say yes. But I'm not, so you'll have to take my word for it, that you don't at this stage, although you will the next time you meet for questioning."

"What do you mean the next time? We're questioning him now." Paisley rapped his knuckle on the table.

"Yes, but only so we can all get on. Ashworth told you what happened, I know you need more detail, and I'll get it to you, but now I need him to look at some faces so we can try and catch whoever is behind this, agreed? Or do I wait until one of our overworked duty solicitors turns up? You heard the Chief, he's going nowhere for the moment. I don't want to waste time arguing with you."

With a sigh, Paisley conceded.

Ed Meredith was cautioned and charged with armed robbery, impersonating a police officer, and advised that further charges may be forthcoming as the investigation got underway.

"Not guilty. I was not armed, to the best of my knowledge until the last one, no one was armed."

"Save it." Meredith shook his head. "This isn't a court room. And right on cue." He glanced at the camera. "DS Louie Trump has entered the room. Thank you. Take a seat."

Meredith leafed through the file and pulled out a mugshot. "Do you know this man?"

Exton was already nodding before Ed answered. "I do. Max Deegan, mediocre thug." Turning to face Ed, he asked, "Was he in on the robberies?"

"I think so, yes. One of the blokes who went in to do the jobs was big. I didn't have much to do with them and was always at a distance. He's the one who slit Tony's throat though. I saw that clearly enough."

"Who's Tony?"

Not wanting that line of questioning to go too far, Meredith answered, "Tony Beresford. He's a former friend of mine. He forced Ed into pretending to be me by threatening his mother and my family. Tony would never have followed through on it, apart from anything else, he didn't have the bottle. Beresford's strings were being pulled by someone else, and that's the bloke we need. He did however challenge Deegan in a layby near . . ." he flipped his hand, "Devon, somewhere. I'll get the detail of where later, and Deegan cut Beresford's throat."

"Where were you when this was happening?" Exton had his pen paused on his pad.

"Taking a pee. I heard some of the shouting and by the time I realised he was armed it was all over."

"And Beresford's body is still in a layby somewhere in Devon?" Exton shook his head, "We'd have heard."

"Nope, because genius here decided to drive it all the way to Bristol. He's in the morgue. I'll get someone to take you if you want to look. PM is underway, and forensics have the car."

Meredith pinched the bridge of his nose. "My wife and daughter are in danger, can we get back to finding the bastard in charge? If you know him, do you know who was pulling the strings?" Meredith slid the photograph closer to Exton.

"Nope. This is out of his league, he's got GBH charges because he can't hold his beer and likes to bully people. Always hung out with a dodgy crowd, although his dad's banged up, so no doubt there's more, but no one obvious springs to mind. I'll have to do some digging, shouldn't take long. Most of his mates have got expensive habits, one of them will—"

"May I interrupt?" Trump turned the file to face him and pulled a sheet of paper. "Take a look at this, sir, Alan Jenkins is an uncle. Son of his wife's sister."

"Bastard!" Meredith held up a hand as he considered this. "Well done, Trump. It fits with him wanting to hurt the girls. Get me a photo."

"Will do." Trump was already on his feet.

"DS Trump has left the room. What do you know about Alan Jenkins?"

"Never heard of him. I'd have to do a—"

"Then you've not caught him yet. You'd know him. Red, does the name ring a bell?"

"No. Never had a name. I don't know how many times I can tell you that."

"But you saw who was with Deegan, right? He was in charge?"

"Yes, absolutely."

"Good, well you might want to consider letting those two lock you up, because there is now a price on your head too."

"Would you like to share?" Exton asked, clearly irritated.

"Jenkins is a bad boy. He wanted to build a crime family, must have read a book on the Kray twins, and he moved to Bristol from his native Gloucester, because the pickings were bigger here. He started a minor protection racket, knocked off some post offices, and did a particularly nasty job at a jeweller's, leaving one bloke blind in one eye. We never proved it, but rumour was he had a not insignificant drugs distribution network set up.

"After I received a tip off, I sent him and half his family down, possibly including Deegan's father, although the name doesn't ring a bell. Jenkins got twelve years, was a good boy for the best part, had a family tragedy and was let out early – aren't they all?"

"But why come after you . . . let's have a look?" Exton held up his hand for the file as Trump reappeared. He and Paisley looked through the images. Both were shaking their head. "Don't know him. Do you?" Spinning the file to face Ed, he pointed at the face of a young Alan Jenkins.

"That's him!" Ed exclaimed. "Although he looks a lot younger here."

"I ask again, why come after you?" Looking to Meredith for an explanation, Exton closed the file.

"Because he thinks I'm responsible for his son's death. Terry Jenkins was part of the outfit that did the jeweller's, the witnesses said he didn't carry out the violence, but he encouraged it. He was twenty-two and wanted to show his father he had what it took. When we rounded them up, Jenkins offered me a bribe knowing Terry wouldn't take to prison life. He said his wife had no idea how he earned a living, and he wanted to save her some grief. I gave a charming refusal, told him where to stick his money and Jenkins junior got eight years. He would have only served four if he kept his nose clean, unfortunately he was a pretty boy."

"He was gay?" Ed joined the conversation.

"Nope, but if you've been inside long enough, you don't need to be . . . Jesus, how innocent are you? You must know what goes on."

"Oh course, I've been to the cinema, but why does him being good-looking matter?" Ignoring the snigger from Paisley, Ed added, "I'm trying to understand why we're all in this shit."

"A lifer took a liking to him, and Terry Jenkins took him on, and paid dearly for it. First, he got his face cut, then . . ." Meredith looked down at the table, "They tried to castrate him. They didn't succeed, but there was a possibility he might be impotent. Despite being told to give it time, he didn't, and he tried to hang himself. Nearly succeeded, but they found him and revived him. In hindsight, they should have left the poor bugger. Now he has little or no mental capacity, lack of oxygen."

Blowing out his breath, Meredith shrugged. "And apparently it was all my fault, not Jenkins' for getting him involved, mine, because I'm not bent." Holding up a hand to silence the next question. "I know this because he wrote me a long letter once he'd received the news. I never read it, he knew they'd tell me though. I was warned he was out, that was two years or so ago. But he never came back to Bristol."

"And then he found him." Exton pointed at Ed.

"He did."

"Why didn't you say all this yesterday?"

"Because I only found out last night."

Looking from one Meredith to the other, Paisley asked, "And you really didn't know each other before?"

"No." Meredith was on his feet. "Interview terminated when Ed Meredith identified Alan Jenkins as being the second man present at the murder of Tony Beresford." Hitting the button to stop the recording, he picked up the file on the desk.

"Wait a minute. You said you were responsible for Terry's death." Ed observed. "Did he die later?"

"No, but Jenkins visited him once, and refused to go again. Told the nurse he wasn't his son, his son had died in Dartmoor."

"Hold your horses, we need more than this." Paisley jumped to his feet.

"Then I suggest you go and find it. We'll cover the Bristol patch, and you do yours, let's see who's the first to pick him up." Giving a false smile, Meredith looked at Trump. "Take these gents and get them a copy of this." Giving Trump the file, he opened the door. "You've got to see the Super in twenty minutes, I'll be in the incident room. Red, stay there a minute."

Exton and Paisley left the room. They whispered to each other as they headed up the corridor.

Trump stopped at the door and waiting until they were a distance away, nodded towards Ed. "What are we doing with him? The story has changed a bit."

"I'm still trying to work that out. As to the story, I think he was confused, your discretion would be appreciated, for a while."

"I hope you know what you're doing, I know he's family, but . . . well."

"Agreed. I hope I know too. See you as soon as you can get away. Flatter your uncle, make promises, and get your arse back down here sharpish. If he offers lunch, you've got a lead you want to follow up."

"Okay, nice to have you back at the helm." Trump grinned, before a grain of doubt surfaced. "You are back, aren't you?"

"I'll let Uncle David fill you in. Get rid of those two, I need a word with Red." Meredith was already closing the door.

Door shut, Ed watched Meredith take a seat. This time on the other side of the table. "I think I should be thanking you."

"Yes, you should. But let me tell you this, if anything, and I mean anything, comes to light to indicate you've lied, I'll turn the other way and you'll go down for a long time."

Ed smiled. "You think I might not go down?"

"Oh, you'll go down, the only question is for how long." Meredith had no idea whether his version of events would save Ed from a prison sentence, but he wasn't going to let him know that. "For now, you stick to my version. Do as you're told, don't ask too many questions, and try and keep out of the way, or I'll hand you over."

"Understood. Can you call Patsy, see if she's got hold of Mum? Hearing your tales of joy and glad tidings have got me more worried than I was before. How do you live with knowing all this shit, and dealing with these people?"

"A lifetime of practice." Meredith called Patsy, but after one ring the ansaphone cut in. "She's on a call. I'd better send her a photo of Jenkins, she needs to keep her eyes open. It's a long shot they'll bump into each other, but better safe than sorry." Leaving a message telling Patsy to check her texts, he got to his feet. "Remember the rules, come on."

15

His head still thumping, Alan Jenkins popped three paracetamol tablets from the blister pack onto his palm and sucked them into his mouth. He chewed them until he wanted to gag and washed the remains away with a bottle of water. Closing his eyes, he waited for the thumping to subside.

"I need to use the toilet." Fiona Meredith's voice was barely a whisper.

"And I need a good night's sleep, and a clear head. Shut up." Opening the car window a little further, he tried to get a lungful of fresh air. What he got were exhaust fumes and the smell of urine. He took another swig of water. Perhaps bringing the old woman hadn't been such a good idea.

"Please don't make me pee myself. There are toilets just inside by the lift."

"If there's a toilet in there, why does it stink like a piss pot out here?"

"How would I know? I'm sorry, I have . . ." Pulling on the door handle Fiona confirmed her suspicion it was locked. Her chin quivered and she blinked back her tears. Too many tears had already been shed over bastard men, she'd not give this one the pleasure. "Please yourself, it's your car." Finding his eyes in the rear-view mirror she tilted her chin defiantly and began unbuttoning her coat.

"What are you doing?"

"I'm not peeing my pants for you. I'll go here." Looking down into the footwell she wondered if she'd be able to manoeuvre herself into position, but found she'd done enough already. The button popped up on the door. She felt no pleasure at this small victory, only relief.

"You bloody dare. Get out of the car."

Exiting the car quickly, Jenkins yanked open the rear door. Holding Fiona firmly by the elbow he marched her to the door. Pushing it open, he scanned the hall and walked towards the toilets, stopping outside the disabled door.

"In there." Following Fiona into the toilet, he glanced at his watch. "Hurry up, she'll be here soon."

"I can't go if you're in here."

"You were going to drop your knickers in my car a minute ago. Get on with it. I'll turn my back."

On the floor above, Patsy stepped into the lift, and smiled at the harassed young mother trying to convince her toddler she wanted to stay in the pushchair.

"She'll be alright once she gets in the car. All she wants to do at the moment is explore, she's used to the car. Lucky for you we're off on the next floor."

"She's a cutie. Do you know what floor the ladies is on in Debenhams?" Patsy smiled at the child.

"Top, next to the restaurant, but there are some on this floor if you're desperate. Mind your toes." Manoeuvring the pushchair ready to exit, the young mother looked relieved her ordeal was almost over. "Here we go, Sasha, nearly home." She soothed the child as the lift announced they had reached level four.

"Thanks, but I'm meeting someone in Debenhams." Patsy smiled as the doors opened. "Safe journey."

Patsy watched her depart and waited for the doors to close. A short red-haired woman with a harassed expression shook her arm free from the man she was with. Wondering if shopping with a child or a man was ever worth it, Patsy looked at the man as the doors closed. Had the child in the pram not launched her doll at him, she wouldn't have realised who it was. The doll hit him on the thigh before dropping to the ground and he stooped to retrieve it. Swooping it up with a smile, he turned to hand it back, as he did so his eyes met Patsy's. Taken aback, Patsy knew she'd allowed her recognition to show as the lift doors shut.

"Shit, shit, shit." Pulling her phone from her pocket she fumbled over the code to unlock it, before she hit the button for the next floor.

As the doors separated, Patsy reopened Meredith's message. She was right. "It is you, Mr Jenkins." Stepping out of the lift, and looking to make sure the coast was clear, she ran to the stairs and back up to the floor above, hid behind a Range Rover, and called Meredith.

"You've arrived, I take it." Meredith stated. "I know you'll be—"

"No time. Is Ed with you?" Keeping her voice low Patsy did her best to scan the car park through the tinted glass of the vehicle.

"Yes, why?"

"I think I've just seen his mother with Jenkins. Put him on." It took only a few seconds to establish that, yes, Ed's mother had a black coat with red collar and cuffs, and her hair was died a deep auburn colour. "Put Meredith back on." Patsy cut off any further questions.

"What I want you to do is get back here. Now." Meredith paced away from Ed. "I'll give the two local boys a ring. They're on their way back down there, they can take over."

"But that's losing valuable time. His mother looked petrified. He'll know I won't go to Debenhams to meet her now, so where will he go? What the hell did he think he could do, kidnap me in the middle of a busy department store with a pensioner in tow? I'm going to have a look round, see if I can find out what he's driving."

"You will not! Patsy, he might have—"

"I'm sorry, I could have sworn you were telling me what to do again. Give me some credit, Meredith, I'm going to try and get his car registration, not rugby tackle him."

Now at the far end of the incident room, Meredith turned his back on the team and Ed. "He might have killed you," he hissed into the phone.

"What?"

"In Debenhams. He could have simply pulled a gun and shot you. Job done. Now, please, I am asking, not telling, please come back to Bristol."

"I doubt that. I'll be careful. I'll call again in fifteen minutes. Hopefully with some useful information you can give the local boys."

Hanging up, giving him no time to argue, she set the phone to silent and put it back in her pocket. Drumming her fingers on her thighs, she wondered if she'd missed Jenkins and Ed's mother. They had been headed away from the lift, and hadn't been on the stairs, so must have come back onto this floor of the car park. There had been no movement of people or vehicles since she'd arrived. Perhaps Jenkins had doubled back. She pulled her vibrating phone from her pocket. It was Meredith, she rejected the call and texted him.

Think I've missed him, I'll come back.

Deciding to go back to her car and drive around the car park before heading for home, she straightened up, only to duck back down as the engine of a large Mercedes, two rows over, roared into life. Whoever was in the driver's seat had been there awhile. There was a screech of rubber as the car shot out of its space. Quickly checking the signs for the exits hanging from the girders, Patsy remained where she was. Unless it was going higher up the car park, the car would have to pass her to get to the exit. Setting the camera on her phone, she inched forward, keeping her head low. Another squeal of rubber as the Mercedes took the bend onto her rank. Facing the camera towards the exit ramp, Patsy readied herself, taking several rapid shots as the car passed her.

Peering at the first few photographs she smiled. Clear shot. Number plate visible, as was the red collar of Fiona Meredith's coat. Fiona was sitting in the rear. Walking briskly towards the stairs, Patsy sent a further message to Meredith.

I was wrong. He was still here, but he didn't see me. Attached photo of number plate, and I believe that's Ed's mum. Now I'm on my way back.

Ignoring the lift, she took the stairs to her car, remembering to pay the parking charge at the machine in the corridor. Ticket clamped between her teeth, she slung her bag onto the passenger seat and started the car as she read Meredith's message.

You'd better be.

Patsy followed the exit signs at a speed which didn't cause the tyres to squeal in protest. When she reached the final exit, there was a queue ahead. Three cars in front, at the barrier, the driver's door was open. Clearly, someone had forgotten to pay their fee before attempting to exit. Sighing, she leaned over to the passenger side and opened the glovebox hoping to find one of Meredith's cigarette stashes. In luck, she rummaged for the lighter. Sitting upright, she glanced in the rear-view mirror as a movement caught her eye. Alan Jenkins was storming towards the line of cars, with a ticket clenched in his hand, his face like thunder. He was the cause of the hold up.

Adrenalin racing, Patsy dropped across the passenger seat again, allowing her hair to cover her face, she shoved her hand in the glovebox, hoping any cursory glance would make the action look natural. As it happened, she needn't have worried. Jenkins was more concerned about Fiona Meredith attempting to do a runner than he was anything around him. Slamming the car door, he shoved the ticket into the machine.

At the sound of the door shutting, Patsy sat up and watched the barrier rise.

"Right, Mr Jenkins, I'm right behind you. What a stroke of luck." Watching his car turn right, she silently cursed the woman in front who fumbled with her ticket. When the barrier eventually lifted for her, Patsy turned right too, her eyes scanning the road for a glimpse of his car. "Lady luck, you are smiling on me today," she murmured, finding the lights several hundred yards ahead were red, and Jenkins was indicating a left turn. Patsy dropped into line several cars behind him. As she waited for the lights to change, she messaged Meredith again.

Stroke of luck, he got stuck at the exit. Now following, will text when I can.

Ignoring whatever reply Meredith had sent she followed Jenkins' car around the corner. Managing to stay several cars behind she followed him for several miles, ignoring her flashing phone, and wishing she knew the area, because then she might have a clue where they were going. At the next red light, she sent Meredith a brief message.

I'm following him, have no idea where I am, other than on the A30 approaching the M5. He might be headed for Plymouth?

The lights changed and Jenkins moved off. The car in front stalled and Patsy was stuck. Looking into the distance, Patsy saw his car move onto the large motorway roundabout.

"Buggeration!" Spotting a layby ahead, she pulled over and called Meredith.

"What the hell are you playing at?" he snapped.

"Doing you a favour. Did you get those photographs off to the local police? I lost him at the motorway roundabout. He's now on the M5 either south to Plymouth, or north to where? Bristol?"

"Trump's on it now. We've found out that Max Deegan is his nephew. So, now we have a proper connection. It's a long story, but I sent him and his son down for armed robbery, son couldn't handle it and tried to kill himself." He paused, "He didn't manage but is now severely disabled. Jenkins blames me, so this is very personal. I hurt his family, now he wants to hurt mine. Tell me you are on your way home."

"I'm on my way home. Where else would I go? I don't think you should work this case Meredith, I think you should hand it over and keep your head down, you're not due back until next week, we could jump on a plane somewhere and wait it out."

"Did you hear what you just said?"

"It was worth a try. I'm going to turn on the Bluetooth, I might lose you. I want to get going."

"Good. Call me back, I need to get on. Love you, Mrs Meredith."

"You too, I . . ." Realising he'd gone, Patsy set up the hands free on her phone. "Damn battery" Cursing, when a search of her bag and the car revealed she didn't have her car charger with her. "Bloody Meredith, I bet you have it." Pulling out into the traffic, Patsy headed for the motorway, wondering if she'd catch Jenkins up if he was headed for Bristol, instantly dismissing the idea as the final lights before the motorway, turned red.

Finally, able to start her journey as the lights changed, Patsy hadn't even joined the motorway before a signpost showed the road to Exmouth was ahead. Remembering that was where Ed's mother lived, she took moments to come to a decision. Rather than get on the motorway, she drove into the services. Buying a large coffee from a machine and an extortionately priced telephone charger for the car, she found the note with Fiona Meredith's address and entered it into the satnav. Pondering whether to update Meredith, she decided against it, and, leaving her phone on silent, she set off.

The journey was picturesque and uneventful. Patsy had just glanced at her satnav which told her she was within minutes of her destination, when Meredith rang.

"How's it going?" he asked.

"Not good, the traffic is miserable. I think there must be an accident or something up ahead. I'm going to stop at the next services as my battery is low. *Someone* must have borrowed my car charger, so I need another. What's happening at your end?"

"Details of Jenkins, his car, and Max Deegan have been circulated across the South, there's an APB out, so fingers crossed he'll be picked up. They are dangerous, Patsy, seriously dangerous. Deegan killed Tony when a good hiding would have done. The sooner you're back in Bristol the better."

"Well, traffic willing should only be a couple of hours. What are you going to do now?"

"Have a poke around some of Jenkins' old haunts. Speak to some of his old contacts, it's a long shot, but either he, Deegan or both were here last night, so might get lucky."

"Good luck. I'll give you a ring in an hour or so."

"Hopefully, you'll be here in an—"

Meredith was cut off. Patsy lifted the phone to find the battery had now run out. She drove on deciding she'd get to Fiona Meredith's house and set up the charger. That stop came up on her sooner than expected when the satnav told her to turn left and her destination was on the right.

Patsy followed the instructions, and turned into Bicton Street, but rather than pull up outside the house, she drove past, glancing at the property. The curtains were still drawn, and she could see the light was on upstairs. Fiona Meredith had clearly left in a hurry. Turning around at the end of the street, she drove back towards the house and slowed as a car pulled up outside. It wasn't Jenkins' car, so she parked in the nearest space available to watch who got out of the car.

Lifting her camera from the pocket in the door, Patsy focused the lens on the garden gate, only to drop the camera into her lap when Fiona Meredith got out of the car and hurried to her front door. Leaving the door open, Fiona hurried inside and returned minutes later with something in her hand and went to the driver of the car.

"Paying a taxi," Patsy muttered as she considered her next move. The arrangement to meet in Debenhams was a safety precaution in case the house was being watched. Given Fiona Meredith had returned in a taxi, Patsy decided to risk going in.

Getting out of her car, she glanced along the road, before hurrying to catch Fiona Meredith before she got back inside. Waving, she called to her. "Mrs Meredith, might I have a word?"

A pale faced Fiona Meredith looked at her. "Who are you?"

"Patsy. We were supposed to meet earlier."

"Do you know where Ed is? Can you contact him?"

"May I come in? Better we chat inside."

Five minutes later, Patsy placed a mug of coffee on the table in front of Fiona Meredith. Fiona's hand shook as she attempted to lift it, so she left it in the puddle she had caused.

"Ed is in trouble, the man you were with earlier thinks Ed is someone else, and he could use you to get to him. I need to take you somewhere safe. I'm guessing you didn't pack a bag as I asked, was he with you when I called?"

"Yes, loudspeaker. How did you know I was with him?"

"I saw you in the car park."

"Ah, he got really angry then. Didn't say why though, but he made me get out of the car at the services and I had nothing. Not a penny. A nice lady in the shop called a taxi for me."

"Did Jenkins give any indication where he was going?"

"Nope, just drove, too fast. I was scared, drove straight through the car park of the services, nearly hit a man with a little boy, stopped and told me if I saw Ed to tell him to call Jenkins, and other than that to keep my mouth shut if I . . ." Her hands flew to her mouth. "I shouldn't be speaking to you. He warned me."

"Don't worry about that, I'm taking you to Ed as soon as you're up to it."

"I didn't pack anything, he let me get dressed, that was it. He was mad as hell, what's Ed done? How long have you been his girlfriend?"

"I'll let Ed tell you what he's done when we get to Bristol. I'm not his girlfriend, I'm his brother's . . . wife." Patsy's eyebrows rose as she thought about this. "It's a long story, Mrs Meredith . . ." Again she paused, she was also Mrs Meredith, this was going to take some getting used to. "We'll talk in the car. Do you think you could go and pack a bag, or do you need a few more minutes.?"

"Call me Fiona. I'll do it now. How long have you been married to John?" Pushing herself to her feet, she lifted her coffee and took a sip. Her nerves had settled a little, but her stomach didn't want anything. Walking to the sink she poured it away.

"A whole day." Patsy smiled at the look of disbelief. "As I say a long story. You go and pack a bag, and if you don't mind, I'll borrow your phone and we'll get going."

Ignoring Meredith's ranting, Patsy explained she was with Fiona, and they would be on the road within minutes.

"It's not safe to take her to our house. What's she like?" Meredith asked

"In what way? I've only been with the woman for ten minutes." Patsy kept her voice low.

"In the, would she cope with Peggy, way."

Peggy had become an integral part of their lives, but she was abrupt, outspoken, and to some far too open to be comfortable around.

"Ah, yes, I think that would be fine. Good idea. Can you call Peggy? My phone is out of battery, and I don't want a conversation with Peggy with Fiona in the car."

"Will do. I'm being serious now, Hodge, no more detours. Straight back this time. No mucking about."

"I think you mean, Meredith. See you later."

Hanging up as Fiona called from upstairs and assuring her that clothes to last her a week would be enough, Patsy walked around the ground floor making sure all the windows and doors were locked. Ten minutes later they were headed back towards the motorway.

16 CHAPTER NAME

Kate Jenkins looked at the clock. It was still only six thirty, she'd been unable to get back to sleep as her mind was full of the possible trouble Max might be dragging Alan into, she was sick and tired of the pair of them. Groaning, she threw back the duvet and headed for the shower.

Pushing the half-eaten cereal away, she pulled the laptop forward. She had an hour to kill, so she might as well get something done. Resisting the urge for a cigarette, she sipped her coffee while the computer loaded. Since they'd had the new digital security systems, it seemed to take an age. Her coffee was almost finished by the time she was asked for her password.

"He won't be checking this today, so I suppose I might as well."

Grumbling to herself, she clicked on the padlock numbered forty-six. A reasonable quality picture appeared of the front of the imposing Victorian villa. A postman was closing the gate.

"Bet that was all junk."

Muttering away to herself, she hit the menu button and found the only starred item was the side alley. Frowning, she hit the play button and smiled as she saw a scruffy vixen followed by two cubs trotting through to the back garden. She moved on to padlock 73.

"Why are those dustbins still out? They got emptied yesterday. Bloody laziness!" There were no starred items. She moved on to the padlock labelled: Office. There were four starred items. "Oh shit, if we've had a break-in and he's off mucking about for Max, there's going to be trouble."

It took her three minutes to watch her husband's arrival, his entry to the office, the collection of money from a safe, and with her fists clenched and her mouth open, she watched him lift the carpet in the corner of the office, remove a floorboard and take out a package. It was impossible to make out what it was. Kate had not been aware her husband had a hiding place in the office.

Stopping the recording, she looked at the time he'd left the office. "So, hubby darling, you went there before going off on your travels. Well, secret hiding places are not acceptable. Let's see how you explain this."

Taking a screenshot, she saved it to the laptop. Alan was not good with computers, he'd been shown time and again how to create a file to save things for future use, but it seemed a step too far. The laptop was full of documents and pictures, none of which had been named.

"Bloody hell. Why is life so complicated? That's it, I'm deleting the lot." Double clicking the first item, she found it was a fishing rod for sale on eBay. "Alan, you don't fish. Why?" Her finger hovered over the delete button, but she relented and made a file entitled: *Alan's Rubbish*, and saved the details of the rod. Within a few moments, she had saved ten items and deleted a further nine. With thoughts of his secret hiding place bubbling away in the back of her mind, she clicked away clearing the laptop, and fighting her craving for nicotine.

Kate was nearing the end of her task when she opened a jpeg and found a photograph of an attractive woman walking towards the camera. She stared at it for a few moments. "Oh, Alan." Slamming the lid of the laptop, she collected her cigarettes and went to her favoured smoking spot. Rather than sitting on the bench at the top of the garden, she paced around it, and smoked two cigarettes, one after the other, before returning to stare at the laptop.

After a few moments, she returned to the task. Opening another file, she named it: *Really?*, and saved the photograph, along with the screenshot of Jenkins at the office, which she consigned to the *Really?* file.

After ten minutes, she had cleared the laptop apart from two documents. She drained her coffee, and opened one of them. Even before she'd had time to read the document one word flew at her and she froze.

Meredith.

Pulling herself together she read the scant information. The document, *Meredith*, contained his home address, his car registration, his mother's address and a list of dates. There was no indication as to why the dates were relevant. The temptation to call her husband was resisted and Meredith joined the photograph in the *Really?* folder. Her hand shook a little as she opened the final document, which she was relieved to find was only an invoice for some tyres.

Her nails drummed out a tattoo as she worked out how to approach the subject of the *Really?* file. If she went in all guns blazing, he'd lose his temper and it could be days before she got the truth out of him. On the other hand, she had to stop him having any form of contact with Meredith. What if Meredith told him? The photograph momentarily forgotten, she covered her face with her hands.

"No, no, no, no."

A thought occurred to her, and she opened Jenkins' email account. He had got that document from somewhere, she doubted he'd typed it himself. Immediately the inbox opened she knew he was hiding something. There were twenty unread emails. Alan didn't maintain his account, a visit there would usually reveal several hundred mostly unread emails, which she would manage once every few months when she had the patience. Alan had been busy, but why? She clicked on the sent folder and found it empty, which given his aversion was not unusual, but a glance at the deleted folder told her he'd emptied that too. "Bastard!"

Returning to the bench in the garden, this time it took three cigarettes to keep her from phoning him. Instead, she called Aretta.

"I'm probably going to be late. I know we have more coming in today, but if I'm not there in time, get on with it. Can you do that?"

Aretta was always amenable, although she had little choice in the matter. She assured Kate all would be well, and Dickie was there to help.

"Why is he there?"

"I don't know. He's just arrived."

"Put him on." Kate lit her fourth cigarette as she listened to the muffled voices. Dickie grunted in her ear, and she blew out a plume of smoke. "What are you doing there?"

"Al asked me to come in, said you had new ones arriving and he couldn't be there. Said you might need a hand."

"Why would I need your help? I've never needed it before."

"I don't know, Kate, I'm just doing as he asked." Not caring if Kate heard his sigh, he looked at Aretta and rolled his eyes. "Have you had trouble here?"

"Never. And he didn't say anything else?"

"No."

"If I find out you're lying to me, Dickie, you'll be out on your ear. Get your arse back round to seventy-three and get the bins in."

"No problem."

"No, I know it isn't. That's why I can't understand why they're still out." Kate hung up and dropped her cigarette into the pot of sand next to the bench. "Something is going on, he's up to something." Singing the words, she hurried back to the house. Tapping the mouse to open the screen without sitting, she muttered, "One more check to do." Opening the recycle bin, she nodded. "I bloody knew it. Ha! You are simply not clever enough, mister."

Dropping onto her chair, she scrolled past the items she'd deleted earlier and opened the first jpeg, then the next, and carried on until she had over forty photographs opened. She clicked through them. Almost all were of two very attractive young women, one of whom looked no older than Terry. She glanced at the wall holding a photograph of her beloved boy.

"Mum's coming to see you later, darling, don't worry."

Kate wanted Terry to live at home. They could afford the nursing staff necessary to help, in fact, it would probably be cheaper than the care home, but Alan couldn't even look at him. On the one occasion he'd seen Terry, he'd wept. It was the only time she'd seen him cry, and she'd found somewhere for Terry to be cared for which was as close to perfect as it could be. Kate visited every other day, but the longing to have him home didn't diminish, if anything it got worse.

Looking at the screen for a moment, she looked back at the photograph. "If he's up to something we wouldn't like, be it a woman or something that could put him away, he's out of here, nothing will put you at risk, and you my darling can come home where you belong." Her phone rang and she blew him a kiss. "Aretta, is it important?"

"Yes, I think so. I have a problem and Dickie is shouting again. No good happens when he shouts."

"Let me speak to him." Kate went to the kitchen listening to the sound of Aretta's shoes clipping against the tiled floor. Squinting, she tried to hear what was being said. Dickie was shouting but his words weren't clear.

"He said he doesn't need to speak to you."

"Tell him I think he does." This time Dickie came over loud and clear.

"It's sorted. Tell her I've gone to do the fucking bins."

"He said—"

"I heard what he said. Has he gone?" Kate massaged her temple with her free hand, a headache was forming.

"He's putting on his coat."

"Tell him I'll see him there." A door banged in the background. "I take it that was him?"

"Yes, he's gone."

"Good, I'll see you later, call . . . shit, is that the time? I have to go. I've got to get ready and make a couple of calls."

It was almost eleven o'clock, Kate had no idea how long she'd stared at the screen of the laptop, but too long to do any good. She called Alan. It rang through to his answer service. She left a curt message for him to call her before making her other calls.,

She went to get dressed. Twenty minutes later, hair done, and face made up she called again. This time her message was to the point. "Alan, if you don't call me in the next ten minutes *you* will be responsible for my actions."

Wanting to speak to him before she left the house, she loaded the dishwasher and emptied the bin. Lighting a cigarette, she walked with the bag to the dustbin. "Come on, Alan, I need to be calm today."

As his car overtook the van in front at ninety miles per hour, Jenkins listened to Kate's message. Groaning, he thumped his forehead repeatedly. What did she want now? She sounded pissed off. Seeing the sign for the services, with no indication, and oblivious to the beeping horns from the cars he had cut in front of, he shot across the motorway, only just managing to make the slip road.

He parked in the disabled space, nearest the entrance, something he'd never have dared to do if Kate was in the car, before hurrying into Taunton Deane service station. He bought himself a coffee and a burger before returning to his car. He'd taken one bite before his phone rang again. It was Kate, this time he accepted the call.

"Hello, babe, what's—"

"Last chance."

Jenkins stared at the burger. "What the fuck does that mean?" Dropping his burger back into the bag, he tried again. "Kate, sweetheart, I'm on the motorway, my handsfree isn't working and I had to stop before I could call you."

"It was working fine yesterday."

"Perhaps the Bluetooth has had a blip. I'll sort it. Now, what do you want, you sounded pissed off?"

"How surprising. Because pissed off doesn't even come close." Her laugh sounded hollow.

"Just tell me, Kate, it's been a long day already."

"Tell me about it. Let's start with you telling me about Meredith."

White knuckles appeared as he gripped the steering wheel. "Well there's a fucking unwelcome blast from the past. What do you mean tell you about him?"

"Cut the crap, you left his details on the laptop. I don't want any more trouble, Alan. I don't need any interruption to our income, think about Terry."

"I do, almost all the time, but you've lost me. Why would Meredith interrupt the income? Kate, I've got to get on, and I have no idea what you're on about."

"You're lying, I told you never to do that again." Her hand was shaking with anger when she hung up.

Jenkins slapped his palms on the steering wheel in time with his cursing. "Fuck! Fuck! Fuck!" Allowing his head to fall forward and rest on his hands, he wondered if phoning her back would be worth it. His eyes closed and he yawned. Wound up and tired, he was a disaster waiting to happen on the motorway, but he couldn't allow himself to sleep, he didn't have long enough, Meredith might go to the meeting place.

Retrieving his burger, he ate it as he called Kate, twice. Each time hanging up before she could answer, if indeed she intended to. That way he had proof he'd tried. Finishing the coffee, he dropped it into the burger bag and opened the car door to dispose of it. There was a bin less than ten yards away, but it was cold, and he was tired, so he simply dropped it on the ground. Pulling the door shut, he closed his eyes and leaned back into the seat, what a shit day, what else could possibly go wrong? He yawned again.

17

Standing, Meredith held his hands above his head, arched his back and yawned.

"You haven't got a clue, have you?" Tom Seaton patted Ed's shoulder. "What if we got you to do a photofit, would that help?"

"No. I was never with them. They were just blokes, dressed like council workers, heads down because of any CCTV. The best I can do is agree that because of his size, one of them might have been Deegan on the Exeter job. But that's purely based on his build."

"This is getting us nowhere. And we're wasting time. I'll check in with Patsy and go and knock on some doors."

"Anyone in particular?" Trump had now spoken to his uncle, and was uncomfortable having to keep tracks on Meredith.

"Some faces from the past. A few who owe me favours, and a few who were tight with Jenkins before he went down. Red, get out the way, I need to get some addresses." Waiting until Ed had moved away from the screen, he dropped into the vacated chair. "Now, who shall we start with?"

Trump pulled his ringing phone from his pocket. "Sergeant Exton. Let's hope he has some news." Having greeted Exton, he listened for several minutes, jotting notes on a pad in front of him. "Thank you. Not sure what use that is, we'll let you know if Jenkins or his car turn up in Bristol." Hanging up, he shrugged at the team.

"No joy, I'm assuming?" Dave Rawlings slumped down further in his chair.

"Not really. He's emailing confirmation of all this, but now we have Jenkins' home address, the address of a seedy gym he owns, the local boys have never had any problems or complaints about, and the fact that Mrs Kate Jenkins runs two hostels in the city and if such a thing existed has a five-star rating from the local authority. Set them up when Jenkins was inside, both registered and licenced by the authorities, all above board. They are both registered in her name."

"Well they would be. I know times are tough on the housing front, but I doubt even Jenkins could swing a CRB check. Glad Kate got herself sorted out, I'm surprised she took him back. Where was I?" Meredith clicked the mouse and pulled the keyboard forward.

"Do you know her?" Tom Seaton picked up the empty mugs. "I can't remember us having much to do with her. I'll make more coffee."

"Only because of the case. She seemed a nice woman, I felt sorry for her. Black with two, now shut up and let me think."

Ed had found an empty seat, and folding his arms on the desk in front, rested his head and tried to grab some sleep. Rawlings had disappeared and Trump stood behind Meredith.

"I'm not going to keep secrets from you, Trump."

"No, I know that. But this will save you repeating yourself. What are we going to do with your brother while we're out tracking this lot down?"

"I have no . . . actually I do. We'll drop him at Peggy's that way he can keep an eye on his mother and vice versa. Talking of which I'd better call Patsy and get her ETA. Peggy was going to stock up on groceries and wanted to be kept informed."

"That's trusting of you. You don't think he'll abscond?"

"No idea. I doubt it, but if he does, I'll find him."

Trump wasn't at all convinced it was a good idea, he thought it better they left him at the station with the others, but he waited for Meredith to make his calls before telling him.

* * *

Patsy took Fiona's arm as they left the service station. The woman looked fit to drop, pale and drawn, and Patsy had noticed the tremor was still there when Fiona had lifted her coffee.

"Not long now, and then you can get some proper rest. You'll like Peggy, she's a bit forthright, but has a heart of gold." She paused for a van to pass before steering Fiona in the direction of the car. Her phone rang as they stepped off the kerb, and she took Meredith's call. "Nearly there."

"How nearly is nearly?"

"Taunton Deane. We stopped for a comfort break. Fiona is a little out of sorts over this."

Checking the time, Meredith asked, "You'll be with Peggy by one-thirty then?"

"Yes, hang on. There you go Fiona, buckle up." Patsy closed the door and walked to the driver's side. "She's not well, Meredith. Lovely lady, but your brother has a lot of apologising to do. How's it going?" Climbing into the car, Patsy fastened her own seatbelt.

"Nothing much to report. Got some unhelpful information on Jenkins' homelife and businesses, I'm off out with Trump now to—"

"SHIT!"

"Hodge, what's wrong?"

"Jenkins is here. He's got a gun, and he's headed this way. Shit, shit, shit." Patsy fumbled as she tried to get the keys in the ignition, it didn't help that Fiona had started wailing.

"Get out of there!"

"I'm trying, I . . . too late, I'm going to put you in my pocket, I won't be able to speak."

Meredith beckoned the others over and putting the phone on speaker, put a finger to his lips before he pulled on his jacket. The next voice was Patsy's.

"Mr Jenkins, I believe."

"Patsy Hodge, fancy bumping into you here. Shut her up before I do, then get out of the car and come with me. We're going for a ride."

"I don't think we want to go—"

"I said get out of the fucking car. I'm happy to use this, I've had a bitch of a day, it might cheer me up. SHUT UP!"

Fiona's wailing dropped to a whimper, a car door slammed, and Meredith listened to footsteps that he assumed were Patsy's.

Covering the microphone on his phone, he issued his instructions. "Rawlings get traffic and an armed unit to Taunton Deane services. Tom, get a car round to the front, I'll meet you there."

Uncovering the microphone, he tilted his ear towards the phone, all was silent. Checking to make sure it was still connected, he gave a sigh of relief when he heard Patsy's voice.

"A Mercedes, very nice. Where exactly will we sit? This model isn't properly designed for more than one passenger."

"You'll manage. Shut up and open the boot."

"I am not getting in the boot. Shoot me now," Fiona stated.

Her voice was muffled but Ed caught it and got to his feet.

"Don't tempt me. Hodge get the tape."

"She's Meredith now, they're married."

Back in Bristol, Meredith pinched the bridge of his nose as Jenkins laughed.

"Even better, ruining the honeymoon is an added bonus!"

"You think you're so clever, you don't know . . . Ow!"

"Fiona, hush, it's best you don't speak."

"Too right. Get the tape and bind her wrists, then you can shut that trap of hers."

"We should let her get in the car first, she's not well."

"Get on with it."

"There, she's secure. What now?"

"Turn around and hold your hands out."

"Where are you going to take us? What good will this do? You won't get away with it."

"If you don't want to be gagged too, shut it! I've had enough of nagging women today to last me a lifetime."

A car door slammed and seconds later an engine roared into life.

Snatching up the phone, Meredith looked at Trump before heading for the door. "Are you coming?"

"I am." Trump managed to catch the door before it shut.

"Me too." Ed was on his heel.

Trump decided against arguing with him, Meredith held the phone to his ear, aware that any noise might alert Jenkins to their presence. Outside, Meredith jumped into the passenger seat and pointed forward, the car was already moving before Ed had closed the door. The four men remained silent as Tom Seaton headed for the motorway.

In the Mercedes, Patsy was also silent, she hoped Fiona Meredith would remain that way too. Patsy hadn't properly secured the tape, and it was only stuck to Fiona's top lip allowing her to breathe normally. Keeping the car at a reasonable speed, Jenkins exited the services, took the next exit for Taunton, but rather than head for town, followed the road around and got back on the motorway. Once on, he quickly accelerated across the lanes and continued at a speed that made Patsy clench her fists.

"Are we going back to Devon?" she asked in a loud voice, hoping Meredith was still listening.

"Shut up. I have to make a call. If you speak, I'll shut you up permanently." Jenkins lifted the gun on his lap for good measure.

"You don't need to threaten me with a gun." Patsy was shouting now. "And slow down, you'll kill us all."

"SHUT UP!"

Jenkins jowls vibrated with the effort of shouting, and his face turned red. When he lifted his mobile and scrolled to a number, Patsy closed her eyes, if she was going to die, she didn't want to see it coming. She relaxed a little when the sound of ringing filled the car. The call was answered.

"Yes, boss?"

"Can you speak? Is Kate around?"

"She's on her way, she's on one too. Gave a—"

"I'm on my way with a couple of visitors, I'll need to bring them to you, but Kate mustn't know. Do you understand?"

"Visitors? Who?"

"That doesn't matter. Where shall I take them? Which house is best?"

"Who knows? How long will you be? She could be paying a flying visit, as far as I know the new—"

"Dickie! Shut up! Why does everybody rabbit on when I'm thinking?"

"Sorry, I—" Dickie rolled his eyes and wondered if he'd get to complete a sentence as Jenkins talked over him.

"I'm going to be a couple of hours tops. Keep an eye on Kate's movements, and I'll call you when I'm closer. If she's with you when I call, answer but don't let on it's me."

"Right."

"Do you understand? Because if you cock up . . . well, you'd better not."

"I got it."

"Is she there?"

"No. Why?"

"Because you seem to have a problem stringing a sentence

together."

"That's because you keep—"

"Dickie, shut up, I've got to go. Don't forget what I said." Jenkins jabbed the hands-free control and the call was terminated.

"Can we slow down now? You're going to get stopped if you don't kill us first, there are lots of police about." Patsy watched two police cars on the other side of the motorway fly past, lights on and sirens blazing.

"They're going the other way. Shut up."

"All I'm asking is—" Unbeknown to Patsy, her phone had died, the charge she'd managed to accrue from Devon to Taunton was spent. She attempted to give Meredith clues for the next twenty minutes until Jenkins was so wound up, he was driving over one hundred miles per hour, and told her he'd aim for the crash barrier if she said one more word. She shut up.

Meredith looked at the screen on his phone. "She's gone," he said unnecessarily. "Trump call Exton and Paisley and tell them the car is southbound, and ask them to find out who Dickie is. Tom put your foot down, at least we know where they're headed." He turned in his chair and looked at Ed. "How will your mother cope with the stress of this, abducted twice in one day?"

"She's a tough old bird, she had to be married to my . . . *our* father. But she'll be crapping herself with worry over me. Shit, none of this should be happening. I'm sorry."

"So you should be. Remember this next time you're tempted to be . . . what's the story now? Blackmailed into breaking the law?" Trump tutted, but seeing the look of hopelessness on Ed's face, added, "At least you're not the cause of his interest in Patsy. It seems to me, his quest for revenge was around long before you met Beresford."

Ed managed a weak smile. "I suppose you're right, and I suppose if I hadn't met Beresford you would never have known Patsy and Amanda were in danger."

Meredith considered this. "Once we catch the bastard, we can find out whether it was the chicken or the egg. We'll know then whether I should give you a good hiding or shake your hand. But first, let's catch the bastard. Tom does this thing not go any faster?"

18

Although Jenkins slowed a little with the two women silent and his call made, he was still driving well over the speed limit. They made Plymouth in record time. Sitting at red lights as they entered the city, he called Dickie again. "I'm here. Which house should I aim for?"

"Whichever you like. Aretta tells me there's been some issue with this last lot, red tape or something, Kate had to go and sort it out. Not been gone long, so if you're quick she'll be none the wiser."

"Just had a thought, I'm coming to yours."

"My what?"

"Your flat. I know Kate leaves the rooms to Aretta and Fati, but the way my luck's been going she'll break the habit of a lifetime today."

"Mine? You can't swing a cat in here, what am I supposed to do with them?"

"Look after them until I find a better place."

"How long will that be? Not that I'm not grateful, but—"

"Dickie, I don't want you to entertain them, just hide them for a few hours while I sort stuff out. Stop bleating and open the back gates. Shut them once I'm in."

Jenkins made no attempt to hide where they were going or confuse Patsy by taking a convoluted route to the house. That was worrying, if he knew so much about Meredith and her and Amanda, he must know she was a private investigator and former police officer. Reaching her bound hands across to Fiona she patted her knee, more for her own comfort than Fiona's. Fiona would be oblivious to the significance.

Despite her concerns, she noted landmarks and street names as they drove into the city. Mutley Plain, that was a name she'd remember, she glanced at the shops and fast food outlets lining the street. A pub situated on an island in the fork of the road appeared ahead, The Hyde Park. Blinking she cleared her mind. An excellent landmark, she could forget the rest and start again here.

Jenkins drove around the pub and without indicating took a left, the street name was obscured by an overgrown hedge. They hadn't travelled far when he suddenly turned again. The gap between the houses was narrow, and Patsy thought it was the driveway of one of the houses, but it was a lane providing rear access to the terraced Victorian villas. After a couple of hundred yards it widened slightly, and Jenkins manoeuvred the car into a small recess before reversing at speed. As the car jolted to a halt, a skinny man with a mop of greasy grey hair stepped out from behind one of the gates pulling it shut as he did so, dropping the stay into its hole, he hurried to the second gate and repeated the process. Jenkins was already out of the car.

"Lock it," he shouted as he folded his seat forward against the steering wheel. "Out!" he ordered, and reaching into the car grabbed hold of Fiona's hands and yanked her forward. She yelped at the pain. "Shut up," he hissed and looked up at the windows of the house. Seeing no one he jerked his thumb at Patsy. "You too, quick now, don't make me angry." He patted the butt of the gun which was now tucked into his trousers.

Jenkins was wrong, he was being watched. Aretta pulled her head back behind the curtain in the second-floor room as he glanced up. She waited a few seconds and leaned forward. A frown creased her brow. Why were those women bound? It was odd enough that they were white, but to be tied up, it had been a long time since anyone, to her knowledge, had been bound. Dickie didn't look happy.

Moving away from the window as Jenkins looked up again, she collected the pile of linen and walked back into the corridor, she didn't want him mad with her ever again. The flexing of her jaw was subconscious as she remembered the punch.

"Why are they tied up? You said guests. I'm not happy about this Al, really ain't happy at all."

"Shut the fuck up. I've had enough whingeing and moaning today. When did your opinion ever count for shit?" Pushing the women towards the rear door, he snapped, "Open the bloody door then."

Dickie led the way through the back of the house and stopped at a door near the bottom of the stairs. He opened the door, before stepping back to allow Jenkins to usher the women in. Following them, he pushed the door shut and flipped the catch.

"Now what?"

"Stop asking questions and answer a few. Who's in?"

"Only Aretta and the girl who caught her hand in the machine."

"Everyone else get off okay?" Jenkins looked at his watch. "What time do you pick the rest up?"

"About an hour, but—"

"Why is Aretta here?"

"That's what I'm trying to tell you. Kate has only got two new ones, she's dropping 'em off here and told Aretta she had to sort 'em out."

"Shit! Why, where's she going?"

"I don't know. How would I know that?"

"When is she coming here?"

"How would—"

"Alright, I get the picture. Right here's what we're going to do. I've got to go and sort something out. I'll leave by the front door, you come out with me, shout up to Aretta you're going out, then scarper back in here and keep those two quiet until I get back."

"What if Kate comes in?"

"Then keep extra quiet. No radio, no telly, no chatting. Got it?"

"Yep, but I'm not happy. What if—"

With a sudden movement which belied his stature, Jenkins sprang across the small sitting room and grabbed Dickie by the T-shirt. Clenching the fabric in his fist, he allowed the momentum to carry him forward until Dickie's head thudded against the wall.

Pressing his forehead against Dickie's with some considerable pressure, he snarled at him, "I said no more questions. I don't care what you don't like, or about your ifs and buts. Do as you're told because I'm nearly at the end of my tether. I need to work off some steam, don't make it be on you." Glancing over his shoulder at the two women, he smirked. "Because I've already made plans for that."

Barely eleven stone, and cowardly by nature, Dickie forced a yellow-toothed grin. "Gotcha."

"I hope so." Jenkins stepped back. "Because I hate my plans being messed up. Now are you ready to see me out?"

"Yep. What about them?"

"You'll be ten seconds. They're tied up. They know not to misbehave, don't you girls?"

Nodding once, Patsy stared him out.

"I like that. I find it's better if there's a bit of fight in them." Turning away abruptly, Jenkins strode to the door with Dickie rushing to keep up.

As Patsy pulled the tape from Fiona's top lip, she listened to Dickie shout to Aretta, and the front door slam at the same time as he reappeared, double locked the door and slid the key into his pocket.

"I need to use the bathroom," Patsy announced.

"So do I. Can I go first? I can't cope with this anymore." Fiona blinked furiously to hold back the tears.

"Shut up! No talking. You heard him. I don't know what you two have done to piss him off, but don't make it worse than it already is."

"You want me to pee on your couch? Because that's what will happen. Come on, Dickie, you don't even need to release me, I'm sure I'll manage." Holding up her bound hands, Patsy looked at Fiona. "Is that alright with you?"

"Not really, but I'll try."

"For God's sake. Stop rabbiting. She could be anywhere." Dickie's eyes darted towards the door.

"This is bloody ridiculous." Shuffling to the edge of the couch, Patsy got to her feet. "Is it this way?" She lifted her hands towards a door opposite before turning to Fiona. "Here let me help you up." With some difficulty, she prised her hands open enough to take hold of Fiona's elbow and pull her to her feet. "If you'll excuse us."

Dickie made a dash for the door. "Wait a minute." He hurried forward and escorted the women through a small galley kitchen and into the bathroom.

Patsy kicked the door shut on him. "Hold out your hands."

Doing as instructed, Fiona moved her taped wrists as directed, until Patsy had removed the tape. She then returned the favour.

"I'll turn my back. I don't need to go. I wanted to get an idea of the layout." Patsy smiled and turned away as she pulled her phone from her pocket. "Damn, it's out of battery again."

"Nor do I. I didn't want you to leave me." Wrinkling her nose at the toilet, Fiona added, "I don't fancy using that anyway."

132

"No." Patsy put her finger to her lips and turned on the tap. As water gushed into the small basin, she looked through the small medicine cabinet. All she found was a disposable razor, a toothbrush, and a pack of aspirin. "It was a long shot. Come on, let's go and see what our charming host is up to." Pulling the flush for good measure, she opened the bathroom door.

"Why have you taken the tape off?" Dickie demanded, pointing a carving knife he had acquired at Patsy's hand. "He'll go apeshit."

"He's a bully. You should try standing up to him, you might be surprised."

"I don't bloody think so. I saw what happened to the last poor bugger who did that." He pointed back to the sitting room with the knife. "Get back out there and sit down."

"Put the knife away, Dickie. You have no intention of using it, it doesn't intimidate me, and in any case if I wanted to take it away from you, I could."

Dickie's eyes narrowed. "You could try." Despite his words he leaned back against the sink as Patsy walked past.

As she entered the sitting room, Patsy heard some form of commotion coming from the hall. A woman was crying. Walking quickly to the door, she pressed her ear to the small gap surrounding it.

"Get away!" hissed Dickie, and when Patsy merely flapped her hand in response, he grabbed Fiona and held the knife to her throat. "Oi." His whisper was harsh. "One peep and she gets it."

Without moving her head, Patsy raised her finger and placed it on her lips.

"Shit," was all Dickie could manage.

A female voice with a strong African accent was attempting to calm the distraught woman.

"Hush now. That noise will do you no good. Come in, come in. A decent meal will help. What is your name?" She asked the question more slowly. "What . . . is . . . your . . . name? Me, Aretta."

The other woman paused her wailing for a few seconds, gave what Patsy guessed was her name but didn't catch, and then spoke quickly in a language Patsy didn't recognise.

Aretta raised her voice. "Woman, be quiet and I will help you."

The gabbling continued and there was a loud slap, after which the woman returned to wailing.

"Fatima, tell me what is wrong with this woman."

A second voice spoke quietly to the woman in what Patsy assumed was her own language, before addressing Aretta.

"She wants her child back. She says the officials took it."

"That's because they won't take children here. What do these people expect?" Aretta exclaimed. "Tell her she must be good, work hard, and once her papers are sorted, she will be reunited with her child."

Fatima spoke quietly, and the woman raised her voice in response. Both she and Fatima were talking at the same time and did so until Aretta shouted, her deep voice echoing through the hall.

"Enough! Tell me what you are saying."

"Nadia is saying she will be good, and she will work hard once she gets her child back. She heard that people in England were good to families with children and she can't believe they have stolen her son. She will die without him. I have tried to explain—"

"Tell her this," Aretta interrupted. "England is good to women who work hard. England will look after her child well until everything is sorted. If she works hard. If she causes trouble or is lazy, she will not get her child back and she will be sent home."

"But that's not true."

"Fatima, you have privileges now. You know how this works, tell her."

Patsy listened to Fatima's calm tones, and the wailing lessened to a whimper. She turned to speak to Dickie, when another voice reached her.

"Aretta. What's going on here?"

"Miss Kate, this is Nadia, she wanted her son to come with her. We have explained she will get him back if she is a good girl."

"Good. This one is . . ." There was a rustling of paper. "Sami. Can I leave them with you? Get them something to eat, show them to their rooms, Sami actually has luggage."

"Of course. This is it?"

"Yes. Some issue with the others. Might be coming tomorrow. I could do without all this messing about, I've got enough on my plate. Mr Jenkins is causing me grief, not answering his phone again, and I want to go and visit my boy. Where's Dickie? He'll have to earn his keep for a change."

"I think he left with Mr Jenkins."

"He was here? When? He's supposed to be on his way to Cheltenham. I bloody knew he was up to something."

"Fatima, take them through to the kitchen. Make tea."

Aretta must have taken the woman Patsy thought was possibly Mrs Jenkins further up the hall, she could hear muffled voices, and a few exclamations, but nothing of any use. Until the woman in charge marched past the door demanding. "Show me!"

A door slammed and Patsy turned to Dickie. "Now unless you want me to start screaming, take the knife away from her throat and tell me what this place is."

"Keep your voice down, sit there." Releasing Fiona, Dickie pointed the knife at the sofa.

Patsy took Fiona's hand and they sat as instructed. "Tell me what this place is. Is it a brothel of some sort?"

"Ha! I wish. No, not a brothel, it's a hostel. Kate takes in female asylum seekers and the like."

"Who's Kate?"

"Jenkins' missus." He frowned. "Who are you two? You're obviously not one of that lot."

"Too long a story, but we're both called Meredith." Patsy wanted to see how much Dickie might know about Jenkins' intentions, but was unable to work out if the look that crossed his face was horror, fear or guilt. "You know about us?"

"No. I don't know nothing. I've heard of Meredith, but he shouldn't have brought you here. That was wrong. Shit. I don't need this sort of shit, I don't."

"You're panicking, Dickie. Why?"

Dickie's response, and the fear in his eyes, told Patsy she'd been right. Jenkins hadn't cared she'd seen where they were because he wasn't expecting her to be around long enough to tell anyone. She swallowed and knew she had to overpower Dickie and get out of the house immediately. She shifted her weight to the edge of the couch. She was about to get to her feet when the door handle turned, and someone attempted to open the door.

"Dickie, are you in there?" Kate Jenkins was back.

Dickie was swishing the blade of the knife about as he paced the small room, his finger held towards his captives in warning. His eyes darted to the door as a key was inserted in the lock and the handle turned again.

"Dickie, stop buggering about and open this door. I know it's locked from the inside."

"I can't Kate. Alan told me to lock it and stay put until he gets back. I ain't pissing him off any more than he already is, not even for you."

"For God's sake. He won't mind if he knows I made you."

"I ain't chancing that." Patsy made to stand up, and Dickie dashed forward and rapped the knife across her knee. "Fucking stay there," he hissed.

"Who's in there with you?" demanded Kate. "What the hell is going on?"

Dickie tried not to mind the blood seeping into Patsy's jeans. "I don't know. Ask Alan."

"I will if I can get hold of him. Who is with you, Dickie? I'm staying here until you answer me."

"My name is Patsy Meredith, and your husband abducted me and my mother-in-law this morning."

"He did what? Dickie, open this door!"

"No. You'll kick me out, and he'll finish me off. You stay there, then when he comes back, he can explain everything to you, because I'm buggered if I know what's going on."

"Mrs Meredith, I'm so sorry. I have no idea what's happening, I'm going to try and find my husband and sort this misunderstanding out." Kate tried to keep the fear and anger out of her voice, she needed everyone to stay calm, she needed to sort this mess out with no fuss. "Are you okay with that?"

"No choice," called Patsy. "Locked in, and this idiot has slashed my leg."

"Dickie! Did you hurt that woman?"

"She didn't do as she was told. I can't have her moving about. Shit, Kate, go and phone Alan. I'm done here, enough's enough, I'd rather sleep rough."

"I'm calling him now. Get something for the damage you've done to Mrs Meredith, and, Dickie, your notice is accepted."

Kate tried to call Alan again, and paced the hall as she listened to the phone ring. She left a brief message before trying again. "Alan, call me please. I have a major emergency on my hands here." Knowing he wouldn't come near the house if she told him she'd discovered the women, she tried again. "Alan, you promised. I don't know what to do

". . . I . . . I." Hanging up, she hoped her ploy worked. Kate didn't cry, if Alan thought she was upset, it might make him call back.

Sitting on the bottom stair, she pulled out a cigarette and lit it. What was he going to do with those women? Where was he going to take them? Kate had no idea why he'd brought them here in the first place, she was in and out of the building all the time, it should have been obvious she'd find out. Unless he'd not planned to abduct them. She nodded, that would be it. Alan was impetuous, never engaged his brain if an opportunity appeared to present itself. It didn't explain why he thought it was an opportunity though. What with this and the pictures . . . perhaps he was having some sort of breakdown. All she had to do was work out where he would take them, then she could find him. Her problem was where to start. Taking a long drag on her cigarette, she blew little clouds of smoke into the air, as she worked out her best course of action.

Getting to her feet, she dropped her cigarette into an empty vase on the shelf above the radiator, and went back to Dickie's door, knocking politely. "Dickie, I've spoken to Alan, he's realised he's made a mistake. You can let them go now." When there was no response, she added, "And about the job, it's still yours if you want it."

"Okay," Dickie called. "Get him to call me like he said he would, then I'll open up. Until then, I'm sorry, Kate, I can't do that."

"Right! I'm going to find him and drag him back here. Ladies, Dickie won't hurt you. I'm so sorry, I think my husband must be having a breakdown."

"Just find the bastard . . . please," Fiona called.

"I will do, I'm sorry."

They listened to Kate's footsteps recede and the slamming of the front door.

"You should have done what she said, it would have been better for you when the police come"

"Shut up!"

"I'm serious, Dickie. Now his wife knows, he's going to have to release us. Wouldn't it be better if you see that this is wrong first? It will be taken into consideration, that and your fear of him."

"Fear? I'm more frightened for you than for me. I've seen what he can do." Dickie rubbed his forehead, trying to unjumble his thoughts and work out what was the best course of action.

Now sitting on the edge of the couch, Patsy readied herself. The blood from the superficial wound on her thigh was congealing and she winced as it pulled open at the tensing of her muscles. She'd disarmed many men during her days on the beat, most of them roaring drunk and angry. Dickie would be easy, if there was only something to distract him.

She sighed dramatically. "All this bloody excitement is affecting my bladder. I need to go again."

"Sit back."

"What?"

Dickie wasn't fooled by her conciliatory tone, he could tell by the look in her eyes she was up to something. "I said sit back. Shoulders resting on the cushions. NOW! You can pee yourself, makes no odds to me, I'm off once Alan gets back."

Patsy didn't move, and Dickie took a few steps to one side, before lunging forward and balancing on the arm of the couch, placing the knife back at Fiona's throat.

"I can see you're up to something. Try it, bitch and she gets it. To be fair, it will be quicker and less painful than anything that bastard has in mind for you."

"Is he that bad?" Patsy inched back. The knife wasn't that sharp, but it would still do some serious damage.

"Worse than you can imagine. He's a sicko."

"Meaning?"

"Ah, shit. Nothing to lose I suppose. When all this over, if you survive, ask Aretta about the two girls who did runners. Only they didn't. He liked them, so he took them I reckon." Nodding as though that were enough, Dickie's eyes revealed his sadness.

"Took them where? What did he do to them?"

"Who knows? They'll turn up dead somewhere, is my reckoning."

"So you don't actually know he did anything."

"Not with evidence, no, only a certainty after what he did to little Mimi."

"Mimi?"

"That's not her real name, but close enough, hers was impossible to pronounce."

"What happened to her?" Fiona asked.

Watching the tear travel one of the creases on Fiona's cheek, Patsy reached out and took her hand.

"She was beautiful. Really stunning. Don't know how old she was, don't reckon she knew herself with any certainty, but around sixteen. Once she arrived here, Alan showed up regularly, suddenly found out how to use a screwdriver and even did the van runs as an excuse. It was funny to watch in the beginning. Then he cornered her in the kitchen, and she rejected him, when he persisted, she kneed him in the nuts. Got away that time."

"What are van runs?"

"They send the girls out to work. Got a few contracts now. The meat packing place, cleaning office blocks at night, and recently they got the sewing job. Sweatshirts and stuff, fakes. You know, like you'd buy at a market. They have to be taken there and brought back."

"Oh right. What happened to Mimi the next time?"

Swallowing, it was clear Dickie was working out whether it was wise to carry on. Rather than speak, he shook his head.

"Like you say, what difference does it make now? Tell us, please."

"No one saw it happen, but one morning she doesn't come down to work. Aretta went to get her, and she was black and blue. Could barely walk. Aretta said it was clear she'd been raped. The girl was a wreck. Aretta and Fatima looked after her as best they could. Alan showed up and said no hospital, told us she must have been out whoring. That's how we knew it was him. That and the fact he told us Kate shouldn't be bothered with it."

"Where is she now?"

"Dead."

"From her injuries?"

"Nope. She recovered from them, the physical ones anyway. To be honest I thought she was getting better, she spoke a little English and used to say good morning and that sort of stuff to me again, and then Aretta found her hanging from the shower rail. The police investigated, evidence said it was suicide." Shrugging, he added, "I don't know any different, but one way or another he killed her."

"And the other two . . .?" Patsy wanted to keep him talking, the more she could find out the more she could use against Jenkins when he showed up.

"Just disappeared. One never came down to breakfast one day, room was empty, no one saw her leave, she didn't tell anyone she was going, but all the doors were locked so someone else was involved, they aren't allowed keys. The other was walking back from the other house. Never arrived here. Authorities put both down as absconders, but me and Aretta think otherwise."

"Why, because of what happened to Mimi?"

"Yep. Alan had shown interest in them, they were both pretty. Like I said, no evidence, just gut feeling, and a knowledge of what he's like." Dickie shuddered. "Now stop talking, I've said enough." He glanced at his watch. "You've only been here fifty minutes, seems like a fucking lifetime."

A sudden knock at the door caused him to jump, and the knife touched Fiona's throat and she screamed.

His hand shaking, he moved the knife away and bellowed at the door, "Who is it?"

"It's me, my friend." Aretta tapped again. "Are those ladies okay?"

"Fine. What do you know about them?"

"No more than you. But Mrs Jenkins tells me you won't let them go. Don't be like him, Dickie. Let them go."

"I can't. He'll be back in a minute, and Kate knows now, so they are perfectly safe."

"You don't know that. Be a good man."

"What is it with everyone telling me what to do today? I'll ring him, alright." Dickie got up and walked to the door. He stood facing the couch as he pulled out his phone and dialled Jenkins. The call went through to the answering service. "He's not picking up. I'll call Kate."

"You know what she wants. She doesn't want prisoners in this house."

"Then she can tell me again. Who knows, she might have found him."

Dickie was about to hang up when Kate answered. "Have you found him?" He placed the phone on speaker and stared at Patsy as she spoke.

"No, I've been everywhere I could think of that's local. Home, the gym, the other house, betting shop, snooker hall. Nothing. Is there anywhere else you think I should try?"

"Not really. He should be fairly local though. He said he'd be back in time for me to do the pick up."

"Bugger. I'd forgotten about that. I'm coming back. This nonsense has gone on long enough. If you don't open that door, I'll get someone to knock it down, the police if necessary." Kate hung up.

"She's right, Dickie. You've been very kind to us, there's no way the police aren't going to find out about this, but we'll both tell them how nice you've been, won't we, Fiona?"

"I'll tell them the truth is what I'll tell them." She pointed at Patsy's leg. "That wasn't being kind."

"That was an accident, wasn't it, Dickie?" Patsy smiled at him.

"Don't fucking patronise me. All smiles and sweet talk. I'm not thick. Stupid, but not thick."

"Calm down, Dickie." Aretta's voice was sharp. "No more trouble. Oh, thank the Lord. Am I . . ."

Her voice faded away. Dickie turned to the door and rested his head against it trying to hear what was going on. Patsy saw her opportunity. The knife was in his left hand, which hung loosely at his side. Edging forward, she braced ready to move. When Dickie's head tilted in the other direction she sprang forward. Several large strides across the small room, and she was able to throw herself at his body, with her right forearm across the back of his neck, and the weight of her body against his, she put her left hand down and around his wrist. While she still had the advantage of shock, she yanked his arm up, clasped both hands around his wrist and twisted.

Dickie yelled in pain and dropped to his knee. Blood ran from his nose following the collision with the door, and the knife fell from his hand.

Kicking it away, Patsy called to Fiona, "Come here quickly, take the key from his pocket."

There was another knock on the door. "Enough of this nonsense, Dickie. Am I calling the police or not?"

"It's okay, Mrs Jenkins, we're getting the key."

"Let me go, I'll give you it." Any resolve Dickie had had was gone.

Releasing his hand, Patsy readied herself, but found it unnecessary, as after having flexed his shoulders several times, Dickie unlocked the door. He stood up, looking at his feet rather than meet Kate Jenkins' eye.

"Thank you." Kate's eyes flared in recognition as she gave Patsy a forced smile. "I'm sorry. Please come into the kitchen, it's warmer." She held her hand towards the hall.

A tall handsome woman, with ebony skin and a proud demeanour smiled at Patsy. "This way please, miss."

Kate turned to Dickie. "Go and pick up the girls."

"What about—"

"Who? Alan? Do you see him? No, nor me. He can whistle, he's got more important things to worry about when he gets back than you. Are you going?"

"I suppose."

19

Throwing an arm into the air, Meredith answered the call. "Finally, what news?"

Detective Sergeant Paisley's voice sounded remote as he replied. "Not much, I'm afraid." He cleared his throat. "I've spoken to traffic nothing on the car. They have an alert on vehicle recognition where it's possible, but not a tickle. He could have come off the main road and gone into the countryside, or be sitting in a car park somewhere, but we'll get him—"

"Do not say eventually. Because that's not quick enough."

"I was going to say, it's only a matter of time." Paisley was lying, but he wasn't in the mood for a battle with Meredith.

"And you have nothing new on him?"

"Nothing. It's like he wasn't living here. Not even registered to vote."

"Which means he was up to something. All you have to do is find out what. Find out where he drinks, eats, buys his knickers, and then find out who with."

"I know how to do my job, sir."

"Then do it quicker."

"Nothing on the phone either I take it?" Seaton joined the conversation.

"What phone?"

Seaton sighed before speaking slowly. "Jenkins will have a phone. If it's on, you can track it."

"Oh right, yes, Exton is on it."

"Well you go and speak to Exton and call me back. We're coming into Plymouth. We'll go to his home address first."

"No need, we have a uniform there."

"Then he can make us a cup of tea. Call me." Hanging up, Meredith looked at Seaton. "Is it me?"

"Nope. Though to be fair, they haven't been back long themselves."

"Patsy and Mrs Meredith have been abducted. They have phones, although clearly not as au fait with them as they might be." Trump was clearly with Meredith on this and he looked at Ed. "Shame your mother doesn't have one, or that might help."

"She does, but only turns it on when she goes out. I doubt she gave it a thought given the circumstances. Are these local coppers really as crap as you think?"

"No," Seaton answered. "It's just with cases like this, time is of the essence and they are not moving fast enough given the personal connections."

"Bollocks! They are not moving fast enough, period. They don't even have him on their radar. With his record and his inability to keep his fingers out of the till, take Red as an example, they don't even know he exists." Meredith scrolled through his phone. "I've got the home address, Amanda told me if I . . . ha! That was easy," He studied the phone and looked up. "Follow this road until the next roundabout and turn left."

Meredith kept giving directions until they entered a rather nice tree-lined avenue. Substantial houses sat behind neat hedges, all had immaculate gardens, most had expensive cars sitting on the drive.

Seaton whistled. "Not bad for an ex-con. Wish my salary would stretch to a place like this."

"And I say again, he wasn't even . . . hang on. It's Einstein." Meredith hit the speaker button. "Anything? We've reached the house."

Paisley sounded smug. "Yep, like I told you, we were working on it. We have a location, and it's not moved for five minutes."

"Then why didn't I get a call five minutes ago? Where?"

Trump tutted, and Ed grinned. Being a police officer wasn't anything like it was on the telly.

"We've got a car on—"

"Stop wasting time. Where?" Meredith was shouting now.

"With all due respect, sir, I—"

"Due respect went out the window when you interrupted my wedding. Now give me the location or put your OIC on. I'm assuming they have officers of a higher rank than you around here."

"There's no need of that. I was going . . . ah shit, if I get bollocked over this, I'm telling them you pulled rank." Paisley gave the postcode and street location, and Meredith put it into Google maps, as did Trump in the back. "As I say there's a car on—"

"We're less than five minutes away. I hope it's an armed response. See you there." Meredith hung up. "Turn around, Tom, take a left."

They arrived on the drab nondescript industrial estate seconds before three squad cars pulled up, their sirens blazing.

"Well, if he's here somewhere, he knows we're coming. I don't understand what . . . I think he might be in charge."

Trump nodded to an officer, who having armed himself with a sub-machine gun, barked orders at the men exiting the cars. His arm swept back and forth as the men surrounded what appeared to be a row of garages.

"Let's go and speak to him."

Meredith got out of the car and was impressed and a little embarrassed when an officer appeared from nowhere, and with his gun aimed at Meredith, shouted at him to hit the ground. Doing as he was told, Meredith shouted that he was a police officer. Another two officers rushed forward and one by one allowed the other men out of the car. Their ID was checked and the OIC was informed. He marched over.

"I've heard we had interlopers interfering. Inspector Dudridge, remain by your car while we secure the building."

"Which building? Because unless it's one of those garages, with your tallyho arrival, Jenkins will be gone."

"You must be Meredith. Shut up and wait there."

Tom Seaton was pleased Meredith couldn't see his grin. Within ten minutes it had been established that no one was coming out, the doors were forced open and the middle garage entered. When Meredith heard the shouts that no threat existed, he walked to join Dudridge.

The garage was empty with the exception of three items. An old desk and chair, and an inflatable double bed. In the centre of the desk sat a mobile phone.

Dudridge picked it up. "I'm guessing this is what has caused all this excitement." Passing it to Meredith, he pulled open the single drawer which was also empty. "Nothing else of interest."

Tapping the screen, Meredith found that Jenkins had numerous missed calls and several text messages from Kate, two missed calls from Max, and one from Dickie. He handed it back.

"I know it's a long shot but get your SOCO guys in here. Unless Jenkins is being unsociable, that's been here for some time. He's either trying to be clever, or something has happened to him." He pointed at a patch of the concrete floor where the dust had been disturbed. "My guess is those dark spots are blood." He went to join the others who had congregated at the door. "Jenkins' phone and signs of a struggle. Anything out here?"

"Nothing obvious. But look at that signpost." Seaton pointed to the large board at the end of the road. It gave the name of the various businesses using the estate.

"Come on, let's go and have a look."

"Look where?" Dudridge clipped his radio back onto his vest and stepped outside to join them. "I'll leave someone here until SOCO arrive."

Meredith pointed at the sign. "FitWorks is the name of Jenkins' gym. We're going to take a look."

"Then I'll escort you."

Meredith nodded, and the group walked to the corner of the road and scanned the buildings on each side of the adjoining street.

"There." Ed pointed towards the end of the rank on the right. "He certainly didn't splash out on the fascia."

A fading yellow tarpaulin, with the name FitWorks, had been strung up across the centre of the two-story brick box building. Below it was the entrance, above it three windows, through which men on various pieces of equipment looked out at them. Dudridge led the way into the small reception area.

Flashing his ID, which given his uniform and the gun slung across his chest was unnecessary, he asked to speak to Jenkins.

"He's not in. Not seen him for a few days." The young girl, with a toned body and enormous breast implants, moved her gum from one side of her mouth to the other.

"No problem. We'll just have a look around." Dudridge walked to the doors on the other side of the small reception area. They didn't open, and he turned to look at her. "Do the honours, don't piss about."

"You're not members."

"This entitles me to a free visit." Dudridge slapped his gun.

"No, that would be a warrant. You got one of them?"

Stepping forward, Meredith smiled at her. "Have you got something to hide, Stacey?"

Laughing, Stacey wobbled her considerable chest. "Nah, it's all on show. How do you know my name?"

"Because you have a label." He pointed at the silver necklace.

"Oh yes. I can be a bit slow. Can you shut the door when you leave? It's bleeding freezing with it open."

"He's got you well trained."

"Just doing my job. Now, I don't want to offend, but if you haven't got a warrant, fuck off, and shut the door on your way out."

As she spoke the door into the gym opened, and a young lad with a holdall allowed his mouth to fall open, before turning his nose up at Dudridge. Catching the door, Dudridge held his hand towards the interior.

"After you, chaps. I think I heard someone calling for help." He smiled at Stacey as the others filed past.

"What's going on, Stace?" asked the young lad.

"You're a fucking idiot." Stacey picked up her phone. "He won't like it," she called as the door closed behind them.

The search of the gym revealed nothing suspicious. It was basic, nearly clean, and stank of the sweat and testosterone of the well-muscled clientele, who did little to disguise their dislike of the unexpected visitors.

"Thanks, Stacey," Dudridge called as they were leaving.

"He said he's going to sue."

"Who did?" Seaton stopped walking.

"Jenkins. The boss."

"Oh, did you call him at home?"

Stacey looked confused, trying to work out why Jenkins' location was important. She shrugged. "How do I know, they're called mobiles 'cos they move about."

"What number did you call him on?"

"His mobile." Her smirk was back.

"Ah, okay, you left a message." It was clear from Stacey's face she had. "Thought so, bye."

Outside, Meredith shook Dudridge's hand. "Thanks for your help. We need to crack on."

"Pleasure. Are you here for the night? I'll buy you a beer later if you are."

"If I am, I'll be looking for the women Jenkins abducted, but thanks for the offer." Meredith increased his pace. "Another time perhaps."

"Good luck. Here, take my card, in case you change your mind. Remember to tread softly, those toes you're crushing might come in useful if they're not limping." Dudridge saluted and turned to his men who were standing around the cars they'd arrived in.

"I'll try." Meredith took the card and slid it into his pocket.

Back in the car, Seaton asked, "Where now? Home address as planned?"

"Yep. Unless they come up with a sighting of his car, and hopefully with Patsy driving. Perhaps she managed to overpower him somehow. But that's wishful thinking. Step on it."

* * *

Patsy asked for coffee and patted Fiona's hand as she took a seat at the large table.

"No problem, do you want something to eat? Not sure what's in, but there will be something edible around." When the two women refused, Kate pulled out a chair and seemed to deflate. "I'm sorry." It was almost a whisper.

"You shouldn't be. I still don't understand it, but whatever is going on, it's not your fault." Fiona smiled. "In my experience, most men are totally and utterly selfish. Now that might be our fault for letting them believe the world revolves around them, but their actions are their own. When it comes down to it, they do what suits them."

"That's very kind of you. I hope, when he turns up, because he will, there will be some sort of understandable explanation." Kate shook her head. "We obviously won't agree with it, and the logic will be skewed, but we might understand what he thought he was going to achieve."

"I know why we were taken, he . . ." Patsy's hand flew to her pocket. "Is there a phone charger I could use? I must let Meredith know we are okay."

148

"Never thought I'd hear that name again." Kate closed her eyes against the conflicting emotions stirred up by the thought of Meredith.

"You remember him?"

"How could I forget the man who changed my life, and not in a good way. Not his fault, I understand he was doing his job, but . . . Anyway, that's in the past. We have to look forward and move on." Again, her voice fell to a whisper. "Although I wasn't expecting it to be because Alan had . . . kidnapped? Is that the right word?"

"Abducted would be better. I'm sorry, Mrs Jenkins, but your husband is a dangerous man. I can only speculate as to what he intended to do with us, but it was certainly not good. He allowed us to see where we were going, and he brought us to a house you own. If we were going to walk away from this, it would take minutes for those dots to be joined. I think he intended to kill us."

Kate threw her head back and grunted a laugh. "Ha! Alan? Kill you? I'm sorry it seems wrong to laugh, but although my husband is many things, I assure you he's not a killer." She shook her head. "No, no, he was probably doing it to frighten Meredith, maybe even try to blackmail him, but not kill you. I can't have that."

Wondering whether to mention what Dickie had told them about Mimi and the others, Patsy shrugged. "But he would have been caught. If he knows Meredith at all, he'd know Meredith would never rest until he'd caught him."

Kate nodded and became animated. "Exactly. Even a fool would know that, and Alan is no fool. He's having a breakdown, had a breakdown, I don't know much about these things. But I know they make people do weird things. It's the only explanation. I knew something was wrong when he got up in the middle of the night and wanted a bag packed."

"Possibly. You know the police are already looking for him. They have the details of his car, and they are building a picture of his movements and associates, I'm sure. It will only be a matter of time before he gets picked up. Then we'll know. Look I'm sorry, I know this has been an awful shock, but I do need to get to a phone."

"Of course. I'm sorry, I don't know if there is a charger here. Here, use mine." Sliding her phone across the table, Kate got to her feet. "That sounds like Dickie is back, I'll check everything is okay. Oh, and his car is still out the back. The police won't be finding him driving that."

As Kate left the room, rather than dial Meredith immediately, Patsy first checked the recent call log. She could see Kate had made numerous attempts to call her husband, judging by the length of each call, most had gone unanswered. A full analysis would reveal the truth, but from what Patsy could see, Kate hadn't had any lengthy contact with her husband for several hours, but numerous calls had been attempted since discovering the women in Dickie's flat.

When she called Meredith, it went through to his answer service.

"Hello, hubby, it's me. I'm safe and well as is Fiona. I'm in Plymouth . . . don't know the address. Hang on . . ." Walking into the hall she could hear voices upstairs, but rather than go in search of Kate, she continued, "Can't find anyone. It's a hostel run by Kate Jenkins. Her husband has pulled a disappearing act. This is her phone, she released us. I'll call again when I have an address, if I don't hear from you first. I have no money, phone's dead, so I'll await the arrival of the cavalry." Patsy deliberately kept her tone light, knowing Meredith would be unbearable by now. Returning to the kitchen, she joined Fiona back at the table.

"I feel sorry for her," Fiona announced. "The wife is always the last to know. Still defending him though, or at least trying to find an excuse. I nearly told her about poor Mimi."

"We'd be wise to say as little as possible. We need to get out of here with no more fuss or bother. We'll keep what we know for the police to investigate. I think we should also not let on that there are two Merediths."

"Why? Don't you trust her? What difference would it make to her?"

"None, I expect. But as you said, she's looking for an excuse, if he does show up, she might tell him, intentionally or not."

"But isn't John on the way?"

"Answer machine, and I don't know where we are."

"Patsy, I'm getting scared again. I reckon we should leave, I'm not good with secrets, especially when I'm mad. My brain engages too late. I don't want to get us in more trouble."

"I'll try Meredith again. If there's no joy, you're right we should get out into civilisation."

Before she could dial a young girl entered the kitchen. Looking shocked at the unexpected guests, she forced a smile and did what Fiona thought was a half curtsey.

Fiona smiled at her. "Hello, did we frighten you?"

The girl's eyes widened, and she tried for another smile. Waving her finger, she said simply, "No English."

"Oh. That's a shame." Fiona turned to Patsy. "She looks worn out poor thing. Look at the bags under her eyes."

Opening a cupboard, the girl lifted two huge saucepans out, and carried one to the sink. Filling it with water, she grunted as she carried it to the hob.

Patsy went to help. "Let me. That looks very heavy." Taking the pot, Patsy placed it on the hob, before pointing at the other. "This one too?"

The response was merely raised eyebrows, so Patsy filled it anyway and was rewarded with a smile. She returned to her seat as the girl busied herself in a walk-in pantry.

Calling Meredith again, Patsy urged him to return her call. The girl had placed numerous vegetables on the draining board, and was proceeding to drag a sack of potatoes across to the sink.

As she began to peel and chop the vegetables, Fiona got to her feet. "I don't think I'll be as fast as you. But let me help." Fiona had to prise the knife from the girl's hand. "More hands make light work," she explained to a blank expression before the girl collected another knife.

Fiona talked non-stop as she worked her way through the pile of vegetables, the girl made a start on the potatoes, dropping them into one of the pots as she went.

Turning to Patsy, Fiona caught the drip on the end of her nose and sniffed. "Onions. Get me every time. What do you think she's making?"

"No idea, but given the variety of veg, I'm guessing a stew."

"That's what I thought, but where's the meat and the stock." Her hands flew to her chest as Aretta answered her.

"It is very kind of you. There is no meat tonight, most of us are vegetarians it saves preparing two meals."

The potato pot was full, and the girl lit the gas as she said something in her own language.

"Bernice thanks you for your help. She didn't have the words to refuse. Please you are a guest, take a seat."

"We're not guests, Aretta, but nice of you to be so polite. Where is Mrs Jenkins? We must be going."

"I do not know, she is speaking with Dickie perhaps."

"I'll go and find her. We should make a move."

"I thought the police would be here banging on the doors and frightening the girls." Aretta turned the gas on under the second pot and said something to the girl who disappeared into the pantry. "Why did you not call them?"

"Because it was unnecessary. They were already looking, now they know where to come. They know . . ."

A commotion and a small scream from the pantry halted Patsy's explanation. She hurried to help Bernice.

Finding the girl surrounded by numerous tins of produce, her hands over her face, and her shoulders moving in time with her sobs, Patsy put her arm around her and helped her to her feet. Bernice was shaking and stumbled back into the kitchen, where Fiona vacated her chair and helped Patsy settle her.

"She knocked over a few cans, why is she in such a state?"

Bernice folded her arms on the table and rested her forehead on them as Fiona patted her back. Aretta spoke softly to her, while adding vegetables to the water. Bernice had stopped crying and simply shook her head in answer.

"She is fine. Tired I expect, she has done a double shift. The cans frightened her."

"How old is she?" Fiona pulled a chair forward and sat stroking Bernice's arm.

"I think about sixteen."

"A double shift at what? Patsy asked. "I thought there were regulations on how long minors could work."

"She wants new clothes, she asked, no, begged for another shift. How else would she get them?"

"Working doing what?"

"Probably she was at the factory." Aretta looked over her shoulder and spoke to Bernice, nodding at the reply. "She has been at the meat factory."

"Well it's clearly too much for her. Whether she begs or not, you should stop her."

"I will try."

"Why is she doing the cooking? That's a lot of food, surely someone else could have done it." Looking at Patsy, Fiona tutted. "This girl is being overworked."

"The others are out at work, they are due back shortly. The food needed to go on. It was her turn. She will be fine after she has eaten and had a sleep."

"I hope you're right." Picking up the phone, Patsy tried Meredith again, and left another message. "I'm going to find Mrs Jenkins, we might go to the nearest police station."

Aretta simply nodded as Patsy left and went to Dickie's little flat, the door was open but she found no one there. Hearing a raised voice coming from upstairs, she started up the stairs.

"Fatima, I don't need this today. Tell her if she hurts herself, she won't be able to get him back. She needs to be good and get stuff ready for when everything is sorted."

Pausing halfway up, Patsy could hear someone crying, and Kate Jenkins' message being barked in a foreign language. Whoever received the message, clearly answered back.

"What did she say?"

"She said she would rather die than be without her son. It was bad enough losing her husband."

"I've had enough. Tell her to get out. Now."

Again, Fatima spoke to the woman. The wailing increased in volume. Patsy was close enough to hear the slap and the gasp of pain. The woman uttered something through more muted sobs.

"She asks where would she go?"

"Tell her I don't care. It's her who doesn't want to be here. She has a choice, she can play the game or bugger off. I've got too much on my plate to be standing here doing this." Hands on hips, Kate stood looking into the room as Fatima spoke to the woman. "Well?" she demanded.

"She said she will obey."

"Good. Tell her she'll be called when the meal is ready, if she doesn't come down, she'll go hungry. I have to go and sort my bloody husband out, so I don't know when I'll be back. I'll expect you and Aretta to keep things running smoo . . . It sounds like the others are back, I want a quiet night here. I haven't been to see Terry, and as for Alan . . ."

Patsy had also heard the door open and moved back to the bottom of the stairs. A line of eight women, of various origins trooped up the hall. A couple of them acknowledged Patsy's presence, most kept their heads lowered and filed past.

Trailing behind, Dickie rolled his eyes. "You still here?" he snapped.

"Obviously, but don't worry, Meredith will be here soon."

"Good."

He followed the girls into the kitchen. Slight bubbles of conversation began to emerge, and Patsy turned as she heard footsteps behind her. Kate looked haggard as she came to join Patsy.

"Has he phoned?"

"Who Meredith?"

"No, Alan. I've left him so many bloody messages, I'm going to kill him when I get my hands on him. He knows I go to see Terry today."

"Sorry, no calls." Patsy held out the phone. "I've left a couple of messages for Meredith, hopefully he'll be here soon, but he may call."

"Would you like to come home with me? I've had enough for one day, I'll wait for him there, although if he doesn't turn up in the next hour, I'll have to go and see Terry."

"With all due respect, that would be possibly the last place I'd want to go. No, if Meredith doesn't show soon, I'll go to the local police station and wait there. You know the police might have picked him up."

"The way I feel at the moment, I'd almost be glad if they have. Mind you, it's going to happen sooner or later, I shouldn't kid myself." Managing a half smile, Kate pointed at the door behind Patsy. "That's the living area, if you want to stay there, it will be more comfortable."

Opening her mouth to answer, Patsy was interrupted by the ringing of the phone in Kate's hand.

"Hello." Kate sighed. "Hello, Meredith, yes she's with me. She's fine. Of course." She held out the phone. "At least yours returns calls." Turning away, Kate walked towards the kitchen.

"Meredith. Nice to hear your voice. Any joy on tracking Jenkins?" She listened to the update. "Well, I doubt he'll come back here. Not now he knows Kate has released us. Are you on your way?" She listened some more, a smile lighting up her face. "And I love you too. Where are the others, you'd not be so soppy if they were in earshot? . . . See you soon." Ending the call, she went to give Fiona the news.

20

Meredith slid the phone into his pocket and walked back towards the car. "Safe and well." He retuned Ed's smile.

"Thank God for that." Tom Seaton beamed. "Are we going to get her, or do you want to go in there first?" He pointed at the glaring neon sign of the pool club.

"Might as well look, as we're here. Don't you think, sir?" Trump pulled open the door and the smell of stale cigarettes wafted out. "I don't think they've heard of the no smoking law." Wafting his hand in front of his face, he led the way in.

At the top of the stairs was a small lobby, created by the questionable erection of sheets of plywood, and a door fitted where the two walls met. A hole had been cut into one of the panels and a desk pushed up against it. On the desk was a half pint mug filled with small change, and a dog-eared diary. The ripped leather chair was empty.

"No one here, should I shout, or are we going in?"

"Stupid question, Trump. Lead the way." Meredith pointed at the door.

The wall in which the door had been inserted wobbled as Trump opened it.

"No expense spared," Seaton murmured.

"Is it safe, do you think?" Ed asked still on the top stair.

"In what way?" Turning to look at him, Seaton smiled. "Will the wall fall down, or will we not be welcome?"

"Both, but more the latter."

"Never know until you try. You can wait here if you're worried."

"No, no. Carry on." Ed's voice didn't match his words. He was right to be concerned.

"Who the fuck are you?" bellowed a large man, sporting a stained shirt. "Members only."

Trump pulled out his warrant card and held it forward. "My membership. We don't want any trouble chaps, we're looking for someone."

Several of the men had abandoned their games, or their pints, and armed with cues, formed a row behind him.

"Never heard of 'im. Now fuck off."

Stepping forward, Meredith smiled. "Well that's not nice. Not when he told us to meet him here."

A frown appeared. "Who did?"

"The bloke you've never heard off. I don't think he'll be pleased." Meredith took another step closer. "Tell the children to get back to their playing." He waved his finger along the line of men. Hearing a gasp behind him, he knew it would be Ed, and saw Seaton step up to join him from the corner of his eye. "We're not looking to cause a mess in your . . ." he looked around the poorly painted room with its worn tables, and stained carpeting, "club. Simply want to ask a few questions and have a look around."

"Well ain't that a shame." A smaller stocky man with a shiny bald head stepped forward, his grin revealed a missing front tooth, which made the adjacent teeth look overly large. "There's a reason it looks like this. Less to clear up when we've dealt with any unwanted visitors." He slapped the cue against the palm of his hand.

"And you are who?" Trump stepped to the other side of Meredith.

"Prince fucking Harry. You got a warrant?" The grin got bigger.

"Well that's not true, because he's a redhead, not unlike us." Ed pointed first at Trump's, and then at his own head as he moved forward to stand next to Trump. He could see this wasn't going to end well, and he'd learned at school that bravado goes a long way when real ability is lacking.

Meredith grinned. "It's getting to be like the O.K. Corral in here. All very dramatic, and unnecessary. Have you seen Alan Jenkins today?"

"Nope," the big man snapped.

Taking his lead, the others simply shook their heads.

"Would you tell me if you had?"

"Nope"

"Then why did he tell us to meet him here?"

"I haven't seen him in months. If he told you to come here it's because he wanted you otherwise engaged. Try his gym."

Watching the big man's shoulders relax, and his cue slide through his hand to rest on the floor, Meredith believed him. He wasn't sure who the men thought he was looking for before, but as it was Jenkins, they'd lost interest. Two of the men walked away to the pool table in the corner.

"Thank you. What about Max Deegan? Where would we find him if we were looking?"

"Saw him in the Tesco on Mutley Plain an hour ago," said a man as he left the line and seated himself at a small round table and lifted a bottle of beer.

"Oi. Button it." The stocky man glared at him.

"Why? He's a prick and I want to get on with my game." He looked at Meredith. "He won't come here, not if he knows what's good for him. All favours used up."

"Think that says it all, don't you?" Cue back in hand, the tallest man stepped forward, and looked Meredith in the eye. "Now fuck off and bother someone else."

"Will do. Thanks for your help, gents." Meredith saluted.

Back in the street, he walked towards a fish and chip shop, the others followed him.

"Shouldn't we be picking up Patsy and Mum?" Ed asked.

"We will do. Just as soon as I've bought her something to eat. She'll be starving. Do you have a death wish, Ed?"

"No, why?" Ed fell into step with his half-brother.

"Two peas in a pod," Seaton observed.

"Agreed, young Ed still has round edges though," Trump answered.

Pulling open the door, Meredith breathed in the fatty air. "Because first you think it's wise to impersonate me, then you get lippy with a bunch of cue-wielding muscle. Can you handle yourself?"

"Well enough. Obviously not to your standard, but I learned, after one too many punch-ups at school, that attack is the best form of defence. Unless you can run really, really fast."

Nodding, Meredith walked to the counter. Order placed, the four men stood to one side waiting for their fish to be cooked.

"Didn't expect to find Deegan here. If indeed we do find him." Seaton yawned. "Next time you get married, Gov, do me a favour and go abroad where we can't get involved. I'm knackered."

"Won't be a next time. Call Exton and update him on both Patsy and Deegan." Turning to Trump, he said, "Might need you to phone Uncle David."

"Why?"

"Because this is all very personal now, and we need to see it through."

"I think we should get the women home, and leave it to the locals."

"Agreed." Seaton nodded.

"But then they are still in danger. Until those two lunatics are behind bars, they're not safe, nor is Amanda. I'm not convinced the local lads will work this case with the enthusiasm it needs. Especially as we have Tony's body in Bristol. He might have been killed down here, but he was found in Bristol. Perhaps a collaboration would suit you better."

Trump laughed. "You mean give you extra men to shout at?"

"I agree with John."

The other three turned to look at Ed.

"I do. I don't know anything about the official way of doing things, but I'm guessing once you cross a border everyone starts getting territorial, but that doesn't help my mum or his girls. John is the best man for the job in my opinion."

"Thank you, Red. It's Meredith, even to you, and all though you don't know shit from sixpence on most things, on this matter you do happen to be correct."

"He's biased." Trump waited until Meredith had collected the two bags containing their food. "I'm happy to pick up Patsy and hear what she has to say before I make a decision."

"Fair enough. Let's go and get her." Meredith grabbed a handful of napkins.

It was getting dark, and a damp mist was settling in for the evening. Ed shivered, wishing he had a warm coat. As they walked back to the car, he lowered his voice, "Are you going to accept that? What if he says no?"

"He'll do the right thing. Trump always does, he . . . bollocks! We didn't ask which house she was at. Here hold this." Passing Ed the bags, Meredith dialled Kate Jenkins' number. It rang for some time before she answered. "Kate, it's Meredith. What's the number of the house Patsy is in?"

"Seventy-three."

"Thanks, I'm going to need to speak to you later."

"I thought so. I'm with Terry at the moment, he's coming home so I needed to make some arrangements. I'll be another hour. I have to go."

Meredith opened the passenger door. "Anyone else want theirs now?" Opening the carrier bag, he held up a carton.

Making short work of the food, the men were soon on their way to Patsy. Seaton had spoken to Paisley, and he and Exton were going to meet them at a local station once they'd collected the women. They arrived at the house ten minutes later.

"Do you think we need to go team handed, Gov?" Seaton asked releasing his seatbelt.

"I do. I don't think Jenkins or Deegan are anywhere near, but it would be folly to ignore the possibility. Once we've done this one, we'll do the other house."

The door was opened by Aretta. "You are the police?"

"We are." Trump showed his ID and stepped over the threshold.

"We have been expecting you. Please come in." Sweeping her arm forward, Aretta allowed the men to file past. "The first door on the .. . Ah, there you are."

Patsy hurried into the hall and put her arms around Meredith's neck. "What took you so long?" She kissed him. "I know we postponed the honeymoon, but this is not what I expected. Life is never simple with you."

"Nor is it boring. But I'm sure he's really sorry." He jerked his head towards Ed.

Raising a hand, Ed smiled. "With knobs on. Where's Mum?"

"Watching the television. This way."

Releasing Meredith, Patsy went back to the sitting room. Fiona was already on her way out, and burst into tears as she caught sight of her son. Ed pulled her into a hug, and led her to a sofa. Sitting with her, he allowed her to weep into his shoulder. "I am so sorry. So, very sorry."

Wiping away her tears, she looked at him. "It's not your fault, son.

They thought you were John. What the hell have you done to your hair?"

"That was my fault. I needed everyone to be sure to get the right bloke." Meredith joined Patsy in the doorway, slipping his arm around her waist.

Looking from one to the other, Fiona shook her head. "Patsy said you were like twins, but blow me down, I can't believe it . . . can I smell chips?"

"You can. We brought supplies. Trump, bring the food." He sniffed. "Did you not get offered anything, I can smell something cooking?"

"Yes, but I couldn't face it, I was so . . . anyway, everything is okay now."

"Almost."

Meredith walked into the room and looked around. A large square room with a bay window looking out onto the street, it was sparsely furnished. Three large sofas, which had seen better days, a table holding the television, and a standard lamp on a threadbare carpet. The once patterned wallpaper had been painted white, and thin sludge coloured curtains hung at the window. It was drab but clean.

Meredith took a seat on the other side of Fiona as Trump handed her the carton. "We're going to have to ask you a few questions about what's happened to you today, and, until Jenkins and his associate, Deegan, have been caught, we'll take you up to Bristol and keep you safe."

He smiled at the woman who had turned his young life upside down. He'd realised many years ago that she wasn't to blame for the destruction of his family life, that honour belonged solely to his father.

Fiona nodded, and he turned to Patsy, who was blowing on a chip to cool it. "We'll give this place a once-over, do the one up the road, and take you to the local station for a formal interview."

Aretta had remained in the hall, and she stepped into the room. "What does this mean, a once-over?"

"We have to search the premises. Both this one and number forty-six." Trump explained. "Mr Jenkins has committed several serious crimes and we need to make sure he's not hiding here."

"I would not let him." Aretta lifted her chin. "He is not here."

"Even so. You are welcome to come with us."

"But Mrs Jenkins never said this would happen."

"I've spoken to Mrs Jenkins, she is with her son making arrangements to bring him home. I'm meeting her later. You can call her if you need to."

Clearly flummoxed, a frowning Aretta shook her head. "No, I will watch you."

"Good girl." Meredith got to his feet. "Red, stay here with the girls. This shouldn't take long." Out in the hall, he pointed at the next door along the corridor. "We'll start here and work our way upstairs."

Aretta tapped on the door. "This is Dickie's flat."

"Is he in?" Seaton put his hand on the knob.

"I don't know. I have a key if it is locked."

It wasn't and Seaton and Trump went into the flat.

Dickie was sitting on the sofa and glared at them. "I saw you arrive. Have you come to arrest me?"

"No, but you're coming with us when we leave. The local boys will want to question you." Trump entered the galley kitchen, which for the best part appeared unused, and turned his nose up at the small bathroom. "All clear. Next room." Wagging a finger at Dickie, he added, "Please stay here until we come for you. You really don't want to get in any further bother."

"I'm going nowhere. Have you got him yet? Jenkins. Have you found him, because he ain't here?" When Trump gave a negative response, he rolled his eyes. "Well get a move on. He'll find a way of blaming me for this."

"Doing our best, sir." Trump pulled the door closed behind him.

Meredith was already in the kitchen. "Evening, ladies, apologies for interrupting your meal."

The quiet murmur of conversation he'd heard on his approach had stopped as he pushed open the door. Eight women watched as he looked inside the pantry. One of them whispered something to another, and Aretta hushed her.

"What did she say?"

"She asked what the handsome man was looking for," Aretta explained.

"Tell her I'm flattered but married." Meredith grinned. He was rewarded by a broad smile and giggles from the table as Aretta translated. "That's better, was looking a bit too glum in here." He looked at the contents of their plates and thought he knew why.

Leaving the women, they moved back into the hall. A small shower room, too small to conceal anything, was given a cursory glance, and the remaining door led to the rear yard. A spotlight came on as Trump stepped outside. A small wooden shed, with no door, housed a variety of mops and brushes. And in the centre of the concreted patch of land sat Jenkins' Mercedes.

Trump tried the door handle with no joy. "I don't suppose you have a key to this too?" He asked Aretta who stood in the doorway rubbing her arms to keep warm.

"No. This is it, I will wait inside before I die of the cold."

Seaton checked the gates, they were securely locked from the inside. "Nothing out here, Gov. They'll have to send transport to pick this up."

Reaching the first landing, Meredith turned to Aretta who was halfway up the stairs. "How many rooms on each floor?"

"Three on this one and the bathroom, two and a bathroom upstairs."

"I'll do this floor, you two do upstairs."

"Wait one moment." Aretta squeezed past the men and pointed at the furthest door. "These are new, arrived today, one of them is very upset. Please be careful."

"Okay, I'll be kind. Please explain to them why I'm here." Pointing up the next flight of stairs, Meredith told the others to carry on.

"I cannot do that, I do not speak their language, Fatima is at the other house."

Nodding, Meredith invited her forward. "You open up and let's see how it goes."

As the door opened, a woman sitting on a single bed with her back against the wall and her knees drawn under her chin, buried her tear-stained face in her knees. On the other bed, a younger woman pulled herself into a sitting position. Her eyes wide, she tried to smile at Aretta.

"Hush now." Aretta stepped back allowing Meredith to enter.

A quick look revealed there was nowhere to hide, but he opened the small wardrobe for good measure. It had been shelved out, only one shelf was empty, one held a few items of clothing, and the others contained linen and towels. He glanced over his shoulder. The bedside cabinet which sat between the two beds had a single drawer and a shelf below.

"Where do they keep their things?"

"In there. They have nothing. Only the things you see. We will help them with that, come."

Beckoning him forward, and pulling a keyring from her pocket, she selected a key and opened the next door along. A large walk in cupboard with a small hanging space was revealed. On the hangers were numerous coats, and several longer garments, on the shelves were various baskets and boxes containing everything from underwear to shoes. It all looked second-hand.

"Will you kit them out?"

"What does this mean?"

"You will give them clothes. Coats and whatever else they need?"

"We will, it won't take long to sort them out. Come." Opening the next door, she led Meredith into a large bay room. There were a further two single beds, a desk with a chair, and a wardrobe. In the corner of the room was another door. Aretta walked to it. "This is Annie's. Look what she has." There was a pride in her voice.

Stepping forward, Meredith peered in. Numerous brightly coloured garments hung from the rail. A vegetable rack contained underwear, socks and scarves, and on the back of the door hung a fur lined anorak.

Aretta pointed to the desk. "You see they have a radio, and . . ." she pulled open a drawer of the desk, "hair dryer, and all that is needed for her." Her hand travelled to her head. "Annie was a hairdresser, she now does our hair. She is very good and works very hard."

"And what were you, Aretta? I'm sorry that was presumptuous, I'm assuming you are also an asylum seeker."

"I was. I got my papers last year. As you would say, I am legal and above board." Aretta lifted her chin, clearly proud of this achievement. "As Mrs Jenkins say, I am good example. I'm good, I work hard, and I am legal."

"But you're still here?"

"Why not? Where would I go? Mrs Jenkins has given me a good home, a job, and I help the others. I don't need a man, mister, if that's what you say."

"No, it wasn't, I was only wondering why you hadn't moved on. If you don't want to, that's fine. Where are you from, and what did you do there?"

"Angola originally. I am not old enough to have worked there, but my mother was a teacher. She taught me skills. My history is long, I am sure you don't want to hear it."

"I'm sure I do. But perhaps now is not the time. Shall we do the last room?"

"Of course."

The room was not as large as the last, it had similar furnishings, and beautiful hand drawn sketches of just about everything covered the wall above one bed. Meredith opened the wardrobe, the array of clothes was not as great as the previous room, but brightly coloured shoes filled its base.

"Someone likes shoes," he commented.

"She has a passion, she worked an extra shift to buy . . ." Aretta had been pointing to the pair that took pride of place at the front of the wardrobe but let her hand fall to her side. "I talk too much. Your friends will want to get into my room. There is only the bathroom left on this floor."

Aretta had been right, Seaton appeared on the stairs. "Didn't you hear me call? One of these rooms is locked, shall I force it?

"No, no. Do not break my door." Aretta hurried to join him.

"I'll finish here and see you downstairs."

Smiling as Aretta pushed past Seaton to protect her room, Meredith entered the bathroom. Functional was the only way to describe it. White tiled walls, white bathroom suite, and a freestanding wooden cupboard. Two faded bath mats hung over the side of the bath and the floor was a bizarrely patterned linoleum. Opening the cupboard, he found a range of cheap toiletries and a stack of old towels.

"At least it's clean," he muttered as he headed back downstairs.

"All clear I take it." Patsy smiled as he walked back into the sitting room.

The girl who had said Meredith was handsome was the only resident brave enough to leave the kitchen and come into the room. Her smile was broad as he entered, and a row of perfectly bright white teeth was enhanced by the deep colour of her skin.

"This is Belinda. She offered us coffee."

"Well it's a shame we haven't got time. Thank you, Belinda." He winked at Patsy. "She thinks I'm handsome."

"Must need glasses."

Belinda giggled.

"Do you speak English?" Meredith ignored his brother's incredulous stare.

"Of course. I work very hard." Belinda's smile returned. "Aretta is a good teacher, but I knew a little before I arrived."

"How long have you been here?"

"Two years and three months."

"And you like it here?"

"I have a bed. I miss my brother, and I don't like working in the meat factory. But I am not beaten."

"Did you expect to be beaten?" Fiona looked horrified.

"In some places this is what happens. England is good though."

"Are you all policemen? You don't look like policemen?"

"Not all, some of us only pretend." Meredith glanced at his watch. "We'd better crack on with the other house. Nice to meet you, Belinda."

"What is the time please?"

"Almost six o'clock."

"Then I must go and sleep, I am working this evening."

"But you haven't long been home." Fiona looked concerned.

"Oh, do not worry. I don't start until midnight. I have time." With one more glorious smile, Belinda left them.

"Another of the girls had done some sort of double shift, she almost fainted she was so tired." Patsy frowned. "I might have a word with this Mrs Jenkins of yours."

"All done, Gov. Shall we move on?" Seaton's head appeared around the door. "Aretta has phoned someone called Fatima who is expecting us."

"Yep. Sooner this is done, the sooner we can get some rest." Blowing Patsy a kiss, he left the room.

"What was Aretta's room like?" Shivering, Meredith pulled up his collar. "I think there might be a frost tonight."

"Basic, but better than the other one. More colourful."

"Describe it."

"Are you serious?" Trump looked at Meredith in disbelief.

"Yes, I'm interested. She's an intelligent woman, she's got the right to stay, yet she chooses to keep on living in that hostel. Don't get me wrong, it was all perfectly clean and functional, but they have next to nothing, I wondered why."

"Probably because she has a roof over her head. I'd imagine it's not easy to get a job or a home if you are a refugee, not without some form of qualification. Rent is not cheap. Even in Plymouth."

"What was her room like?"

Trump sighed. "Single bed with a pink headboard. Ikea style bedside cabinet, and chest of drawers. Walk-in cupboard with clothes, shoes and bags. Small television on a small table. Curtains at the window, carpet on the floor, and a fake sheepskin mat next to the bed. Is that enough information?"

"Did you look in the drawers?"

"Strangely enough no, wasn't expecting Jenkins to fit in a drawer."

Seaton touched Meredith's arm. "What were you after? What did you think we'd find, we could always go back in there?"

"I don't know. She's obviously some sort of . . . housekeeper, matron? Whatever, there was a lack of homeliness in the other rooms, I wanted to know if hers was better."

"Not somewhere I'd like to live, but certainly better than the other rooms." Trump exchanged a glance with Seaton.

The door to number forty-six stood open and Fatima gave a short bow as they climbed the steps.

"Welcome. I understand you want to do all the rooms. Where would you like to start?"

"Bottom to the top."

The house was slightly larger and had a different layout to the other property, but it was furnished in the same manner. One of the rooms was clearly unoccupied, and Fatima explained that three women they were expecting to arrive that day had been detained for a longer period. She didn't know why. Where Aretta was big and bold in stature and in personality, Fatima was small and quietly spoken. On the way back to the other house, Meredith observed that their personalities seemed to affect the women who lived with them. There was no talking or giggling in Fatima's house.

"I was going to ask how the older woman got her black eye, but to be honest, I think we've got enough on our plate, and I'm not sure our interfering in any way would help," said Trump. "They have a clean and tidy place to live, they have food in the cupboard, and are working, I'm not convinced upsetting the applecart would be welcomed."

"No. You might be right." Meredith's frown deepened. "You take Red and his mother to the station, keep him away from the action, and I'll call a taxi and follow with Patsy and Dickie."

Aretta gave him the card of a local taxi firm, and they awaited its arrival in the kitchen. Dickie remained in his flat. An argument of some sort broke out upstairs, and Aretta left to deal with it.

Glancing over her shoulder, Patsy sighed. "Finally, alone."

Smiling, Meredith grabbed her hand. "Nice sentiment, Hodge, and I know we're newlywed, but this is neither the time, and certainly not the place."

"Do you want to hear what I have to tell you?"

"Of course."

"When Dickie got in a panic, he told us Jenkins had been rough with some of the girls. Sexually. One young girl, Mimi, appeared to have killed herself. Two others disappeared. The story was they'd jumped ship rather than wait for permission to stay. Dickie thinks otherwise but wouldn't elaborate. That information needs to be passed on. I didn't say anything earlier because there was always someone around, and I didn't want to alert anyone before they were questioned."

"Bastard. He's going away for a long, long time!" He got to his feet as the doorbell rang. "That'll be the taxi. Let's get Dickie down to the station."

21

By the time they got there, Fiona's interview was well underway. As a courtesy, Trump was allowed to sit in with Exton.

Paisley came to the reception to collect them. "Who's this?

"This is Dickie . . ." Meredith looked at Dickie.

"Bird."

"I'm guessing Dickie isn't your given name?"

"Richard. My dad thought he had a sense of humour."

"Richard Bird. Lives at one of the hostels for some reason, and was party to holding two women against their will. In his favour, they are prepared to say how kind he was, pressured as he was by fear of his employer, and that he subsequently released them. Go soft on him, IF and only, if, he gives you a full account of his knowledge of the actions of Alan Jenkins. Including the disappearance of a young girl named . . ." He turned to Patsy for confirmation.

"Mimi. Don't look at me like that, Dickie. What? You thought I'd forgotten, or wouldn't tell?"

"I'm a dead man." Running his hand through his greasy hair, Dickie sighed. "But looking on the bright side, one way or another, I'll be rid of him."

Paisley was yet to speak and looked around the group. It looked like it was going to be a busy night. "Come on. This way."

"I'm assuming no news on Jenkins or Deegan?"

"Nope, but everyone who can is working on it. Chief Super has caused quite a stir. He's insisted you lot are party to anything you want to be party to." He turned to look at Patsy. "I'm afraid that means you'll need to wait to be interviewed. Given what DCI Meredith has told me, I think it's best we speak to Mr Bird first."

Nodding at the recognition of his status, Meredith agreed. "Best course of action. Where's Seaton and my brother?"

"Seaton is in the incident room, waiting for you, and the last I heard, the other one was snoring in the canteen."

"Good, Seaton will interview Hodge, won't take long she's ex-job, I'll sit in on this one." He jerked his thumb towards Dickie.

Holding open the incident room door, Paisley asked, "Modern girl then, not taking your husband's name?"

"Yes, that is, I don't know, haven't given it much thought. Certainly not for work."

"Modern," Paisley declared as he let the door shut. He called to Seaton, "Tom, your boss has got a job for you."

Within minutes, Dickie had been cautioned and the interview was underway. Having had enough of being in Alan Jenkins' debt, not to mention the continual bullying and threats of violence, he answered each question honestly and with as much detail as he could. He'd liked Mimi, and he was pissed off that although the other girls knew it was Jenkins who liked to knock women about, Kate had been fooled into thinking it was him.

The interview with Patsy was, as Meredith predicted, short and precise. A blow by blow account of what happened from the time she'd seen Jenkins in the car park, followed by a less detailed explanation as to why she was meeting Fiona Meredith. When they were done, the recording was placed in a sealed envelope, signed by them both and handed over for typing up.

It wasn't long before Fiona reappeared, although she looked better now that she was out of the house and therefore Jenkins' clutches, her skin was pale and she looked exhausted. "Where's Ed?"

"Sleeping somewhere. Shall we go and find him?" Holding out her hand, Patsy's smile was warm.

"I think so. I could do with some sleep myself. I . . . Oh here he is." Her shoulders relaxed at the sight of her son.

Exton approached them with a pad. "Looks like this one might take a while. I'm taking orders for food, what would you lot . . . Hang on." Tucking the pad under his arm, he pulled his phone from his pocket. His eyes widened as he listened. "You're sure? Okay, okay. Where? We're on our way." Without stopping to explain, he tossed the pad onto the nearest desk and ran from the room.

"He's going towards the interview rooms. Rude not sharing. I'll be back." Seaton hurried to catch him up.

Minutes later they both appeared with Paisley, Meredith and Trump.

Meredith pulled Patsy to one side. "They've found Jenkins."

"Found but not apprehended?"

"He's well and truly apprehended. He's dead."

"What? How?"

"Shot. But that's all I've got. We're going with them." He jerked his head towards Paisley who was pulling on an overcoat.

"So am I." Patsy lifted her own coat from the back of the chair in front of them.

"You can't. Don't give me a hard time, we're only just married. Take those two and get us all booked into a hotel somewhere local."

"We're staying here?"

Meredith looked at his watch. "I don't fancy a midnight drive back to Bristol. Your car's been taken into Taunton somewhere, so I think that's the best option." He looked at Trump. "You coming or heading back to Bristol?"

"I'll come and see what's what with Jenkins. But if you don't mind, I'll get back to Bristol, and come back tomorrow if I'm needed. With Jenkins dead, I'll sleep easier in my bed. Tom?"

Seaton rubbed his hands over his face. "I'll go back with Louie, whatever time that might be. Don't like sleeping in strange beds. Just book for you lot, Patsy."

Irritated, but knowing Meredith was right, she wasn't a police officer and therefore it would be wrong to even attempt to go with them, she nodded.

"I'll pick up some toiletries and stuff, and call to let you know where we're staying. My phone should be charged by now." She held out her hand. "Credit card. I've got nothing with me, it's all in the car."

"Thank you." He leaned down and kissed her before giving her his card. "Keep an eye on him." He nodded towards Ed. "He's not out of the woods yet."

"I will, and I know these things can take an age, but please keep me informed. I have a vested interest."

Looking over his shoulder as Paisley called out that they were leaving, he agreed, "Will do, and on that note, you can let Amanda know she is released from Sherlock's clutches."

"If she wants to be of course."

"What does that—"

"You're wanted. Go." She pushed him away. "Don't forget, I want information," She said as the door shut behind him.

"What's going on? What's happened?" Ed asked.

"Jenkins is dead. Shot. That's all they know."

"Good riddance to bad rubbish, that's what I say. I know you shouldn't speak ill of the dead, but that man . . ." Fiona was lost for words.

"Agreed, and I don't think we know the half of it." Patsy shrugged. "We're going to be staying the night, so we need to pick up some bits to tide us over. I'll get a hotel booked and we'll need to go shopping."

"Oh God, I'm sure we don't." Ed grimaced.

"Yep, and you're coming with us. You've been released into my custody, so no nonsense."

"What does that mean?" Fiona looked from one to the other.

"Long story which Ed can tell you another time. For now, let's find a hotel and you can get some proper rest."

Having managed to secure the only two rooms available at the Crowne Plaza near the Hoe, Patsy managed to grab a lift to the local shopping centre, Drake Circus, from one of the detectives who was heading home for the night.

Ed groaned as they entered. "Why couldn't we go to a chemist and pick up some deodorant and stuff, why do we need to shop?"

"Stop moaning, you sound like a ten-year-old." Fiona linked her arm in Ed's and pulled him in. "You'll need a shirt, underwear, socks. I can't believe you sometimes."

"I was hoping we'd, that is you and me, would be up and on our way home now Jenkins is dead. I could cope with smelly socks for the couple of hours that would take. But if I have to shop. I don't want a shirt, I want something comfortable that's likely to get some wear."

"Stop moaning. What . . ." Fiona was jerked to one side as Ed spotted something of interest.

"How long are we going to be here?"

"That depends on how fussy you are. We're lucky Meredith isn't here, he hates shopping too, but if he has to do it, he goes to town."

"Give me five minutes." Shaking off his mother's arm, Ed ran to a shop situated behind an escalator. Patsy and Fiona followed him.

"Ha. This should be interesting."

Ed had gone into a hairdresser. He was speaking to a young stylist with false eyelashes so long Fiona commented she was surprised she could see anything. Patsy was watching Ed in action. She couldn't hear the words, but she could see that his mannerisms and gesturing were charming the girl into doing something she wasn't comfortable with.

"He's a chip off the old block that's for sure," she murmured.

Grasping the girls face between his palms, Ed placed a kiss on her forehead and was rewarded with a dazzling smile and a slap on the arm. Grinning, he returned to them.

"She can do me straight away but no promises on what might happen. It needs at least twenty minutes with some sort of toner on, then a half an hour for a new colour blah, blah, blah, an hour and a half at most. I've told her that's okay." His eyes met Patsy's. "It is okay, isn't it?"

"Go on then. We can always grab a coffee if it's necessary." She flapped her hand towards the girl. "Get on with it. Your mum needs a lie down."

"Ah, well that's the other thing." Patting his pockets, Ed sighed. "No cash."

"Then you'll have to wait until we come and collect you. I've only got Meredith's credit card."

"Good, I'm glad he'll be paying to put this right."

"You always manage to get out of it." His mother chuckled. "What do you want if you don't want a shirt?" She rolled her eyes when he told her a T-shirt and hoodie would suffice. "I wish you were more like John in that department, he looks so smart. I like you in a suit."

"Excuse me. We shut at eight-thirty. If you want that sorted, you've got two minutes to get in the chair."

"Be gentle with him," his mother said with a giggle as Ed allowed himself to be led away.

* * *

"Here?" Trump leaned between the front seats at the rank of garages. Several squad cars blocked the entrance to the area, and a uniformed officer was taping off the forecourt.

"Someone has been very clever, or we're losing our touch, Meredith observed. "There's Dudridge, he didn't get his pint."

"Is that whatshername from the gym? Stacey?" Seaton pointed at a girl wrapped in a red blanket sitting on the step of an ambulance.

"It is." Meredith walked over to Dudridge. "Fresh or did we miss something?"

"We didn't miss it. Not as such. He's not been dead long according to the ME, but he was probably there when we visited." He pointed to the garage they had inspected. "All of these are rented by the gym. Young Stacey and some of the other staff use the one at the other end of the row to store their bikes while they're working. When Stacey finished her shift, she came to collect her scooter and found Jenkins. Shot through the forehead."

"Did we check the other garages?"

"When you say we, I suppose you mean me. We checked and they were locked. We didn't break in, didn't know there was a connection. It would be nice to think he wasn't there at the time though. Right, I'm off. I only came to this shout because of the location. That offer of a pint remains open if you're around later."

"Thanks." Meredith went back to the car where Exton was handing out overalls. Meredith slipped the covers on his shoes and looked at the ambulance, Stacey was on her feet, pacing around and smoking a cigarette. "I'll have a word with Stacey first."

Throwing away the stub of her cigarette, Stacey walked towards Meredith. "Have you got any smokes? That was my last one."

Pulling a packet from his pocket, Meredith joined her in lighting up. "Bit of a shock for you, Stacey. You okay?"

"Understatement. I crapped myself. I didn't see him at first, I'd put my gear on, and me helmet, it was only when I put the light on, I saw him. He looked like he was smiling at me." She shivered. "It was disgusting."

"Was the garage locked when you got there?"

"Yes. At least I think so. It's always locked so I didn't try it, just put the key in the lock."

"Who else has keys?"

"Most of us. Jenkins obviously, he has keys for all of them. Justin, he's the manager, he's got keys for all of them too, I think. Then Amy, Tom and Harry. They've got bikes too, cycles. I do enough exercise without cycling up the hill every day."

"I'm assuming you didn't notice anything else unusual as you approached or in the garage itself?"

"Nope. But I wasn't looking. Not much to see around here at night."

"No cars, vans, people walking dogs?"

"No."

"What else is stored in the garage, your bike and . . ."

"Just bikes. There's an old fridge from the restroom in the corner, got put there when it broke down, but nothing else. The spare and damaged gym equipment is stored in the middle one."

"When the lights came on, other than your bike and a dead body, all you saw was a fridge. Nothing other than the body was unusual?"

"Fuck me. That's enough, ain't it?" Closing her eyes, Stacey shook her head. "A McDonald's wrapper."

Grinning, Meredith patted her on the back. "You see. Was it there when you arrived for work?"

"Nope, I don't think so. It was light then, so I'd have noticed."

"Okay. One last thing, what's the far garage used for?"

"Shagging is my best guess." She screwed her nose up. "Only Jenkins had a key to that one, Amy saw him letting a prossie out of there a while back. A couple of days later, he was there when Amy arrived for work, and he opened up the door and pointed at a bed. Asked her if she wanted to try it out. She pretended she didn't hear him and walked away."

"Sensible girl. I thought you said Justin had keys for all of them."

"Oh yes. Well you'll have to speak to him about that. Ugh. I never thought about that. Disgusting! He's not a letch like Jenkins."

"Don't go anywhere, I'm going to have a look in there and I'll be back."

Stopping on the threshold of the garage, there wasn't much to see. Stacey's scooter was leaning against a wall rather than on its stand, presumably how she'd left it, the fridge in the back corner as she described, and a blue crate containing several evidence bags sat a few feet in front of him. One of which contained the fast food bag.

At the rear of the garage, a forensic officer was shining his torch methodically up and down the wall before lifting his camera and taking a series of photographs. Each flash highlighted the splatter of blood and tissue from Jenkins' wound. Another FO, with her back to him, obscured his view of the body, all Meredith could see were the feet. The tread of Jenkins' shoes looked remarkably clean against the mess on the wall. He watched as she pushed herself to her feet and arched her back.

"I'm getting too old for this," Alice Boyd complained to her colleague. "My old bones won't take much more of this." Pulling off her gloves, capturing one inside the other, she added, "Get him to the morgue."

"Any signs of a struggle?" Paisley dared to cross the threshold.

"DS Paisley," she turned to face him and saw the row of spectators. "Oh, I see you've brought the football team. No, no signs of a struggle." She pointed at the ground by the feet of the body. "This floor is reasonably clean, but there is dust and a little debris, had there been a violent struggle, or the dragging of feet let's say, it should be evident, and it's not." Lifting her hand, she scratched her forehead where tell-tale signs of grey ate into her auburn hair and framed her face. "Might find more when I've done a full examination."

"But he saw it coming?" Meredith asked.

"Unless they were quick on the draw, I'm guessing his killer was no more than five feet in front of him." Cocking her head, she asked, "Have we met?"

"Never had the pleasure." Meredith walked forward, his hand out. "DCI Meredith. He's connected with a case I'm working on in Bristol."

Shaking his hand, Alice Boyd smiled. "Nice to meet you too. Call me Alice, everyone else does. Not a lot more I can say until I get him back. Bullet entered here," she tapped the middle of her forehead, "and exited here." Tipping her head, she pointed at the back of her skull. "We've recovered what's left of the bullet. It's safe to presume that was the cause of death. No signs of poison." A smile twitched as Meredith grinned at her.

"I like you, Alice."

"Then you have impeccable taste. Now, much as I'm enjoying this chat, I was hoping to get home at some stage tonight. I won't be doing him until tomorrow."

"Nothing else you can give me?"

"Hmm, I shouldn't without confirmation, but it appears there was a slight upward trajectory, indicating the gunman was either shorter than the deceased, or the gun was being raised when the trigger was pulled, hence my comment on being a quick draw."

"Thanks. Have a pleasant evening. One thing, could you get someone to work the takeaway bag. I'm not sure what Jenkins was doing in here, but I'm guessing it wasn't to eat a burger."

"I'll see what I can do."

"Thank you." Turning away, Meredith walked to Paisley. "I've already arranged to speak to Kate Jenkins later this evening, do you want me to break the news?"

"When was that arranged?" Paisley was clearly miffed.

"When Patsy used her phone to call me. I was going to question her about Jenkins' possible location, now it will be his possible assailant. You're welcome to come."

Paisley thought about his wife and the steak supper he'd been promised. Having been away the night before, and this was already going to be a late one, he shook his head.

"You carry on. I'll have a word with this Justin bloke and get the names and addresses of the other key holders. What time are you seeing her?"

"Didn't get that far. She was going to see her son. She's in the middle of arranging to bring him home or something. I said I'd call. I'll do it now." Pulling out his phone, he listened while the ringing stopped and an automated voice asked him to leave a message. He asked Kate to call him. "Can't do much until I know where she is. I'm going to find out where we're staying, have a shower, and then get over there. This isn't likely to get out before is it?"

"Wouldn't have thought so, but you've tried." Paisley held his hands palm up. "Not your fault she's not answering her phone."

"He might be a lowlife, but she's still his wife."

"I know, but don't tell me she didn't know he was knocking those girls about. She runs those hostels, and yet . . ." He let the sentence trail away.

With the surprise of Jenkins' demise, Meredith hadn't considered the investigation into Dickie's allegations about Mimi and the others. He pursed his lips. "I'll ask her about that. Now we know Max Deegan is back in the area, I'm assuming you've got someone on that."

"Of course."

"Good. We'll catch up later and see how far we've got. Now I need to track down my wife." He returned Trump's grin. "That warmed the cockles."

When his call came in, Patsy was trudging back towards the hair salon with Fiona, both laden with shopping bags.

"I occasionally like an impromptu shopping trip, but all I want to do now is have a hot bath, something decent to eat, and to sleep."

"Me too. I think this has been the longest day of my life. I hope the beds are comfortable. I don't know why I said that, I reckon I could sleep on the floor. I'll probably keep Ed awake snoring. Do you . . ." Fiona stopped speaking as Patsy's phone rang.

"It's Meredith, two minutes." Patsy excused herself. "Hi, we've finished shopping, and on our way to the hotel in five."

Meredith gave her a brief summary of Jenkins and got the details of the hotel from her.

"We're heading for a taxi now, see you there." She omitted the part about having her fingers crossed that Ed would still be in the salon. Putting the phone back in her pocket, she increased her pace.

"You look worried. Was everything alright?" Fiona was struggling to keep up.

"Yes, it was definitely Jenkins, and Meredith is on his way back."

"Is that why you're hurrying now?"

"No, I'm sorry, habit."

Slowing, Patsy's eyes were fixed on the salon fascia. As they approached, she scanned the interior and smiled when she saw the stylist still working on a customer mainly obscured by her body. The feet sticking out from the gown told her it was Ed. The two women took a seat and waited for the stylist to finish. When she had, Ed spun the chair to face them.

"What do you think, ladies?"

"Ooh, I like it." His mother smiled.

"Perfect." Patsy looked away. Auburn suited him even more than his natural colour. Getting to her feet, she smiled at the stylist. "Well done, I didn't think there was much hope. How much do we owe you? We need to make a move."

"Are we in a rush?" Ed pulled off the gown.

"We are. Meredith is on the way back and your poor mother is fit to drop. Some of us have been trudging around shops while you've been being pampered." Patsy walked to the small reception desk and slid Meredith's card into the machine. "Take these, and the ones your mum has. I think you can do your bit now."

Ed smiled at her. "You look flustered. Why?"

"Not flustered, thrown by the resemblance. Again."

As they climbed out of the taxi, Seaton's car arrived, and an exhausted looking Meredith climbed out and waved. Leaning into the car, he bid Seaton and Trump goodbye and slamming the door, waited for the others to join him at the entrance to the hotel.

"Nice hair, but I think I preferred the proper red," Meredith called as Ed approached him laden with all the bags. "Did I pay for that too?"

"Yep. But you'll get it all back, don't worry."

They checked in, and Patsy sorted the bags out. When Meredith explained he still had to go out, it was agreed they would eat separately and meet for breakfast the next morning. Their rooms were opposite each other on the second floor.

"That's handy. I can trust you, can't I?" Meredith looked at his brother.

"Of course. Knock if you feel the need to check."

Fiona grabbed her son's arm. "Why would he not trust you? You've got some explaining to do."

"See you in the morning." Patsy ushered Meredith into their room and shut the door. "You look at the room service menu, I'll run a bath and sort this shopping out, then you can tell me what's going on."

Opening the menu, Meredith skimmed it as he undressed. Lying naked on the bed, he watched Patsy sort through the shopping.

"You know we're on our honeymoon, don't you?"

"Oh no. You don't get away with it that easily. This is work, a honeymoon is a sunny beach somewhere."

"But we can practise."

"We can," she laughed, "but first a bath and an update. I thought you had to go back out?"

"I do. But that's not been booked in yet." Sitting up, he reached for his phone. "Actually, I'd better try and call her again."

"Her?" Patsy removed her own clothes, and folding them, placed them into one of the shopping bags.

"Kate Jenkins. She doesn't know he's dead yet. I'll have the goat's cheese, and the ribeye. You order while I make the call."

Unsuccessful, Meredith dropped his phone on the bed and went to the bathroom while Patsy completed their order. He gasped as he stepped into the bath, but after a few seconds he lowered his body into the water, dunking his head under. When he surfaced, Patsy stood watching him.

"That's my bath, shove up. How come you got the short straw?"

"I chose it. I feel sorry for the woman. Her world is about to be shattered for the second time. I'm not sure how bad the son is, but she was making arrangements for him to come home. I hope she wasn't relying on Jenkins for help. If she doesn't call back by the time we've finished eating, I'll have to go in search. Won't be nice finding out from the news, or worse, one of his associates."

"Do they have any idea who did it?"

"Shut up and get in. Did they say how long room service would take?"

"Half an hour."

"Plenty of time. Come here."

22

Placing his plate to one side, Meredith tried Kate Jenkins again. It was the third time since arriving at the hotel. Sighing, he looked at Patsy. "Still no answer."

"Do you think something might have happened to her?"

"It's a possibility. I have two choices, either phone the local boys and pass it over to them or go and track her down."

"Where would you start?"

"I've got five locations. Home, the two hostels, Jenkins' office or the care home. I doubt she'd be at the gym. If she is, she'll have seen the news." Swinging his legs off the bed, he picked up the two plates and put them on the tray, which he carried outside and placed in the corridor for collection. When he came back Patsy was pulling on her jeans. "Why are you getting dressed?"

"Because you've decided to go looking, I'll come with you. My duty as your new wife."

"You don't need to do that." His phone alerted him to an incoming message. Reading it, he nodded.

"No. But I will. You can thank me later. One thing, how are we going to do all this travelling around? We have no transport."

"That's where you're wrong. They delivered your car to the station, if you have the keys, we just need a taxi and we're off. I would like a whole night in bed. Do me a favour, go and give Ed our telephone numbers and tell him we'll be out for an hour or so."

"An hour? When did you become an optimist?"

"Nearly funny, Hodge. Go and tell them." Looking at the clothes hanging in the open wardrobe, he asked, "What should I wear, a shirt and tie, or the rather fetching jumper from Marks and Spencer? Since when did I buy jumpers in Marks and Spencer?"

"Shut up and get dressed. It will suit you." Jotting their numbers on the hotel notepad, Patsy went across to Ed's room and tapped on the door.

Yawning, he pulled his mouth back into a smile. "I was nearly asleep. What can I do for you? Has something happened?"

Patsy heard Fiona asking if everything was alright, and stepped into the room. "Everything is fine. We're off out for an hour or so to see Kate Jenkins. I wanted to leave you our numbers, in case you need to contact us."

"How are you staying awake?" Fiona was already in her bed. The television was on a low volume, and she pointed at the screen. "I'm going to watch the news, if I can stay awake long enough, then I'll be out for the count until tomorrow morning." She looked thoughtful. "Give my condolences to Mrs Jenkins. He might have been a bastard, but he was still her husband and the father of her son."

"I will. Been a hell of day for all—"

"Look." Ed had taken a seat on the edge of his bed, and pointing at the screen, called. "That's where he died." Lifting the remote he increased the volume."

"...and yet another fatal shooting has been discovered in the city. Police were called to this garage on the industrial estate where the body of man was found late this afternoon. Police have confirmed the fatality, but are not releasing the identity of the victim until the next of kin have been informed. This is the third shooting in the last twelve months, the other two were related to gangs involved in drug smuggling. There is speculation . . ."

Lowering the volume again, Ed asked, "Has she not been told?"

"Not as yet no. And now that's out, we'd better get going." Patsy placed the sheet of paper on the dressing table. "Call if you need anything. Sleep well."

Hurrying back to her own room, she told Meredith of the news report, and he lifted his tie.

"Then we'd better get going. I'll do this in the taxi."

Having collected Patsy's car, they decided the home address should be their first port of call. As they pulled onto the drive, it appeared the house wasn't occupied. It was in total darkness. A security light came on as they approached the front door.

"I doubt she's in bed, but I'll give it go." Meredith pressed the bell several times and they listened to the chimes echo in the hall. He tried again after a few seconds, and leaving Patsy at the door, walked over to the front window and peered inside. "Nothing I can see. Let's go around the back."

As they travelled up the side of the house to the back garden, various security lights came on lighting their way. They looked in all the windows as they passed.

"Nice house," Patsy observed. "They must be making decent money. Look at the view over the Tamar."

Glancing over his shoulder, Meredith nodded. "Yep. Not bad. I'm more interested in getting my hands on that though." He tapped the kitchen window, and Patsy walked to join him. They both looked at the laptop. "Wonder if it's his or hers?"

Walking to the back door, Patsy tried the handle. "Oh. For a criminal he's not very security conscious." She pushed open the door.

"How fortuitous. We'd better go in and make sure she's not been murdered in her bed." Pulling out his phone, he placed his fingers to his lips and dialled Kate again. There was no sound in the house, and as the answer service picked up the call, Meredith hung up and replaced his phone. "Just checking she's not avoiding us. "Now let's have a look at the laptop."

"Should I remind you that you have no warrant. I'm assuming they'll ask for one if Kate doesn't allow a search, but you could bugger things up if there's anything incriminating on there."

"No, you needn't remind me. Get it going if you can, I'll make a call."

As he tried first Exton and then Paisley, Patsy switched on the laptop.

"Paisley, it's Meredith. I'm not getting any joy getting hold of Kate Jenkins. I'm at her place now, and the back door is open . . . yes literally open. Something is amiss, I'm going in. Have you got a warrant for the home address yet? . . . Well, chase it up and let me know." Hanging up, he glanced at Patsy. "Any joy?"

"Give me a chance it's not booted up yet."

"Well, while you sort that out, I'm going to have a look around."

Leaving Patsy sitting at the breakfast bar, Meredith made his way from room to room on the ground floor before going upstairs, giving each room a cursory glance to make sure nothing untoward had happened to Kate Jenkins.

The second largest bedroom had clearly been designed with their son in mind. Signed photographs of him with several high-profile footballers were arranged along one wall, his team's scarf pinned above the door, and an Xbox was set up with a selection of games. Meredith sighed, from what he understood, Terry Jenkins wouldn't know what it was, let alone be able to use it.

Having checked the final bathroom upstairs, he went back to the main bedroom. Although he believed Jenkins was too smart to leave anything incriminating lying around, and being careful not to leave his fingerprints, he searched through the cupboards and drawers.

"Ahem!" Patsy appeared at the door. "You're being naughty, Meredith."

"Perhaps. Did you find anything?"

"No. Need a password. Tried their names but need some ideas. To be honest, it's best handed over to the technical chaps."

"That could take forever. They've not even got a warrant yet. Ah bollocks, we'll take it with us."

"What? Meredith, what the hell are you up to?" Hands on hips, Patsy looked on as Meredith selected a drawer and emptied the contents onto the floor.

"Need to make it look like a break in." Striding across the room, he took a bedside lamp from the table and threw it on the bed, before scattering the contents of the drawer. "If you don't like it, don't look. But Max Deegan is still at large. I doubt he knows about Jenkins yet, unless he did it of course. Either way I want him off the streets so I can relax."

Being careful not to leave fingerprints in the wrong places, he moved from room to room disturbing things. No damage was caused, and as Patsy pointed out, if the house had been burgled there would have been more of a mess.

"Not if they knew what they were looking for." Entering the kitchen, he picked up the laptop. "Time to go."

Back in the car, he called Kate Jenkins again. "Kate, I've been to your house, the rear door was open, and you've had unwelcome visitors. Please call me, it's urgent that I speak to you."

He called Paisley again. "Someone's been having a poke around the Jenkins' residence. No damage, and not much mess, they were clearly

184

looking for something, the question is whether they found it. I'm going over to the nursing home to see if she's there. If not, I'll go back to the hotel."

They hadn't been in the car five minutes when Paisley called back. Meredith hit the speaker button.

"We have had a call from Max Deegan. Doesn't sound good."

"Explain." Meredith rolled his eyes.

"This came in about forty minutes ago. Different station, and the duty sergeant has just sent it over."

"What—" Meredith was interrupted by the voice of an emergency operator, he lowered his head and listened to the call.

"Police. What's your emergency?"

"I want to hand myself in, but I want a deal."

"Hand yourself in for what?"

"Loads. I need to speak to whoever is in charge. Tell them it's Max Deegan, I know they're looking for me."

"This is a big organisation, sir. You'll need to be more precise. I think it would be best if you go to your local station and speak to the officers there. This is an emergency service and not—"

"It is a fucking emergency. I'm going to be killed, I haven't got time to muck about. Now let me speak to—"

"Who has threatened you? Please give me your location, sir."

"Not before I've got a guarantee that . . . fuck! I've got to go. I'll call back, speak to whoever's in charge and tell them I'll not hold back for the right . . . shit!"

The operator asked if he was still there several times before there was a click as she terminated the connection.

"You're tracking the number?" Meredith drummed his fingers on his knee.

"On to it. All I know at the moment is it was a pay as you go."

"Do we know if it was definitely Deegan?"

"Nope. Would need someone who knew him to verify that."

"Has someone checked his home address? I'm hoping you're going to say yes, but it might be worth sending someone back round there to see if he's appeared, and—"

"If it is Deegan, we've missed something. It means there is someone higher up the ladder than Jenkins. Otherwise why would Deegan be getting jumpy? It does indicate he knows about Jenkins' murder though, don't you think?" Patsy mused. "We need Deegan alive to find out who. Have you found out anything about Jenkins' contacts down here worth a look? It's Patsy by the way."

"Evening, Patsy." Yawning, Paisley apologised, "Sorry about that. I'm sleepwalking at the moment. No connections I've been told about, I'll make sure someone double-checks. Then I'm going AWOL for a couple of hours or I'll be no good to anyone, they know to keep you in the loop should anything happen. In the—"

The rest of Paisley's words were lost. Meredith cut him off as his phone vibrated. It was Kate Jenkins.

"Meredith? Are you there?"

"I'm here. You're a difficult lady to get hold of."

"Yes, I'm sorry. I'm with Terry. I always put my phone on silent, so I'm not distracted. I've not listened to your messages, but I'm assuming it's urgent given the number of times you've called." Kate sighed, already resigned to more bad news. "Have you found Alan?"

"Yes, but I need to speak to you. Where are you?"

"Still at the nursing home, but I can leave and meet you somewhere, Terry is sleeping now."

"Stay there, I'll come to you. I'm almost there." Glancing at the satnav, he added, "Five minutes."

"I'll meet you in the car park. This place is a bit of a warren. As you enter, turn left and park as near to the signpost as possible, I won't miss you then. Alan is alright, isn't he?" A note of concern had crept into her voice.

"Sorry? What did you . . . You're breaking up, Kate. If you can hear me, I'll see you at the signpost." Hanging up, Meredith tutted. "I should have told her to go home. Not the sort of news you want in a car park."

"Maybe. But given Deegan's call, the sooner she hears it from us the better. He might take it upon himself." Swivelling to look at Meredith, Patsy asked, "Do you think she might be in danger? Criminals in this part of the world seem to attach their animosity to the whole family, and not restrict it to the wrongdoer."

"Who knows. Perhaps Kate will have some idea. Here's hoping."

23

Standing under the signpost, smoking a cigarette, Kate Jenkins looked tiny as Meredith pulled into a parking space. "I hate doing this, even with a lowlife like Jenkins. It's always the bloody family who take the brunt."

"I know what you mean. Be gentle, Meredith. I know there's lots of questions you want her to answer, but pace yourself." Patsy climbed out of the car and looked at him across the roof. "Put your phone on silent too." Taking her own advice Patsy silenced her mobile.

As Meredith mirrored her actions, he muttered, "Never done this before, have I?"

Patsy hurried to keep up with him. "You look as knackered as I feel. It wasn't personal."

They had almost reached Kate and ignoring Patsy, Meredith called to her, "Kate, over here. Don't hurry with that, I'll join you." He pulled out a cigarette and lit it as he reached her. "How's your boy?"

"He's well, thank you." Kate smiled. "I think he understands he's coming home for good. I've packed all his stuff into boxes, usually when he comes to visit it's just an overnight bag. I'm sure he knows this is different. He's been smiling all evening, bless him." Her eyes glistened and she blinked rapidly. "He's asleep now, so I had a break and picked up your calls. Where is Alan? Have you arrested him?"

"No. Look is there somewhere we can talk . . . in private?"

"They have a small café, but that will be closed. There's a reception area, it will be quiet at this time of night. Why? What's happened. You're worrying me, Mr Meredith."

Throwing his cigarette into a nearby bush, Meredith took hold of her arm and started to lead her towards the entrance of the building. "Let's go and find a seat."

Pulling her arm free, Kate turned to Patsy. "I'm not stupid, something's wrong. You tell me - has something happened to Alan?" Rapidly tapping her fingertips together, she stopped walking. "I don't need any more crap at the moment. My boy is coming home."

Holding her arm towards the building, Patsy nodded. "It's not good news, Kate. But better delivered somewhere more comfortable." To her surprise Kate took off at a trot.

"Bastard. He always manages to put a spanner in the works. Well if he's got into another fight because of that temper of his, he'd better not expect me to visit him." Glancing over her shoulder, she snapped, "Well come on. I've got things to do."

Kate had already sat herself on a small corner unit in the reception area when Patsy and Meredith entered the building. She gestured at two chairs on the other side of a walnut coffee table. "I'm sitting, get on with it."

"You go, I'll grab some water." Patsy walked to a sideboard on which sat several jugs of iced water, and a tray of glasses.

Lowering himself into the chair, and with elbows on knees, Meredith leaned forward. "There's no easy way to say this, Kate, I'm afraid Alan is dead. His body was found in a lock-up near his gym earlier."

"Don't be ridiculous. Why would someone shoot him? Are you okay?" Kate moved quickly to avoid the water flying from the glass in Patsy's hand, as Patsy tripped.

"Yes, sorry about that, the rug got me. Here take this one, it's still full."

Kate returned her attention to Meredith. "More to the point, why there? Why would he arrange to meet someone dangerous in a lock-up?" Snorting a laugh, a smile flashed momentarily. "Mr Meredith, you know my husband, you know about his past, do you think he'd be that stupid? No, no. It wasn't him." Getting to her feet, she placed the glass of water Patsy had given her on the table. "Take me to the body. I can stop this nonsense. You never know, I may even be able to tell you who it is."

"I can do that, Kate. But I saw him. It's Alan, you need to accept that." Meredith watched her lip quiver, and standing, he took her by the shoulders and pushed her back onto the couch. "Take a breath."

"You're wrong." There was less conviction this time, so she looked to Patsy for reassurance. "You've seen him recently, was it him?"

Although she hadn't seen the body, Patsy could see telling Kate this would only complicate matters, so she agreed, "It was him, yes."

A blink allowed the first tears to escape. "You're sure? It's not like Alan, not like him at all. I . . ." She fell silent for a moment. "What happens now?"

"Now, unfortunately, we need to speak to you. A formal identification isn't required, they'll do that from his fingerprints, but if we're to catch who did this quickly, we need to see if you can help in any way. We can take you to the station, but I think you'd be more comfortable at home. I don't think here is appropriate." Meredith's eyes travelled to the porter who had halted his journey with a laundry trolley to speak to the receptionist about Plymouth Argyle's chances in the next match.

Throwing her hand into the air, Kate shrugged, she didn't care.

"Did you listen to any of Meredith's messages?" Patsy moved to sit next to Kate, who looked at her as though she had only just appeared.

"What?"

"I'm sorry, Kate. But your back door was open, we went there to find you first. Someone appears to have been searching for something." Patsy held up a finger. "There's no damage, a little mess, but it's not clear whether anything was stolen."

Throwing her head back, Kate stared at the ceiling and offered it a silent scream. It was the most surreal thing Patsy had ever seen. The sinews on Kate's neck bulged, her head vibrated with the effort and her face reminded Patsy of a gargoyle on the local church, but it was the silence that was concerning. Shooting a worried glance at Meredith, Patsy put her arm around Kate's shoulder.

"Let it go, Kate. You're a strong woman, you can handle this. It won't be easy, but Terry needs you."

As though a switch had been flicked, Kate stilled, and straightened her neck. She held out her hands. Her voice was calm. "What have I ever done to deserve this? Why, even though things can never be perfect, why when they start to sort themselves out does the shit always fly my way?"

Opening her mouth to respond, Patsy held her tongue as Kate continued.

"Do you believe in karma, or is it Buddhism? One of those Indian things anyway, where you have more than one life, and if you've been bad in a previous life you pay for it in the next? Well that must be me. I must have been Genghis Khan or Myra bloody Hindley, the amount of shit that's come my way. What next, cancer, an earthquake? Because let me tell you, bring it on." Studying Patsy's face for a minute, her glare softened. "You're right. I can deal with anything life chucks at me, I will always have Terry, I will always survive for him. Take me home please."

Getting to his feet, Meredith held out his hand. "Come on. Is there someone we can call to be with you?"

"No, I'll be fine. I'll call my nephew if I need anything. I have to say goodbye to Terry. I won't be long."

Watching her disappear through the double doors behind the receptionist's desk, Meredith pursed his lips. "I need to caution her and ask her if she wants a solicitor. She could know something that incriminates her. Bollocks, I should have taken her to the station."

"Or wait until the morning," Patsy suggested. "Why not give her the choice when she gets back?"

"Yes, I'd better call this in. Wait for her, I'll have a smoke while I wake Paisley up."

Lighting his cigarette before making the call, Meredith noticed the missed call and the waiting message. He listened to the message, and throwing his cigarette away, he ran back into the building.

"What's happened now?"

"Long story short, they found Deegan in the same condition as Jenkins, I've got the address. We'll see her home and . . . follow my lead."

He watched Kate allow the doors to swing closed behind her. Rounded shoulders and head down, she looked even more diminutive as she walked back to them. "Kate, you look all in. Let's leave the chat until tomorrow. We'll take you home, make sure all is well and come back in the morning. Come on." Placing an arm around her shoulder he led her back to the car.

Once home, Kate walked around the house with them. Her tone flat as she repeatedly told them that nothing appeared to be missing. They returned to the kitchen, where Kate located her cigarettes and opening the back door, lit one and stared into the darkness.

Filling the kettle, Patsy asked again, "Are you sure there is no one we can call? I hate leaving you on your own."

"No. I'm fine, thank you. I need to be alone to get my head around this, I don't want someone fussing over me." She looked over her shoulder. "Terry's coming home tomorrow, whatever else happens. I promised and I keep my promises."

"Good for you. But you should know, you may be cautioned and you'll be asked if you want legal representation, that all takes time," Meredith explained

"You said we could do it here." Kate spun around to look at him. "Why do I need a brief? I've done nothing wrong, I'm not going to pick up the can for Alan. I might have to inherit debts or tax or whatever, but surely to God they can't blame me for kidnapping or …" Flapping her hand in frustration, she pointed the cigarette at Patsy. "You can tell them. I had nothing to do with this. I was the one who let you go," swinging her hand to Meredith, "and you, you know better than anyone I'm not involved."

Meredith held his hands up. "No one is accusing you, Kate. It's procedure."

"Well unless procedure says I can't be interviewed here, then that's what's going to happen. I've had enough. You," jabbing the cigarette at Meredith again, she ground the ash that fell onto the doormat, "you, be here, got it?"

"I will be. I promise. Now, is there anything else, if not, we'll make a move?"

"No. I'm sorry. It's been a bit of a day." Kate gave a weak smile. "Master of the understatement." She flapped her hand towards the hall. "Go on. I'll see you in the morning. I know you said I didn't need to see him, but I think I will."

"Yes, it might help. Sleep on it. Bye, Kate. Don't forget to lock the door." Patsy looked at the kettle. "That's boiled if you want a drink."

"Thanks. If I do, I doubt it will be tea. See you tomorrow."

Patsy and Meredith had reached the hall, when she called to them, "The laptop is gone. It was here this morning."

"Bollocks." Meredith cursed quietly before turning back. Raising his voice, he asked, "What's gone? A laptop? Whose was it?"

"Ours. We both used it. Neither of us very much, but anything you do these days you need an email address so there it sits. It was definitely there when I left today." She pointed at the empty breakfast bar.

"Clearly what your visitor was after. Would your husband have had anything important on there?" Patsy asked. "Important as in valuable to someone else?"

"I doubt it. He could hardly use it really. He knew how to . . . this makes no bloody difference, does it? Who am I to say what he was and wasn't up to? What did I really know about him?" Her voice broke and she turned back to face the garden as she cleared her throat. "That's it, go now. I need to be alone."

"You have my number."

24

Pulling up outside the hotel, Meredith leaned over and kissed Patsy. "An hour at most. Go and warm the bed up. Nothing can be achieved tonight, I'll have a quick look, get the basic details and be back before you're asleep. Give Amanda a ring for me, let her know it's safe to go home."

"I doubt that, and I doubt I'll last five minutes. I think the motion of the lift might send me off." Patting his chest, she warned, "One hour. Any more and we will have our first married row. If it is Deegan, the threat to us is gone, whoever killed them can wait until tomorrow." Lifting the Jenkins' laptop from the footwell, Patsy opened the door.

"Absolutely. Agreed. Get out of the car, the quicker I go, et cetera." Blowing her a kiss, Meredith pulled away as the door closed.

Back in their room, Patsy stripped off and climbed into bed. Sleep proved evasive. Her eyes were sore, her throat was dry, and throwing back the duvet she went to the fridge and got some water. Running her fingers along the laptop, she pondered trying to get into it again, but telling herself that sleep was more important, she returned to bed. Her resolve lasted ten minutes and collecting the laptop she studied the information she had on her phone about Jenkins, hoping for inspiration.

Several miles away, Meredith was cursing as he attempted to find a parking space anywhere near the latest murder scene. Giving up, he blocked the drive of a property several houses away from the scene and left a note on the dash.

One of the uniformed officers guarding the gate to the relevant property walked towards him. "You can't park there. It might be needed for an emergency vehicle. Move it please, sir."

"DCI Meredith. I won't be long." Having reached the officer, Meredith forced a weary smile.

"Sorry, sir. I'll need to see some ID. The name's not familiar."

"Because I'm from Bristol." Coming to an abrupt halt as the officer stepped in front of him, Meredith sighed. "I forgot my ID."

"Then you won't be going in. You reporters have got some neck."

"I'm not a reporter. PC 23547. What's your name?"

"Wilcox."

"I haven't got time for this PC Wilcox, it's been a long day. If you don't—"

"Meredith, get a move on. Forensics want us out."

Paisley sounded wearier than Meredith.

PC Wilcox stepped aside. "Apologies, sir."

"None required."

Joining Paisley, Meredith followed him into the small modern block of apartments that had been squeezed into the space between two imposing Victorian properties. They walked through the spotless hall and up the stairs to the first floor. On each end of the landing was a door. To the left, an officer, writing notes, was speaking to a pale-faced woman, who was leaning against the door frame for support.

The door to the right stood open, and a series of flashes illuminated the hall. Taking a paper overall from the officer guarding the door, Meredith looked at the silver metal tiles placed around the blood on the floor, and noted the blood smears on the otherwise pristine white walls of the small hall. Pulling on shoe covers, he stepped forward.

"Not quite as neat as Jenkins then? May I?" He pointed to the first tile. "Tell me what you know, Paisley." Stepping carefully onto the second tile, Meredith looked at the interior of the mostly open plan living space. "Very nice, I bet this didn't come cheap."

"The occupant of the flat above was coming home after dinner with his girlfriend. As they reached this level, Deegan opened the door and called for help. He was plastered in blood, and they helped him back inside. He was dead before they'd completed the 999 call."

"Did he say anything?"

"Help me."

"Seriously?"

"Yep. Didn't have time to say anything else. He died as they got him to the couch."

"Do they know him?"

"Don't think so, you'll have to ask Jeff. He interviewed them. That was him we passed."

"Will do." Coming to a halt at the edge of the granite breakfast bar, Meredith looked at Deegan. Slumped on the white leather couch, head resting on the back of the sofa, he stared unseeing at the ceiling. His clothes were soaked in his own blood from mid-chest down.

"Single shot to the chest, sitting on that couch over there." Alice Boyd pointed a gloved finger to a patch of blood to the left of the body. "Probably nicked an artery. Can't tell you anything else until I get him examined. Are you trouble, Mr Meredith? You've only been here a day, and look what happens."

Turning with a smile, Meredith held out his hand. "Hello, Alice. Not my doing." He pulled his hand back as Alice held up bloody gloves.

Pointing to several areas on the highly polished floor, Alice explained, "Blood in significant quantity, there, there and there. If you look to the left of the body, there is a circular blood splatter. I think that's where he was shot. I'm guessing the bullet is in the back of the couch. He got to his feet and grabbed a tea towel."

Pointing to an evidence bag on the breakfast bar containing a blood-soaked cloth, she turned neatly on her tile.

"Blood pooled at his feet, and got smeared, he staggered, do you see the droplets?" She waved her finger along the trail of blood. "And stopped here, and here, before entering the hall. That will be a nightmare to process because he and the neighbours then walked the blood back and forth, as did the paramedics and the first officers on the scene. However, we might get lucky if you lot bugger off and let us get on." Her lips twitched into a smile.

"Received loud and clear. Has anyone done a proper search?" Meredith turned to Paisley.

"Brief rather than proper. Nothing of interest as yet. No laptop, phone, address book, or interestingly, car keys. Just those on the breakfast bar." Two door keys attached to a silver ingot shaped keyring, sat to the left of the evidence bag. "If it was him who shot at you in Bristol, how did he get here?"

"Train? Taxi? I was more interested in the gun he used. What's he done with that?"

"Not here. Not unless there's a secret compartment somewhere, which we can look for once the wonderful forensic team have done their job."

"Enough flattery, we'll do a thorough search. Now get out. The sooner you go, the sooner we'll be gone."

"We're out of here. Thanks, Alice." Leading the way back to the landing, Meredith stripped off the protective overall. "Where's your mate Jeff gone?"

"I'm not psychic. But given I can smell smoke, I'm guessing having a fag outside."

"Let's join him."

Lighting his own cigarette, and after a brief greeting, Meredith fired a series of questions which the officer answered without reference to his notebook.

"None of the neighbours are friends with him. It's nodding terms only if they happen to pass on the stairs. Only one of them knew his name, and that's because his post got placed in her box in error. No one saw anyone coming or going this evening. There are no security cameras outside or in the communal areas. They don't think he has a significant other but couldn't swear to it. They think he moved in a year ago. All in all, bloody useless. There's no love thy neighbour in this block."

"And I take it they didn't see anyone leaving as they arrived home? Must have been a close-run thing if he was still walking."

"No. Not on the property, but they were in a taxi and took no notice of anyone who may have been in the street. I've already put a call in to the taxi firm so we can speak to the driver, and we've started the door to door with the immediate neighbours." Jeff Pinner pointed his cigarette to a neighbouring doorway, where a uniformed officer was speaking to a man holding a baby. "More officers due to arrive any minute."

"Thanks." Grinding out his cigarette, Meredith yawned. "Not much more I can do, I'll head back to the hotel. Keep me informed."

"You seem to attract trouble, Meredith. Did I hear you were leaving? Me too, fancy that pint?"

Turning to face Dudridge, Meredith held out his hand. He was about to refuse, but Paisley got there first.

"Good idea. I can tell you what Dickie has been telling us. I think we've got a major murder investigation about to hit us."

"You'd better talk fast. One pint, I can barely keep my eyes open. I'll drive." Pulling his keys from his pocket, Meredith pointed at Patsy's car. "It's tiny, but it works."

25

Gasping as Meredith climbed into bed and pulled her close, Patsy turned to face him. "You are freezing, and you smell of beer. What happened to one hour?"

"I went for a drink to find out what Dickie has been telling them. It appears Jenkins was some kind of sadistic psychopath. They reckon they will be looking for at least three girls, probably their bodies."

"We had a lucky escape. Poor old Kate, this will knock her for six. What else is news?" Shuddering, Patsy rolled over and pressed her body against his.

"Deegan was alive when he was found, but only for seconds, he died almost as soon as his neighbours got there. Needless to say, so far no one has seen anything. Jenkins kept a lot of secrets from Kate. Dickie knew he was up to something, but no detail on the robberies. Kate is absolutely in charge of the hostels and Jenkins only threw his weight around when she wasn't there. Apparently, he said Kate was the only person who Jenkins was frightened of, and anyone speaking out of turn in front of her about his business got a good hiding, or more."

"Was he into more than just the robberies for income?"

"Looks that way, Dickie reckons he always had something on the go. Kate has two interests, first and always foremost, her son, and then the hostels which finance their home and his care. Whatever else Jenkins got up to, he made sure she was kept happy and at arm's length from his own interests. Interestingly, Deegan stepped out of line once, about a year ago. Dickie didn't know what he'd done, but Jenkins gave him a good seeing to at the gym. One of Jenkins' mates who was there said Deegan was lucky to be alive, and told Jenkins he'd thought he was going to kill Deegan. Jenkins said if it was anyone else, he would have, but he was family, and family matters to Kate."

"Why is that interesting? Other than the fact that he would happily have killed him if they weren't related."

"Because that's what Julia said to me when I told her about Ed. She told me to be gentle with him, as he was family, and family matters."

"It does, that's why you didn't leave him in a cell. You're an old softy on the quiet."

"I think you're right. Either that or I'm losing my grip. I don't know the man. He's lied, cheated and ruined our wedding. He's had me chasing all over the country and I'm now neck deep in another force's crap. He doesn't deserve any more consideration than the next man. But there he is, tucked up and sleeping soundly next door."

"You like him." Patsy laughed. "And he is your brother."

"I do not. I have a misplaced sense of loyalty that's all. Now shut up and go to sleep."

"'Night, Meredith. Husband. I'll tell you about Kate in the morning."

Groaning, Meredith hugged her a little too tightly. "Tell me now."

"Get off. Kate called me, she does want to see the body and she's asked if I'd go with her, because she couldn't get hold of Deegan. Poor woman."

"How did she get hold of you? Does she have your number?"

"Didn't, but she does now. She called the hotel. I said I'd ring in the morning. I'll go with her, you never know, it might prove useful in picking up a clue as to how to get into the laptop. I had no joy there."

"I might come with you, we don't know for certain it was Jenkins who was after me and mine. And, as there is still a killer on the loose, we shouldn't take our eye off the ball. Shame about the laptop, I'll hand it over to Paisley tomorrow. Back to the subject of Kate, she's got more trouble coming her way. Asylum seekers can't work, so that little money spinner is coming to a halt. I knew that asylum seekers couldn't work, but it didn't occur to me while we were there because I was so focused on finding Jenkins. Dudridge pointed it out earlier when we were discussing the case. I think she'll be prosecuted."

"Well she must have known, and some of those girls were like zombies they were so tired, I think she has more than taken advantage of them, poor things. Is it wrong I still feel a little sorry for her? Forty-eight hours and her life has been turned upside down."

"As my mother used to say, she didn't actually but it sounds good, cheats never prosper. And nor should they, however good a job they hope to do with what they've gained. But given the circumstances, I hope she doesn't go to prison for any length of time, but only for her son's sake. Last question then sleep. Did you get hold of Amanda? I bet she's glad to be sleeping in her own bed tonight, she should be safe, whoever is doing this is definitely in Plymouth."

"She was very chipper, and glad they are both out of the picture. 'Night, Meredith." Snuggling down, Patsy chose not to mention that she didn't think Amanda would be sleeping in her own bed that night.

"'Night, Mrs Meredith."

"That has a nice ring to it."

"I know. Shut up. 'Night, Hodge."

"'Night."

* * *

The next morning, they ate breakfast with Ed and Fiona. Now rested and knowing that they were almost certainly out of danger, Fiona talked almost non-stop.

"I'm sorry for the trouble he's brought to your door, John, and so is he. But then, if he hadn't you might have lost Patsy or Amanda, or both." A shiver ran down her spine at the thought. "Do you think he'll go to prison? That would be such a shame, especially as you haven't got to know each other yet. I think you'll be really close when things have settled."

Watching the two brothers exchange a glance, Patsy banged the table. "Do you know your eyes even twinkle at the same thing?"

"Stop being dramatic, Hodge. In answer to your question, Fiona, I don't know, I doubt it. I think there are bigger fish to fry, including whoever killed Jenkins and Deegan. Fingers crossed all will be well and he can go back to picking daisies for a living."

"That's so good to hear. I'd be on my own if anything happened to him. He's all I've got."

"Now you're being dramatic, Mum. Let's change the subject, I don't even want to think about it."

Pushing away his plate, Ed looked at Meredith. "What happens now?"

"We're out of here as soon as. I've got to drop a laptop off to the local boys, I'll get clearance that they are happy for you to be released until it's decided what charges will be brought against you. I'm hoping I'm not expected to babysit you. I am supposed to be on my honeymoon. But, my . . . our sister, Julia, is still in Bristol and has sent me a text long enough to be a novel, asking questions about you, and whether she is likely to meet you. For some reason now you've turned up, she wants to."

"Ah, isn't that lovely, Ed. A proper family at last."

"We don't live in each other's pockets, but they are always on the end of a phone. Julia lives in deepest darkest Wales, miles away from civilisation now, and Ann is currently living in Canada." Lips twitching, Meredith looked at Ed. "She won't know what she's missing." He slapped his breast pocket as his phone vibrated. Glancing at the screen, he got to his feet. "Excuse me."

Watching him wander off into the foyer, Patsy smiled. "He likes you. I know it's difficult to see, his sense of humour is not always obvious, but he does."

"I'll take your word for it. How long before we know what they're going to do with me, do you think? The hotel has a pool and you can buy swimming shorts in the little shop, I might go for a swim."

"No idea. Why don't you do that anyway, once Meredith goes he'll be a couple of hours if not longer."

Getting to his feet, Ed patted his mother's shoulder. "Come on, Mum. I need you to pay for the shorts, and there are some nice loungers around the pool, you can read one of those magazines about what posh people get up to."

They waved goodbye to Meredith who raised a hand in acknowledgement before turning away to continue his call. Pouring more coffee, Patsy carried them to the lounge area, and waited for Meredith to join her.

"Not good news, I take it?" she asked as he dropped into the chair opposite.

"Two different guns. Alice is an early riser, she's examined both bullets and they were fired from different guns, I've asked them to contact Sherlock and compare them to the bullet recovered at the scene where Deegan shot at me." He slurped his coffee. "That's cold."

"It is now. Shall I order a fresh pot?"

"No, I'm going to get to the station, they say there's nothing on the door to door, no one heard the shot, must have had a silencer, which is why I think it might be the same one as used in Bristol."

"But that means Deegan was shot with his own gun."

"Exactly." Getting to his feet, Meredith stretched and yawned. "I'm still knackered. Come on, wife, back to the room, I need the laptop."

As they exited the lift, Patsy's phone rang.

"Kate Jenkins." She stopped walking to take the call.

"Make it lunchtime, I'll come with you, and . . ."

Meredith's own phone rang. He continued his journey to the room. When Patsy joined him, he was pulling on his jacket, the laptop sitting on the corner of the bed.

"News?"

"Yep, one of the neighbours questioned in the house to house went to put rubbish in the bin and caught sight of something foreign. It was a gun. Complete with silencer. Exton's waiting for me at the station."

"You'd better get going." Patsy lifted her coat from the hanger.

"Where are you going?"

"The morgue. Kate has called them, she definitely wants to see him, and they'll be ready for her at nine fifteen." Holding her hand up, Patsy stopped Meredith's protest. "She has her son coming home today, she couldn't do it later. Yes, I know there's a killer out there. Yes, I'll be careful. Yes, I'll explain to Kate, again, that she could still be in danger. Has anyone told her about Deegan yet? I'm assuming she won't be required to identify him?"

"Doubt it, fingerprints will do that, and not next of kin. Get the job done and call me. I'll let you know where I . . . bugger, only one car, I'll have to get a cab."

Tossing him the keys, Patsy lifted her bag. "No need, Kate is picking me up. You can take mine."

Meredith's phone was ringing again before they left the room. He answered it as they walked to the lift. "Meredith." He listened to the call for a few seconds. "Okay, hang on a minute." Grabbing Patsy by the lapel of her jacket, he pulled her forward and kissed her. "You go on, I need to take this, and I forgot the laptop. Be. Careful."

"Yes, husband."

The lift opened and Patsy stepped in, leaving Meredith to resume his call as he went back into the room. Kate was waiting by the reception desk and waved as Patsy emerged.

"Blimey, were you already here when you called me?"

"On the way, I had to pick up a few things from the shop. Once we've done this, I'll drop you back and go and collect Terry."

"Sounds like a plan. I hope he brings you comfort, you mustn't know if you're coming or going."

"I'm okay. But only because I have Terry to focus on. He's more important than anything and keeps me busy." She touched Patsy's arm. "Thank you for your consideration though, you're a good person. Given the circumstances, it's surprising you're even speaking to me."

"It wasn't you who took me hostage, it wasn't you who shot at Meredith, and it . . . I understand it wasn't you. Why would I hold you responsible?"

They'd reached the car park, and Kate pointed the remote at the car.

"Some would. I'm grateful. Now, let's get this done before I change my mind."

They travelled the few miles to the mortuary in relative silence as Kate navigated the traffic. Patsy had no idea if Kate had been told about Deegan and was wondering if it would be kinder to warn her about the investigation into the asylum seekers working, before she picked up her son. She felt sorry for the woman and was torn as to whether to tell all so she was forewarned, but she also wondered if having Terry close would be a solace. Whatever the outcome, it would take months to go to court. She kept her mouth shut.

A lanky man in scrubs met them at reception. Introducing himself, he led them into a small office and offered them a seat. They both refused, and his voice was low and kind and he explained Kate wouldn't be in the same room as the deceased due to the nature of his death and the on-going examination.

Kate frowned. "What difference does that make?"

"In some cases, once the offender has been caught, they demand a second examination. It's unlikely in this case, but it's still early days. I'm sorry, Mrs Jenkins."

"I see. What if you don't find them quickly, are you saying I won't be able to bury my husband?" Kate's chin quivered.

"Not at all. I'm sure the police will agree to release the body fairly quickly in this case."

"You keep saying that. What does that mean, in this case?" She looked from the pathologist to Patsy.

"Your husband was shot in the head. There is no question that the shot was intentional, or the cause of death." He reached out a hand to pat her shoulder, but she stepped out of the way.

"Let's get it done." Taking hold of Patsy's elbow, Kate stepped forward, hesitating, when she realised she had no idea where to go.

"This way." The corridor was eerily silent as they followed him almost to the end. He stopped at the last door but one. "In here, please. I'll be one minute."

Drawing in a deep breath, Patsy stepped into the small room behind Kate. A vase containing silk flowers stood on a wooden table beneath a small narrow window near the ceiling. Several chairs were against one wall. On the opposite wall was a long thin window, a curtain hung on the other side of it. It was drawn back, and the pathologist's eyes acknowledged them.

Kate gave a gasp and took hold of Patsy's hand. Behind the pathologist was a table holding her dead husband. Giving her a nod, he took hold of the top of the sheet.

"Are you ready?"

Kate returned his nod, and Patsy watched her body stiffen. The sheet was removed, and her response was almost a whisper. "It's him, that's Alan." She looked at the floor as the sheet was replaced.

Waiting until the curtain had been drawn, Patsy put her arm around Kate's shoulder. "Let's go. You were very brave, there must be somewhere we can get a coffee."

As though Patsy had somehow punctured her, Kate's knees buckled, and her body collapsed on top of them. A low groan vibrated in her throat, trapped behind clamped lips. Patsy gave her a moment, but when the groaning continued, she fetched a glass of water from the table, and knelt beside Kate.

"Here, take a sip of this, and when you're ready we'll find something stronger." She lifted Kate's hand and placed the glass into her palm.

Once again, her touch caused a change in Kate. Lifting the glass to her lips, Kate emptied it, and using Patsy's shoulder for support, she got to her feet.

"I'll be fine. It was the shock, you know. I never thought anyone had lied, but there was always a chance they were wrong. That it wasn't him. But it is, and I accept that. I need to get a grip and get on."

Stepping forward, Kate reached her hand for the door. The jerky movement contradicted her brave words.

"Kate, this has affected you more than you realise. I think you should take some time and gather yourself. I'm not sure how much care Terry requires, but you need to look after yourself first. He's safe where he is. Let me take you home."

"Are you suggesting I can't look after my son?" Kate was incredulous. "He comes first. Always. If I didn't think I could cope, then I wouldn't have done it. I'd have left him there. You underestimate me, Patsy."

"No, I don't. I have no doubt about your capabilities. I was only suggesting that perhaps another twenty-four hours may be beneficial for you."

Pulling the door open, Kate took a determined step into the corridor where the pathologist waited to show them out. "What will be beneficial to me is having my boy at home. Please leave it at that, I don't want to fall out with you."

Aware of the effort it was taking Kate to walk calmly and steadily to the car, Patsy didn't push it, but made a decision.

"Kate, let's go and get Terry together, I'm sure I can help, even if it's carrying his bag or something. I'll grab a taxi once you're home and settled."

Kate waited until they were both in the car before responding. "There really is no need." Her head cocked to one side. "Why are you helping me? What do you hope to achieve?"

"Nothing." Her retort sharper than intended, Patsy decided to explain. "Kate, you have had a massive shock, first your husband abducts two women, then he is found dead, and it all happens just as you are finally bringing your son home to live with you . . ." Patsy hesitated, and Kate jumped in.

"But there's more. Spit it out, Patsy, things can't get much worse." Fixing Patsy with a stare, Kate grasped the keys in her lap making it clear they were going nowhere until Patsy provided more information.

"There's no easy way to tell you this, Kate, but Max Deegan was also murdered last night. Also shot." Although Kate's expression didn't change, Patsy caught the intake of breath. "I'm sorry, Kate, I have no idea if you were close to him or not, but that's why the police are concerned about your safety, that's why I was suggesting it might be better to leave Terry where he is until the police . . . or you, have some idea who is responsible."

"What else?"

"What do you mean?"

"Patsy, I have lived with a liar and cheat most of my life. I know when people are lying to me, and I know when they are telling half-truths. Tell me what else, and for the record, I have never been involved in my husband's illegal activities. I have of course benefited from them, but whoever held a grudge against him and Max, will not have an issue with me."

"How can you say that? Look at what Jenkins . . . sorry your husband, was going to do to Meredith's family. He was prepared to kill me and Fiona Meredith yesterday, and he had plans for Amanda, Meredith's daughter too, why? To hurt Meredith. To make him suffer."

Lowering her head, Kate considered this. "Yes, I'm sorry. That I would never have turned a blind eye to. But Alan won't suffer now if I'm killed. He's past feeling." Swallowing, she composed herself. "So, while I appreciate your concern, nothing can be gained from killing me, except I suppose some form of twisted pleasure. I'm happy to take that risk and bring my boy home. But tell me what else."

Frowning, Patsy held her hands up. "Is that not enough?"

"More than, but there's more, I can tell. Don't mess about, Patsy."

"I'm sorry, Kate, you are clearly a perceptive woman, I can't say any more."

"Get out of my car."

"What?"

"Get out. Don't sit there pretending you care about me and what might happen, you clearly don't give a shit. GET OUT!" Kate covered her face, and her whole body shook.

Patsy remained where she was.

Hands falling back to her lap, a look of pure hatred on her face, Kate stared at her for a while. "It's Meredith, isn't it? He sent you to spy on me. For what reason God only knows, but you're here because he wants you to, what? Get more information about Alan's activities out of me?" Fumbling in her pocket, she located her cigarettes and lit one waiting for Patsy to answer.

"No. He didn't."

Blowing smoke at Patsy, Kate gave a laugh. "And I'm supposed to believe that?"

"Believe what you want, Kate. I'm not a police officer, I don't need to do things I'm not comfortable with, and Meredith, my husband, would never place me in danger. I believe you are possibly in danger. For the record, Meredith didn't want me to come alone. He wanted you to do this later so he could come too. May I have a cigarette please?" Holding out her hand, she took the cigarettes from Kate, and opened a window.

"Then what? I believe you about Meredith, but what else aren't you telling me?"

"Oh bollocks, look I'll tell you, but if you run you will make matters worse. I—"

"Run from what? What do they think I've done?"

"The hostels, you're making the girls work. That's illegal. And as they can't earn under their own names, I'm guessing you are contracted to supply staff, the onus being on you to ensure they are eligible to work. Is that how it works? You just send an invoice once a month?"

"Weekly. Seven days to pay, if they don't pay on time, they get no staff until they do. Had my fingers burnt there, learned from that mistake."

"So, you do know it's illegal?"

"I didn't. I moved here when the boys were sentenced. I wanted to be close enough to visit as often as I was allowed. I sold the house in Bristol and bought number forty-six. It wasn't much, but I could let out the rooms and earn some extra income. It was tatty, worse than it is now, and I struggled to get any interest from anyone other than undesirables. I decided that if I had to deal with people," holding up her fingers, she made speech marks, "with issues, it would be best to stick to women. That's how I found Aretta." Kate smiled.

"She applied for a room." Stating the obvious, Patsy ignored Kate's raised eyebrows.

"Of course. She was so . . . so . . . It's difficult to explain, subservient but superior. Called me Miss throughout the transaction and complimented me while all the while telling me what a shit hole I was trying to let." Kate gave a laugh. "Really pissed me off. I told her if she wanted a room, then she would have to help decorate it."

"And she did."

"Yep. I lived there too then. We did her room first, then mine, then worked our way around the house cleaning, decorating and buying cheap, but decent furniture. Aretta only received a basic living allowance and I received her rent direct from the local authority, so I paid her for her help. Not much, but enough for her to buy what she needed, and then wanted. It was mutually beneficial. I realised taking in female asylum seekers would be the easiest course of action. I got paid direct, they were grateful and would help out for pocket money. It worked. We let the rooms one by one."

"Aretta helped find the girls?"

"No, for the best part you don't have to look. The council are desperate for reasonably priced places, Aretta's strength was her knowledge of African languages. She could communicate with them. Then we found Fatima. Not only did she speak good English but her linguistic skills complemented Aretta's and number forty-six was in demand. An inspector came around and gave me advice on what I needed to do, to have more beds in the rooms on a temporary basis. Up to that point I'd only had two sharing when there was an overlap."

"Okay, I understand that, but how did it go from mutually beneficial to . . ." Not wanting to use inflammatory language, Patsy chose her words carefully. "To sending them out to work for you?"

"The demand was so good, I had to move out. I had the biggest room, and if I went, I could put three girls in there and rent a little flat and still make a little profit. I had little or no savings, I bought the house for cash with the money from the Bristol sale, and had forty thousand left over. That was slowly getting eaten up by buying the stuff needed to do the house up. And buying a van. I got fed up with having to pay someone else to deliver stuff."

"And you sent them out to work to boost your income?"

"No!"

"What then?"

"I decided to use what little money I had left to put a deposit on seventy-three. Had to pay a high bloody interest rate too because it wasn't for domestic use. I asked Aretta and Fatima for help. They are both intelligent women and were happy to help me sort number seventy-three out and get the income coming in, and I would pay them. Although we called it a reward."

"Halfway through the job, Fatima's papers arrived. She was free to stay in the UK, she had a two-year permit and could work. She took a job in the meat factory. Capable of much more of course, but decent jobs are hard to come by when you might disappear at any moment."

"Her idea?"

"No. She was approached by her boss. He could see she was hard-working, did more than she was paid for, and helped out with some of the other women who couldn't speak English. Her boss asked if she had any friends and she spoke to Aretta. Between them they put a proposal together."

"Which was?"

"They were both happy working for me. They liked our arrangement, and they liked living in female only accommodation, I've never had the details, but both had had a rough time at the hands of men before arriving here. They wanted me to employ them as what they called house mothers. They were quite cute, they didn't ask for much in comparison to what they did, and if they didn't declare it, they could claim benefits and pay for their rooms."

"Cheat the system." Patsy's tone wasn't judgemental.

"For a while. I wanted to get out of my little flat, I wanted to have a home for the boys to come back to, so while they ran the houses, I also took a job for a while, as I needed to save another deposit. I was moaning about it one day, and Aretta suggested some of the girls could work. Fatima had told her that some of the girls at the factory shouldn't have been working and yet they were. We went to see the bloke who owned it. Long story short, Patsy, because I can see you don't approve, if any of the girls wanted to work to buy extras, shoes, clothes, phones, they could."

"And you took the money."

"Not all of it, no. Obviously their hourly rate isn't brilliant, and I do have overheads, the van, the petrol, the organising." She shrugged at Patsy's sigh. "It's true. Don't judge me, Patsy. They get a safe and secure home, they get fed, they get ferried to and from work. They can come and go as they please within reason, they can save or spend their money on whatever takes their fancy. Most of them save it. Most of them know, one day, they will either be able to leave and make their own lives, or they will be deported, either way they need money. This way they get it."

"Okay, I'll accept you don't force any of them to do anything. But if this was all set up by Aretta and Fatima, how come you get the big house with the posh car, and they get a room in a hostel?"

"Because we have a plan." Kate looked away from Patsy as she lit another cigarette. "When Terry got injured and was released, I needed to have more time, I needed to have a home for him. We set a goal. A three-year plan. At the end of which they would own one of the houses, and I would be mortgage free."

"How?" Patsy opened the window a little more and took a cigarette.

"I already owned forty-six outright. I paid the deposit for seventy-three and financed the furnishing and maintenance. For three years they would continue to run the houses as before, arrange the work for the girls, and make sure they were where they should be when the authorities wanted to check on them. All profits would be ploughed into clearing the mortgages. That's where we got the three years from. When both were paid off, I would sell forty-six or not, and they would get seventy-three, and do with it as they will. It was a win win, for everyone."

"But not the women sent out to work."

"Rubbish! You want to do some homework, Patsy. Their normal life waiting for a decision on their future would be worse. This way they are able to save, buy some luxuries, and be safe." She wagged a finger at Patsy. "You should hear the tales they tell about what happened to them. With us they are safe. So, don't bloody judge me."

"But they weren't always safe, were they?"

"Not all of them."

Watching Kate closely, Patsy searched for signs she knew the girls had been abused or worse by her husband.

"You're talking about Mimi, I suppose. That was bloody Dickie. He took to her, and I'm guessing she rejected him. Poor little Mimi, she was always troubled. I told Alan he had to get rid of him or I'd call the police, and he wouldn't hear of it. He said he'd sort him out, and I should steer well clear of the police because I didn't want them poking . . . But you know why I wouldn't want that."

"What about the others who went missing?"

"Missing? Who have you been talking to?"

"Does it matter?" Patsy's tone was cold. "The bottom line, Kate, is you were working a scam, whatever your justification, and even though you might not have forced them. But when a young girl kills herself, and several others who had mysterious injuries disappear overnight, surely to God you were suspicious. Because you should have been. Because it was your husband, and not Dickie who was doing the damage. Dickie was kept around so you would blame him."

Patsy released her seatbelt. "You know what, I'll get a taxi."

Opening the door, she turned to Kate. "I can't believe I felt sorry for you because you must have known, and that disgusts me. Leave your son in peace, don't drag him into this sordid mess that is your life." Slamming the door, she walked away from the car.

Kate's mouth opened and shut several times, her brow furrowed, and closing her eyes, she tried to remember as much as she could about the events Patsy had thrown at her. Her mind was elsewhere when Patsy took the call from Meredith, and as Patsy slipped the phone back into her pocket, Kate gave a scream that reached Patsy through the open window of the car.

Headbutting the steering wheel, the horn sounded, and Kate repeated the action again and again until Patsy pulled her from the car.

Once again on her knees, Kate allowed the tears to flow. "I didn't know." She told Patsy, wiping the blood away from her forehead. "I didn't know."

Kate vomited, narrowly missing Patsy's feet.

26

Still protesting as the door slammed and trapped her words, Kate was driven away in the police car. Turning to Meredith, Patsy took his outstretched hand.

"Can we go home now?"

"We can in a couple of hours. A few bits to tidy up, but then we're done."

"What bits? I thought you were sure it was her." Emotionally drained, Patsy climbed into the passenger seat of her car, happy to allow Meredith to drive. "I got the gist but start at the beginning."

"The code to get into the computer was Terry's date of birth. The first thing to raise suspicion and put Kate in the frame, was the document containing all the information on me. That was opened at a time when Jenkins couldn't have been there, then put into a newly created file called 'Really?'. Jenkins was on his way to Ed's mum at that time, same with the photographs of you and Amanda."

"Kate knew what he was planning? I don't believe it, she seemed so genuine."

"Don't they all? To be fair, and her interview should reveal more, she might not have known what was planned, but she certainly had seen the documents, so her pleading ignorance when she found you at the house was rubbish."

"I thought she looked shocked when she saw me. But she had a reason for wanting us out of there pronto." Quickly explaining what Kate had told her, Patsy said, "Tell me about the gun."

"Also on the laptop are the video recordings from various security cameras. The one at Jenkins' office shows him taking something from a compartment under the floorboards before setting off to Fiona's. The whiz kids can also prove that Kate watched that. An hour or so later, she appears and pulls back the carpet, she clearly didn't know what she would find, but she examined it in full view of the camera. It was a gun. A gun that matches the calibre of bullet used on Jenkins. Of course, they need to find it to prove that."

"If that's the case, she must have had it when she found us at the house, and therefore when she went off in search of Jenkins. The timing is going to be crucial though. When she went looking for Jenkins she wasn't gone long, I don't think it was long enough to find him, kill him, and get back to the house. If she managed that she's a great actress. If I was asked, I'd say she still had no idea where he was at that time."

"Unless she can prove she ditched it, she had it when Jenkins and Deegan were shot. But I doubt she was intending to kill you, if she was, she was hardly likely to pick you up at the hotel."

Turning to face Meredith, Patsy gripped his arm. "I don't know how she did it, but she did. I've remembered what she said. Can't believe we didn't work that out before." Tutting, she returned to her former position.

"Worked what out?"

"When we told her he was dead, she said who would shoot him? Do you remember? She never asked how he died. We missed it because I dropped the water."

After a moment Meredith began to nod. "You're right. We're losing our touch. Think, Hodge, what else did she say?"

Closing her eyes Patsy replayed the meeting in her mind. "Why would anyone shoot him? Why would he arrange to meet someone dangerous there? Double bluff, because he didn't, he arranged to meet his wife. You have your murderer, Meredith. Poor Terry won't be coming home anytime soon, poor man." Tutting, Patsy looked at Meredith. "What will happen to the hostels and Aretta and co., if she is convicted?"

"No idea, but I'm sure it will be worked out. Oh yes, I reckon she also took Ed's ill-gotten gains from Jenkins' car."

"Well that adds up for reaching their three-year plan, and I suppose once she realised he had put her plans in jeopardy, leaving a trail to anything else was to be avoided. I know it wasn't Shakespeare, but whoever wrote, what a tangled web we weave, when first we practise to deceive, was spot on."

"Marmion. The poem was called Marmion, it's about the battle of Flodden. I did it for English Lit at school."

"Well I never, you are cultured, Meredith, who knew?"

"Don't be cheeky, Hodge. It doesn't suit."

"I'm sorry, who wrote it?"

"Can't remember." He grinned. "Do you want to come to the station with me?"

"Yes. But not really, I've had enough of this case. Whatever happens, husband, we are going home tonight. I'm going back to the hotel to pack up our meagre belongings and check out before we are charged for another night. Can I do the same for Ed and Fiona? As you are the only one with any money you are paying, not sure if Ed can pay you back . . . how did you know she took the money? Or that it was Ed's?"

"During her interview, Fiona said Jenkins had taken a bag from her house, not sure whether she knew what was in it, she didn't offer that information. But there was a holdall in the boot with Jenkins' overnight bag and it was empty. I asked Ed what was in it, and he told me. Pleased he was honest with me, to be truthful, he could have lied and said nothing of value. I doubt anyone would have gone to the trouble of testing for prints even if the bag had been there."

"You didn't answer the question. Shall I check them out, and if I do, are they free to go?"

"Probably. Keep them with you until I'm finished, I'll make sure the coast is clear. Do you want the car? If so, I'll go to the station, and you can drive to the hotel. I can get a lift back."

"That would be good, if you're delayed, we can do some sightseeing or something."

An hour later, Ed dropped the plastic carrier bags containing their belongings into the boot.

"Where would you like to go? Given it's Meredith's credit card, I think more shopping is out, but we could find somewhere nice to have lunch." Starting the engine, Patsy turned to Fiona in the back seat. "You choose."

"Can we walk along the Hoe? I haven't done that for years, fabulous views, and there are a few restaurants there. That should kill a few hours." Tutting, she added, "I can't believe that Kate. What will poor old Aretta and the others do now? Out on the street, begging, no doubt. Poor people."

"I don't know. I don't even know if they'll be told anything very quickly."

Ed joined the conversation. "If they were part of the scam, won't they get picked up too? You said Kate told you it was their idea."

"But can we believe her?" Starting the engine, Patsy asked, "Do you think we should give them the opportunity to leave, or should we let justice take its course?"

"Well how long would that take, they could be locked up for months, and deported. They were helping those girls, tell them to run, Patsy." Fiona nodded defiantly.

"Ha! I don't think I can do that, but I can let them know Kate might be detained for a while. I doubt she'll be remanded in custody, because of Terry. But at least they'll know who to call to find out what's happening. Does that sound like a plan?"

"Yes. Let's go."

Pulling up in the only space near either house, Patsy cursed, "Bugger, double yellows." Leaving the keys in the ignition, she instructed, "You two stay here, I'll pop in and give them the lowdown. Won't take long, but if a parking warden turns up, drive around the block. Should only take ten minutes."

Having left her jacket over the back of the car seat, Patsy shivered as the chill wind caught her as she hurried along the street and up the steps of number seventy-three. Ringing the bell, she wondered whether it was wise to go to the Hoe, only Fiona had a decent overcoat with her. Dismissing her thoughts, she smiled as a surprised Fatima opened the door.

"Hi, Fatima, may I have a quick word? Is Aretta around, might be best I tell you both at the same time?"

"Come in, come in. Tell us what? Aretta is not here, she is shopping." Fatima led the way to the lounge and offered Patsy a seat. "May I get you something?"

"No thank you, I'm not stopping, this won't take long, is Aretta going to be long, because—"

"I will call her. One moment." Fatima's foot tapped as she waited for Aretta to answer. "Ah, Aretta, greetings. The lady, Patsy is here. She wishes to tell us something but is keen that you are here too. How long will you be?" Listening to the answer she turned to Patsy.

"Another ten or fifteen minutes. Aretta asks what this is about?"

"It's about Kate Jenkins, she's been arrested and—"

"Arrested? By the police?" Fatima screeched. "I must tell Aretta."

She spoke quickly and a little incoherently to Aretta, who was asking questions to which Fatima had no answers and kept repeating "I don't know" or "How would I know?" Eventually Fatima fell silent and listened to Aretta. Hanging up, she smiled at Patsy. "Aretta is on her way. She will abandon her shopping and come directly. She says you must wait for her because I am useless with the information. She said five minutes."

"In which case, I will have a cup of tea."

Checking her watch, Patsy placed her mug on the chipped coffee table. "I really do only have ten minutes or so, if she's not back then, I will tell you, and you can tell her."

"That is acceptable."

After five minutes, Patsy decided to tell Fatima what had happened, she was more than capable of passing on a message.

"I'm sorry, Fatima, I'm going to have to make a move. You'll have to give Aretta the details. I'll leave you a telephone number for the police station."

Fatima looked horrified "I'm sure she will be here soon."

"Perhaps, but I must go. As I mentioned Kate Jenkins has been arrested, I can't give you all the information, but they are serious charges, and she is likely to be held for at least two days, although it might be longer. If you need to contact her, or find out what is going on, then unless she has a solicitor, you must phone the police on the number I give you. Do you understand?"

"I do. And we have a solicitor. Where have the police taken her?" Fatima pulled her phone from the pocket of her tunic and found the number she wanted, the call was answered as Patsy told her the name of the station. She spoke quickly and with authority to the receptionist answering the call.

Patsy was taken aback. Her brief but previous meeting with Fatima had not revealed this steely determination and authoritative side. Listening to the one-sided conversation, it was clear the solicitor had already been summoned to the station. Getting to her feet, Patsy smiled at Fatima.

"Well it seems you have everything under control. I'll—"

The door to the lounge banged open and a breathless Aretta

entered. "What is happening? Why has she been arrested?" Lowering herself into the nearest armchair, handbag on her lap, she gripped the handles as she caught her breath. "I must get a bike or learn to drive. I am not fit enough to run up those hills," she managed between gulps of air.

"As I was explaining to Fatima, I can't give you many details. I suppose the real reason I came is to warn you that one of the charges Kate is facing, will be about the supply of illegal labour. I am sure you know that unless you have the appropriate paperwork you are not allowed to work here. I know that you have worked hard and helped Mrs Jenkins with this . . ." winding her finger in search of the right word, Patsy settled for the least inflammatory, "arrangement. I don't pretend to be an expert, nor am I able to predict what might happen to you, but I simply thought that if you knew what was happening, you could prepare yourselves, or perhaps make other arrangements."

"Other arrangements. What does that mean?" Aretta asked.

"I don't know. That's down to you, you could sit tight and see what happens, or perhaps you might not do that." Patsy stepped towards the door. "I've said more than I should, I'll leave you two to discuss what you think is best."

"Run away and abandon her, is that what you mean? Never." Aretta lifted her chin. "Never would I do such a thing."

"No. We will stay." Fatima didn't sound as convinced as Aretta.

"Good. I wish you both luck."

"When they know she didn't shoot anyone, how long do you think it will be before she comes back?" Fatima asked, halting Patsy's next step.

"It depends on whether she did or not. I believe the evidence is quite damning."

"Then the evidence is wrong," Aretta announced.

"Your support and belief in Kate is touching, Aretta, but these are serious charges, and as I say the evidence would suggest that she was involved. But . . ." Patsy had reached the threshold and turned back to face them. "How did you know—"

"Sit down please, Miss." Aretta pointed to the sofa with the barrel of the pistol. "You have given us yet another problem to solve."

Not moving, Patsy held her hands up. "Not me. Never been a problem to anyone. If you think she's innocent, perhaps she is, that will all come out in court. Now, I must—"

"Why do you take us for fools? I said, SIT DOWN!" Aretta's voice bounced off the walls.

Walking to the sofa, Patsy sat on the edge of the seat, and looked at Aretta. "Why are you doing this? What can you possibly gain from holding, or worse, hurting me? I can do nothing to help you, in fact, it will simply get you into deeper trouble. I like you, Aretta, it's why I came here, listen to me now. If you let me go, I can help you sort this mess out."

"Why do you people speak to us like we are fools? Because our skin is a different colour, because we don't speak the Queen's English? Let me tell you this, we speak it better than some of your countrymen I have met. And the men . . ." Aretta made a guttural noise in her throat, and for a moment, Patsy thought she was going to spit on the carpet. "The men think we are here to be used and abused."

"Not all men are like that. And I'm sorry. Did Alan Jenkins hurt you?"

"He hurt everyone he ever came into contact with. He will rot in hell. His soul will never find peace."

"Did he hurt you, you personally?" Patsy looked at Fatima. "Did he hurt you? Are you telling me one of you killed him?"

"We are telling you nothing. I will find a safe place for you until Miss Kate comes home," Aretta answered.

"That might be days, weeks even. You can't hold me that long. Half the police force will be looking for me, people know this is where I was coming." Shaking her head, Patsy got to her feet. "I can't believe I came here to help you. I'm leaving and leaving now. Shoot me, if you will, but I'm not going to be locked in some bloody cupboard for weeks." Taking a step forward and looking Aretta in the eye, willing herself not to look at the gun, she asked, "Do you think it's fair to kill me?"

Patsy took another step forward and seeing the hesitation in Aretta's face and her eyes darting to Fatima for support, she took another and now had her back to Aretta, her eyes looking towards the front door and freedom.

Behind her with a nod from Fatima, Aretta flipped the gun, catching it neatly by the barrel as though the move had been practised. Raising it, she lunged forward bringing it down on Patsy's head.

Patsy screamed out and fell to her knees stunned.

Aretta rushed forward and placing her foot in the centre of Patsy's back, pushed her to the floor. "I swear if you move, I will shoot. Don't make me do that," she hissed, beckoning Fatima forward. "Help me take her to the kitchen."

"And what then?"

"Then we will think. The girls will be back within the hour. Quickly now, take her arm."

Groaning as she was lifted by the arms, Patsy screwed her eyes shut against the pain, aware the two women were speaking, she fought to hear the words above the ringing in her ears. Opening her eyes, and keeping her head hanging forward, she allowed the two women to half drag her forward as she focused on the tiles on the floor. By the time Aretta kicked open the kitchen door, Patsy was back in control of her faculties, but maintained her floppy posture.

Once in the kitchen, Aretta hooked out a chair from under the table with her foot, and Patsy grunted as she was dropped onto it. Her chin still on her chest, she watched their feet.

"We need to secure her, but do we do it here?" Aretta mused. "What is in the shed?"

"Nothing. Rubbish. How can we leave her there?"

"Well we have to do something with her. Just until Kate can tell us what to do."

"But the shed? Can we not put her in one of the rooms, at least then we can feed her and let her use the toilet?"

"You want her in your room? Go on. How will we get her up two floors, she is a dead weight?"

"I don't know, but we must try. Please, Aretta, we have come so far, please remember she came here to help us. She is not one of them."

Hearing Aretta sob, Patsy almost looked up. Instead, she readied herself to take some form of action.

"Forgive me, it is fear taking over my brain." Aretta rested a hand on Patsy's shoulder.

Patsy forced another groan.

"We will have to move now, one flight at a—" Aretta's hand was snatched away as the doorbell rang. "Who can that be? Will you go, or shall we ignore it?"

"I don't know. What will I say?"

Fatima was panicking, Patsy watched her feet shuffle from side to side. She willed Fatima to leave and give her a chance against Aretta, who had now placed the gun on the table, but Fatima had other ideas.

"I will go if it rings again. Let us wait a minute more."

"We should either move her or bind her. She won't remain like this for long." Aretta waved at the dresser. "Get me the tape."

Patsy's heart sank. Her only hope was that Ed would call Meredith when he couldn't find her.

27

Bored, Ed opened the glove compartment and pulled out a packet of mints. "Do you want one?" Turning towards the back seat, he held the packet towards his mother.

"No, thank you. You shouldn't go poking about in their things. It's rude."

"Probably." Ed turned back and put a mint into his mouth. "But it is also rude to say I'll be five minutes and then take twenty."

Fiona looked at her watch. "Don't exaggerate, it's only been fifteen. I expect those girls were upset and she's comforting them."

"Which is lovely, Patsy is a lovely girl. But she could have dropped us off somewhere other than a side street first." Putting his hand on the door handle, he opened the door. "I might go for a wander."

"Don't you do that, she might . . . that's Patsy's phone." She looked at the glowing screen in the cup holder. "It says it's Meredith."

Snatching up the phone, Ed answered it. "Brother, how goes it? I'm afraid your wife has abandoned us. Can I take a message?"

Patsy had left her keys in the ignition and his voice was broadcast in the car.

"Where is she? Abandoned you where?"

"Calm down. You sound agitated. We're in the street where Jenkins brought Patsy and Mum, Patsy has gone to tell . . . thingy and someone else that Mrs J has been taken in."

"Shit. Go and get her, I'm on my way."

"What do you mean go and get her? What's wrong, don't tell me there was a Mr Big after all?"

"Not a mister, no. If Kate is telling the truth, she found Jenkins' gun at his office and when she got to the house and found Patsy there, she gave it to Aretta to get rid of. Kate's in this up to her neck, but so is Aretta. Kate was with her son at the time Deegan was killed, but if I'm right — look you don't need to know this now. Go and get her. Now! I'm on my way."

"Oh my." Fiona leaned between the two chairs. "I can't believe that Aretta did it, can you?"

"Who knows, but if she did and she has a gun, how am I going to help Patsy? Shit!"

"Don't let on you know. Just tell her there's an emergency or something. Go on, hurry up."

Hesitating for only a few seconds, Ed got out of the car and went to the boot. Moving their bags, he lifted the carpet and took out the wheel brace. Sliding it up the sleeve of his sweatshirt, he took off for the house. Taking a second to compose himself, he rang the doorbell. The chimes echoed around the hall.

When no one came, he dropped to one knee and gently lifted the letterbox. All doors onto the hall were open, and he caught the shadowy movement from the door at the end. Unless they were deaf, and Patsy wasn't, they were ignoring him. Standing, he glanced to the side of the property. A gate led to an alleyway between the two houses. As he approached it, he prayed it was open. It was, and squeezing past several bins, he made his way to the back of the property.

Halting at the corner, he peeped into the yard at the back of the house. It was empty except for a shed which was padlocked. Two windows flanked a door on the rear elevation. Creeping to the first window, he looked in. The curtains were drawn, and he made his way to the door, weighing up whether to knock again or just go in if he found it to be unlocked. He settled for the latter, hoping that having surprise on his side would definitely be a bonus.

He placed his hand on the knob and pressed his ear to the glass. Hearing muffled movement, he turned the knob and gently pushed open the door, relieved to find it didn't squeak, he moved into the small lobby and paused again to listen at the door to the kitchen.

"Look in the cupboard. I know there was tape there last week, I used it to tape the carpet on the stairs. Stop panicking, Fatima, calm yourself. We need to secure her."

"But it is not here. Perhaps you put it somewhere else." Fatima opened another cupboard.

"Why would I put it with the dishes? Oh, Fatima, come and watch her, I will look."

Ed pulled in a breath and opening the door strode into the kitchen. Taking in the scene, he shouted. "Oh no! Has there been an accident? I rang the bell, now I can see why no one came."

Two steps and he was by Patsy's side. He lifted her head, and she looked at him for a second before closing her eyes again. Knowing she was fully aware of what was happening, he turned to the others. Fatima had frozen and stood looking at him open-mouthed. Aretta was talking non-stop as she walked towards him, her eyes darting to the table.

"I am so pleased you are here. She took a fall, so difficult to move, we didn't know whether to call an ambulance. Is she awake yet? I was looking for a bandage."

This time Ed caught her eye movement and spotted the gun, allowing the brace to slide down his sleeve he caught the end neatly in his palm and gripped it tight. "Leave it!"

Aretta's mistake was to look back at him, it lost her the seconds she needed to snatch up the gun. As her hand found it, Ed lifted the brace and brought it down with all his might, there was a sickening crunch as the metal crushed several bones. Pulling back her hand as she screamed, Aretta backed away.

Picking up the gun, Ed held it by his side while threatening them with the brace. "One more move, and you'll get this on your head."

Patsy got to her feet, wincing as her head protested at the sudden movement. "Thank you, Ed. Shall I take the gun?"

"Please."

Looking at Aretta, Patsy shook her head. "You silly woman, take a seat. You too, Fatima. Ed give the police a call please."

"No need, they are on their way. It's how I knew you were in trouble. Kate Jenkins told them Aretta had taken it upon herself to kill Jenkins. Don't know who did Deegan yet, but she was with her son."

"No. She would not. I did it at her request." The expression on Aretta's faced changed from horror, to evil, as she hissed, "She told me it would be okay. That they would never suspect me, that she could protect me. If that is not the case, I will finish her. She will never see her son again, and lucky he will be. An evil family." Aretta spat out a curse in her native language.

Fatima's nerves had given in, and she sank to her knees. "No, no, no, no."

Inspector Dudridge stepped through the back door, sub-machine gun in hand. "You can do your talking at the station." Stepping to one side, he allowed Meredith, Exton and a uniformed officer to pass him. "All yours."

"All under control." He rolled his eyes at Meredith. "You again. Shall I take that?" Taking the gun from Patsy, he saluted. "They've got the warrant, they'll be here team handed any moment. See you back at the station."

Aretta stepped forward, her chin held high as she was handcuffed, but Exton had to lift and half carry Fatima out into the yard.

"Come here." Meredith pulled Patsy into his arms and looked at the angry gash with a grimace. "Will you ever stop doing this, Hodge?"

"I was being kind. I thought it was all over. Anyway, where were you? Ed had to save me." Patsy grinned as Ed waved the brace. "Do we have to go to the station now? Can we go home? I'll give a statement tomorrow and send it through."

"First we need a visit to the hospital, that looks like it needs stitching, and then home."

"You didn't argue or make some excuse to stay involved." Patsy pushed herself away and looked up at him. "What's going on?"

"Why should something be going on? Now, stop making stuff up and let's get you to the hospital."

He put his arm around her shoulders and walked her through to the hall.

They found Fiona pacing up and down outside. She waved the car keys at them.

"I didn't like to stay in the car with these in . . . Oh Patsy, what did they do to you?"

At the hospital, Patsy was seen quickly, and her wound stitched. She accepted the sandwich Fiona had purchased for her.

"Thanks, I'll eat it in the car. I want to go home. I want my own bed, and some peace and quiet."

"Ah."

"Ah, what?"

"We're dropping Fiona home as planned, but I've said Ed can come back with us to meet Julia. Sorry."

"An agreement and an apology within a couple of hours.

Something is going on." Patsy turned to Ed. "Do you know what he's up to?"

"No idea, but I'm happy to arrange this another time, Patsy. I've caused you enough grief."

"Don't be silly, of course you must come and meet her. But let's make a move, Meredith can tell me all as we walk to the car."

"Thanks, Patsy. I'll make this up to you both, I promise. Not sure how, I'm glad it wasn't only me who ruined your honeymoon week though, takes the pressure off a bit."

Patsy stopped walking, "Why who else has?" Holding back a smile as Meredith punched Ed's arm, she put her hands on her hips. "Tell me, Meredith. I'm not moving until you have."

"Okay. Get in the car though. It's nippy out here."

Seatbelt fastened, Patsy put her hand over his as he placed the car in gear. "Start talking."

"Looks like we've got a serial killer in Bristol. They've located the first body and it's with Sherlock. It had a coin in its mouth and three hands."

"There were three hands?"

"Yep. So, two bodies, although one of them is missing a lot of bits. Hence I need to get back."

"Why you?"

"Because they wrote to me."

"Who did?"

"Whoever killed them."

"Wrote what?"

"Letter to me at the station, here, look." Pulling his phone from his breast pocket, he handed it to Patsy. "Check the photographs."

Patsy opened and enlarged the photograph to read the typewritten note.

DCI Meredith, you disappoint me. You ignored my last letter, and so now I've done it again. I need to be stopped, but are you man enough? To help you this should give you a good start. I buried her under the Aldi car park in Henbury. Pure luck, it was being tarmacked the next day. You'll find Karen Cardly in the bottom right hand corner. The latest one, you'll have to find yourself.

"Oh my God. Is your life like this all the time?" Ed leaned forward. "I don't know how you cope."

"A stiff drink, and the love of a good woman . . . Wife." Meredith patted Patsy's knee. "You see, Hodge. I have no choice. The letter was opened two days ago, Karen Cardly was reported missing in Bradford-on-Avon in 2015. That's why this one was taken seriously. They investigated, went to the location, dug it up and found her. They are trying to find the first one now."

"What first what?" Hand still over her mouth, Fiona leaned forward to join her son.

"He says I ignored it, I didn't, but someone did. There might be a record of it, rephrase, there'd better be a record, I . . . who's that?" Meredith looked at his phone.

"Exton. I'll put it on speaker."

"Hello, Exton, you're on speaker phone," Patsy warned him.

"Hello all. Brief update for you so you can all sleep easy in your beds tonight. It would appear that Kate had had enough. She found the stuff on the computer, the gun at his office, and when she found Patsy and Mrs Meredith locked up at one of her houses, she knew Jenkins would have to go, permanently, and concocted a plan with Aretta. Kate arranged to meet Jenkins at the garage, but Aretta went instead so Kate would have an alibi, and she did the deed willingly. Later, when Deegan showed up, Kate told him there was a contract out on him, Jenkins had already been killed, and that he should lie low. Fictitious, but he believed her, and she said she'd send the girls with money."

"I take it, it was them at the door when he was on the phone?" Meredith asked.

"Yep. He let them in, and they didn't even need to use the gun they'd taken. Once he realised it was them, he put the gun on the breakfast bar. That part was from Fatima. Aretta picked it up and shot him where he sat. Neither of them cared about the lives they have taken, only that they were caught, and that Kate Jenkins seems to have set them up."

"Why did they kill them so willingly?" Patsy asked. "However much they thought they owed Kate, it seems pretty drastic."

"Because both men had abused some of the girls at some time or other. Aretta took a beating when she tried to defend Mimi, which reminds me, the two girls who disappeared are alive. Fatima got them out after Jenkins took a shine to them, but she never told anyone for fear of reprisals from him."

"Yes, but can she prove it? I hope so." Patsy sighed.

"Aretta said she kept a diary, and when we read it, all will be revealed. Although she's told us to get on with it, we're awaiting a search warrant, so we don't fall foul. That's about it, safe journey, good luck with the letter writer, Chief Super told us to leave you alone unless it was desperate. No peace for the wicked. I'll buy you a pint if you have to come down for the trial."

"Thanks, glad you're on the Chief Super's buddy list, might keep him off my back for a while. How's Kate taken all this, now she knows her passing the buck won't work?"

There was a short silence, and they heard Exton's intake of breath.

"You'll find out soon enough. She says she had thought her husband's quest to ruin you was ridiculous, she didn't blame you, she blamed Deegan, it was him who had taunted his cousin into becoming involved in the robbery. But now, she says, she realises it was all your fault, Terry, the murders of her husband and Deegan, the exposure of her illegal labour operation. Told us to tell you to watch your back, she'd get you one way or another."

"Nice, I'll add her to the list. We'll let you go now. Sew that case up tight."

"Will do. Nice working with you, and apologies about the wedding again. Bye all."

Exton ended the call, and there was silence in the car for a while, it was broken by a notification that Meredith's phone had received a message.

Checking the screen, Patsy asked, "It's from Louie, shall I open it?" Meredith nodded and Patsy read the message. "First letter found, you won't believe this, brace yourself, copy to follow."

"What does that mean? Why doesn't he just say what he means? Bloody drama queen."

Ignoring him, and opening the next message, Patsy read silently while he complained. From the corner of his eye, he saw her hand come up to her mouth.

"What?" Meredith demanded.

The action wasn't lost on Ed either. "Read it, Patsy, I'm not involved and you've got me hooked."

Meredith, I've killed one for you. Won't be easy to solve, but you're super cop, aren't you? You have three months to find her or I do another. Let's see if you're as clever as you think? If not, I will gift them to you on a regular basis. Happy hunting.

"My God. Do these people really exist? I thought they made them up for films."

"Unfortunately, Fiona, real life is sometimes far more unbelievable. Does he say when that was sent, and more to the bloody point where the hell it's been?"

"Nothing else. I'll ask him." Patsy's fingers tapped out the message, as Ed directed Meredith where to turn off for his mother's house. "There it's sent. So much for us having a few days of married life together." Leaning her head back against the seat, she closed her eyes. "You owe me big time, Meredith."

"I know, I'll pay, but let's leave that discussion on how until we're in private. Don't want to make Fiona blush."

From the back seat came a giggle. "Too late for that."

ABOUT THE AUTHOR

Having worked in the property industry for most of my adult life, latterly at a senior level, I finally escaped in 2010. I now work as a consultant for several independent agencies, but I dedicate the bulk of my time to writing and, of course, reading, although there are still not enough hours in the day.

I began writing quite by chance when a friend commented, "They wouldn't believe it if you wrote it down!" So I did. I enjoyed the plotting and scheming, creating the characters, and watching them develop with the story. I kept on writing, and Meredith and Hodge arrived. In 2017 the Bearing women took hold of my imagination, and the Bearing Witness series was created. I should confess at this point that although I have the basic outline when I start a new story, it never develops the way I expect, and I rarely know 'who did it' myself until I've nearly finished.

I am married with two children, two grandchildren, two German Shepherds and a Bichon Frise, and we live in Bristol, UK.

I can be contacted here, and would love to hear from you:

Website: http://mkturnerbooks.co.uk/

https://www.facebook.com/mkturnerbooks

www.ingramcontent.com/pod-product-compliance
Lightning Source LLC
Chambersburg PA
CBHW051456170626
46811CB00002B/512